The Sharp Q

Rachel Brimble

"Shit! Jamie?" I manage to splutter before slapping my hand over my mouth.

My heart lodges in my throat and I start to choke. And then I watch in slow-motion horror as he leaps towards me and proceeds to clap me on the back. No matter how hard I try, I can't catch my breath and I expel spittle over his suit, hacking like a forty-a-day smoker.

Someone pushes a glass of water into my hand and once I find a scrap of air between coughs, I gulp down the liquid. And even though my breathing finally regulates, I cannot find the strength of character to look at him. Not Jamie. Not now. Not here.

"Hannah?" Mr. Baxter is pushing his way toward me. "Are you all right? My goodness, come and sit down."

I feel the weight of Jamie's hand lift from my shoulder as Mr. Baxter leads me away from twenty pairs of staring eyes to the relative privacy of a vacant corner. I drop into a chair.

"What happened? Did you choke on a satay stick?" he asks.

"I'm fine, really. Something took me by surprise and I started to choke, that's all."

"Something took you by surprise?"

"Or someone."

I snap my head up at the sound of Jamie's rich, velvety voice. Good God, he is something else. My heart threatens to cut off my air supply once more, but I manage to swallow it back down to my chest where it belongs.

"Jamie," I whisper.

"Hello, Hannah."

He smiles down at me from his incredible six feet two inch height and I feel trapped. His smile reflects his amusement and I notice that the dimple in his left cheek is still there. Only now it's shadowed amongst the faint grey of his stubble and fifty times as sexy.

The Sharp Points of a Triangle

The Sharp Points of a Triangle © 2009 by Rachel Brimble

All rights reserved. No part of this book may be reproduced or transmitted in any form or by any means, electronic or mechanical, including photocopying, recording, or by any information storage and retrieval system, without permission in writing from the publisher.

This book is a work of fiction. Characters, names, places and incidents either are the product of the author's imagination or are used fictitiously, and any resemblance to any actual persons, living or dead, events, or locales is entirely coincidental.

An Eternal Press Production

Eternal Press
P.O. Box 3931,
Santa Rosa, CA, USA,
95402-9998

To order additional copies of this book, contact: www.eternalpress.ca

Cover Art © 2009 by Amanda Kelsey
Edited by Pam Slade
Copyedited by Barbara Legge
Layout and Book Production by Ally Robertson

eBook ISBN: 978-1-77065-013-8
Print ISBN: 978-1-77065-021-3

First eBook Edition * January 2010
First Print Edition * January 2010

Production by Eternal Press
Printed in The United States of America.

The Sharp Points of a Triangle

To Mum,

Your ongoing support means the world to me — I love you,

Rachel x

Rachel Brimble

Dedication:

To Nan Pedwell — because you knew how to laugh with the best of them.
We love & miss you.

Chapter One

I've done it. A whole year of exceedingly hard work, less sleep than I thought humanly possible and a brain so fried I'm not sure it will ever fully recover, and I have reached my professional goal. I, Hannah Lauren Boyd, am now officially the youngest female Independent Financial Adviser in the South West. I blow out a breath. What an accolade.

I lean back in my chair and contemplate my rosy future—until my gaze falls on the photo sitting on my desk. Mark. A deadbeat boyfriend who is absolutely, unequivocally no longer wanted and I have to get him out of my house. I pick up the frame and slowly open the back, like I'm pulling the pin from a grenade. I slip out the photograph and run my finger over its surface. Two years. It's not a lifetime in anybody's book but still I feel as though I've been tied to a sinking ship for far too long. It's time to cut the anchor and sail on alone. New career, new singledom.

With the help of Oprah Winfrey and a mountain of self-help books, I have finally woken up and accepted that a romantic partnership does not involve picking up skid-marked boxers from the bedroom floor or listening to a partner's declarations of undying love after ten cans of beer and a chilli kebab.

But it's not just these two minor misdemeanours that have me ready to close the door on the Mark Hardy chapter of my life, it goes deeper than that. You see, Mark has never understood how hard I have worked over the last six years to be the best I can be. He's never realised that if you want something, you have to go out there and get it for yourself. So because of this incomprehension, he never left me alone to study unless I threatened him with death or at least removal of some body part or another.

I slowly nod my head. Oh, yes, it's time to wave a cheery goodbye to him and embrace whatever exciting things life has in store for me.

Turning off my computer, I hitch my bag onto my shoulder and head out the door.

Forty minutes later, I pull into my driveway and turn off the engine. Dropping my head onto the steering wheel, I inhale long slow breaths, summoning the strength to get out of the car and do what has to be done. But then the door is yanked open and Mark is grasping my arm.

"Our new neighbours have arrived," he announces. "So far I've only seen the removal men coming and going, but let's hope they're about the same age as us. It would be great to have a couple of new best friends living right next door, wouldn't it?"

I groan inwardly. It's six o'clock in the evening and he is still dressed in his uniform, of pyjama bottoms and England T-shirt that I'd left him in at seven-thirty this morning. It makes me want to cry. The sooner I tell Mark he's out of here, the better. I look at him.

"Let's go inside, shall we?"

"What's wrong?" he asks. "Bad day?"

I sigh and pull my handbag from the passenger seat. "No, Mark. A fantastic day, actually."

He steps back as I get out of the car and slam the door.

"Are you sure? Because you've got a face like a smacked arse right now," he says.

"Gee, thanks."

I walk through the front door with Mark at my heels chattering on and on about the mystery of our new neighbours, like an incessant Jack Russell. Snapping and yapping on about some irrelevancy to which I have zero interest. I head directly to the fridge and extract a bottle of Sauvignon Blanc.

"You're having wine? Now?" he asks.

I turn, swinging the chilled bottle to and fro in my hand. "Yes. Do you have a problem with that?"

"You've only just got through the door," he says, tapping a finger on the face of his watch. "And it's barely six o'clock."

"I need a drink, okay?"

"You need it? Whoa, AA alert," he says, waving his hands in the air.

Rolling my eyes, I turn to the cupboard and take out the largest wineglass I have and proceed to fill it to the brim. It depletes a third of the bottle. Perfect. I take a hefty gulp, wipe a hand across my mouth and then turn back to face him feeling more than ready.

"I don't want to do this anymore, Mark."

"Drink? Yep, I thought so. We'll get you booked in somewhere, don't worry. There are so many places for alcoholics…"

"Us, you moron. I don't want to do us anymore."

"What did you call me?"

It just slipped out. I swallow back the apology that automatically bubbles across my tongue. I will do this. This time I will do it. "So I need you to get any stuff you have hanging around my house and leave. Preferably in the next half an hour."

He sticks his head out and tilts it to the side as though I've hit him with some complex mathematical problem. "You want me to leave?"

I nod. "Yes."

"You're breaking up with me?"

"Yes. Please don't make this any harder than it has to be."

"Now? You're breaking up with me now?"

"Yes."

For a long moment he says nothing. I sip at my wine resolutely ignoring the nervous thump, thump, thump in my chest. The seconds slowly tick by and then bang, the explosion detonates.

"But you can't!"

"I can."

"No, you bloody well can't! You can't just waltz in here and announce we're finished like this. Bloody hell, Hannah. We're happy enough. What's the matter with you?"

I stare at him incredulously. "We are not happy, Mark. You may be but I'm not," I say, my voice rising with each word. "And don't you dare act as though this is some sort of shock. I've been telling you for weeks that I don't want to go on like this."

"No, you haven't."

"I have."

"When? Tell me, when you have said that you don't want to be with me anymore!" he demands.

I put the wine glass down on the counter top for fear of launching it at his head. "I told you five weeks ago the love has gone for me, and I can't see the point in us dragging out the inevitable. How could I have possibly made myself any clearer?"

He waves a hand in the air. "Oh, that was just you sulking."

"Sulking? What should I have said? Fuck off out of my house, you lazy bastard? Would that have got through to you?"

He walks to the wine rack and pulls out a bottle of red. "Looks like I'd better join you in an early glass of wine the way things are going."

I lunge forward, snatch the bottle from his hand and grip it to my chest. "No."

Our eyes lock and there is a long, long pause. I sigh. "Look, there's no point in getting drunk, it won't exactly help the situation, will it?"

"Too bad, you started this."

"Mark…"

"No, Hannah." He crosses his arms. "What if I don't want to go?"

"You don't have a choice. This house is mine. If I want you to leave, you have to go."

"Really?"

I look at him. "Yes."

"You think so, do you?"

"Yes."

He nods a few times, obviously trying to pluck an obstacle of mass obstruction from thin air. I wait.

"Well, where am I supposed to go?" he cries, throwing his arms up.

I arch an eyebrow. "Your mother's? Your friends?"

"But I don't want to go back home."

I grimace as his customary whine finally surfaces. I knew it would rear its ugly head eventually. "I'm sorry but that's not my problem. Just get your stuff together and go. Please."

He pushes himself away from the counter. "Fine. I'll go but this isn't the end of it."

I pick up my wine glass and take a mouthful. "Don't threaten me, Mark."

"Oh, I'm not threatening you. All I'm saying is you'll soon want me back, looking for my forgiveness and another chance to climb aboard the Marky-Mark Machine of Manly Motion."

I swallow back the sudden bitterness in my throat when he gyrates his pelvis in my direction. Our sex life has never exactly set the world on fire and it's incredibly sad that he doesn't recognise the complete absence of it for the last three months, as a screaming announcement of a problem.

I force a smile. "Well, I'm glad you've still got your sense of humour at least."

The slight soars over his head and hits the wall behind him.

"Right, if that's the way you want it," he huffs. "I'll go upstairs, grab a few things and get out of here, but don't even think about asking me to come back when you change your mind."

"I won't change my mind, Mark."

He marches out the room and I squeeze my eyes tightly shut. It's done. I'm not sure the message has got all the way through but at least it's been said. My shoulders lift a little higher and my breathing flows through my lungs a little smoother. Don't get me wrong. There is absolutely no part of me enjoying this. It's just something I have to do or risk losing myself to him forever. I can't allow that to happen. I just know there are bigger and better things right around the corner for me, and there is a huge chance being with Mark will make me miss them.

His footsteps clump back and forth across the ceiling as I walk to the freezer and take out a box of Lemon Chicken with Rice for one. By the time I've pierced the lid several times with a fork (a little harder than strictly necessary), Mark comes back into the kitchen.

"All done," he says.

"Good. You've got everything?" I ask.

"There are a few bits still up there, but like I said, I'll be back."

"Mark, you're not listening to me, mmmph..."

I am unable to finish my sentence because his lips are now welded to mine. A short struggle ensues before I manage to prise my hands between his chest and my flattened breasts, in order to push him away.

"What the hell are you doing?" I yell.

"What? It's just a little something for you to remember me by," he snaps. "What happened to you today to make you so damn angry, huh?"

I shake my head. My body is humming with suppressed rage.

"Just get out, Mark. I want you out of here right now."

He picks up his bag. "Fine. See you around."

When I hear the front door slam behind him, I turn back to the counter and pick up my wine glass. It trembles against my tender mouth but somehow I manage to take a sip, before sliding to the floor and pretending I don't notice the tears slipping slowly over my cheeks.

I've done it. Mark is gone. I'm on my own again. But this time it feels different. This time my heart isn't lying in a thousand pieces on the floor. This time it's me making the choice to be alone, not somebody else deciding it for me.

****

A week later, I am sitting at my desk frowning over a sheet of performance tables when Mr. Baxter, my boss, pokes his head around the door.

"Hannah? Will you come into my office, please? And when Miss Willoughby finishes on the phone, can you ask her to join us too?"

"Sure."

Walking next door, I wait in front of Miss Willoughby's desk until she replaces the phone in its cradle.

"Mr. Baxter has asked that we join him in his office."

"Oohh, that means he's ready to tell us all about the trip," she says, scrambling out of her chair.

"Trip?"

Her cheeks redden. "Oops, I'd forgotten he hadn't told you. I'm sure it doesn't mean he has more trust in me than you, Hannah. I think he wants it to be a surprise, that's all."

Let me explain, that even though Mr. Baxter is barely five feet tall, as round as a bowling ball and ejects gas when over-excited, Miss Willoughby holds a torch, no that's wrong—a frigging thousand watt light bulb for the man—and views my presence as a continual obstacle, preventing her from getting her leg over.

"But what are you talking about? What trip?"

She opens her mouth to answer, but then Mr. Baxter appears behind me. "Are we ready, ladies? Come along now."

Miss Willoughby quickly brushes past me. She is so excited I'm left wondering, whether Mr. Baxter's impending news is causing her clitoris to contract.

Once we are all seated in his office, Mr. Baxter leans forward on his elbows and folds his hands together. He sits there with the widest, most absurd grin on his face. So we wait. He grins at me, then at Miss Willoughby, then at me. This goes on for so long that cold perspiration breaks out on my spine and images of Jack Nicholson breaking through the door in 'The Shining' come to mind.

I swallow. "Are you all right, Mr. Baxter?"

"Ha, ha, ha!" He claps his hands together and leaps to his feet. I jump so high in my chair that I actually feel air pass beneath my arse. "Am I all right?" he cries. "Am I all right? You are going to be over the moon when you hear what I have to tell you, my dear."

I laugh, albeit nervously. "I am?"

I snatch a glance at Miss Willoughby, whose face is so red she looks as though she's about to self-combust.

"Shall I tell her what I've been up to, Miss Willoughby? Or will you?" he asks, his eyes dancing.

"Oh, Mr. Baxter, don't tease Hannah like that!" Miss Willoughby cries. And believe it or not, there are actual tears in her eyes.

"Okay, okay....." He draws in a long breath. "We are going away, Hannah. On a business trip."

My heart begins to thump hard in my chest. "Business trip? Us?"

"Yes, dear. Us. But not any old business trip. After such a successful year and the acquiring of so many wealthy new clients in the last twelve months, Callahan's are official guests at the annual conference, 'Financial Planning for the Entrepreneur'..... Great business minds of the past and future come together to eat, drink, discuss and negotiate."

Miss Willoughby clasps a hand to her chest. "Oh, Mr. Baxter," she breathes. "How wonderful."

Ignoring her, Mr. Baxter continues, "For a whole five days, we will mingle and socialise, learn and devour everything there is on offer."

My eyes widen. "Five days?"

"And four nights."

"But why didn't you mention this before?" I say. "How do you know I don't have plans?"

Mr. Baxter holds up a hand. "Show her the brochure, Miss Willoughby. I'm sure you'll be a little more enthusiastic when you see what The Laurels has to offer, Hannah. It won't be all work and no play, you know."

I take the brochure from Miss Willoughby and flick through the pages. The Laurels is a fourteenth century manor house, set in exquisite, landscaped gardens. There are deer grazing amongst the emerald green grass and the sun glints from the water of the outdoor pool, but still, five days? With the Munchkin and the Wicked Witch of the West?

"So, I'll leave you to book the rooms, shall I, Miss Willoughby?" asks Mr. Baxter.

She eagerly leans forward, her pen poised above her notepad. "Three rooms with breakfast, is that correct?"

"Two rooms, Miss Willoughby, two rooms," he smiles.

Two rooms? He can't possibly be suggesting I share a room with her? Or worse, him? I slowly turn to Miss Willoughby who is looking at me with the exact same terror etched across her face. We simultaneously snap our heads around to face Mr. Baxter.

"I really don't think..." I begin.

"Mr. Baxter, I need a room of my own..." Miss Willoughby says.

He raises his hands. "Ladies, ladies. There will be no sharing rooms. One room is to be booked for me and the other for Hannah."

Oh, shit. I swallow hard as I watch from the corner of my eye, as Miss Willoughby slowly turns again to look at me. I am too terrified to meet her gaze. I feel like I am taking her husband away for a dirty weekend.

She gets to her feet. "Right. I see. I'll get on and book the two rooms then."

Mr. Baxter stands up. "Good. Good. Where would I be without you, Miss Willoughby?"

She manages a pinched smile and marches from the office.

Chapter Two

The photographs of The Laurels did not do the place justice. The house is absolutely breathtaking and I feel extremely self-conscious, bouncing up the circular driveway in my battered Ford Fiesta. I should be trotting up side-saddle on an immaculate chestnut mare. I park my car and Mr. Baxter pulls in beside me. We both get out and gaze up at the house. I am a sucker for anything historical and The Laurels is nothing short of magnificent.

"Lovely, isn't it?" asks Mr. Baxter.

I nod. "It's beautiful. Look at the architecture, the windows...God, how many windows are there?"

Mr. Baxter chuckles. "A lot, my dear. A lot. Shall we go in?"

Grabbing our bags from the cars, we make our way up the stone steps and into the lobby. I suck in a breath. There are rich rosewood tables holding stunning displays of pink and white lilies along one wall and antique gold chairs with jade green seats positioned around a handsome fireplace on the other. I look above me and gasp at the huge chandelier, its crystals dangling like icicles as they catch the light. And in the centre of it all is a huge staircase, splitting off in two directions inviting the hotel's guests to venture to the upper level.

My grin widens. God, I'm going to enjoy this trip.

Mr. Baxter approaches the reception desk.

"Hannah?"

"Mmmm?"

He smiles at me. "Do you have the booking information?"

"Pardon?"

"The booking details, dear. This lovely lady here needs our confirmation."

I stare at him for a second before my brain clicks into gear. I blink. "Right, yes, booking confirmation. Um, just a minute it's in here somewhere."

I rummage about in my bag while Mr. Baxter and the receptionist wait. I glance up apologetically and see Mr. Baxter is looking at me with sympathy, but the receptionist's lips are sucked into such a small O, I'm reminded of a dog's crinkled rear-end.

"A-ha. Here it is."

The receptionist gives a small smile. "Lovely. Thank you."

We go through the particulars and after a few efficient minutes, she hands us key cards to our rooms. "I hope you both have a worthwhile conference and please feel free to ask for anything you need. Your bags have already been taken to your rooms. Enjoy your stay."

I look down and see that indeed our bags have vanished. Efficiency is obviously the hotel motto. Mr. Baxter touches my elbow.

"How about a quick drink?" he suggests, glancing at his watch. "We've got another hour before the introductory drinks and chit-chat."

"Great."

We walk into the lounge and I take a seat in such an enormous leather armchair, I instantly feel remarkably tiny. I realise Mr. Baxter is sure to take the identical seat opposite me, and find myself wickedly looking forward to the prospect. But as I settle back against the butter-soft leather, my phone rings and burning heat scalds my cheeks. I really should have changed my ring tone to a romantic concerto when I knew I was coming here. Instead, I have the husky tones of Jon Bon Jovi screaming to all and sundry that I give love a bad name.

I scramble for my bag and after what seems like a fortnight I locate the phone.

"Hello?" I hiss and roll my eyes at the couple sitting to the left of me. Then I do a double take and look at them again — is that the Queen and Prince Philip?

"It's me."

"Who?" I say, turning my attention back to the phone.

"Mark!"

Oh, great. "Why are you ringing me?"

"To make sure you're not still angry with me, but by the tone of your voice I'm guessing you are."

I sigh. "Mark, we're finished. You make it sound as though we've had a lovers' tiff, for crying out loud."

"Why are you being so stubborn?" he whines... "You know we're meant to be together."

"No, Mark. We're not. Goodbye."

I snap the phone shut and promptly switch it off. Damn him. Now the romance of The Laurels has disappeared right along with my fantastic mood. I drum my fingers up and down on the arm of my chair. Why was I stupid enough to think Mark would disappear with no hassle? But then before I can ponder that question any further, Mr. Baxter returns from the bar and places a glass of champagne in front of me. I decide for the next five days at least, Mark Hardy no longer exists.

I take a sip of my drink, savour the burst of bubbles at the back of my throat and watch Mr. Baxter struggle with the height of his chair.

"Phew. Well, here we are then," he beams, finally heaving his butt into the seat. "Here's to a fabulous five days of negotiation."

I touch my glass to his and sip. "Here, here. So...I assume anyone who's anyone will be here?"

"Certainly. But I didn't bring you here for star spotting alone, my dear. You are here to face head on the challenge I am about to set you."

I slowly place my glass on the table in front of us. "Challenge?"

"Oh yes," he says, his eyes ablaze. "There is an extremely successful and wealthy gentleman attending the conference, and it's your job to secure him as Callahan's client. You have just as good a chance of turning his head as anyone else here. His name is Malcolm Jenkins, he's forty-eight and worth an estimated eight million pounds."

I swallow. "Oh, my God."

Mr. Baxter laughs. "Now, take a deep breath and finish your drink. I have complete faith in you. We could take a quick look at the itinerary while we're waiting," he suggests, reaching into the inside pocket of his jacket.

"Itinerary? I didn't see one with the other information we received."

"No...no, the itinerary came directly to me."

He pushes some stapled papers across the table. I put down my glass and pick them up. I run my gaze over the timetable. Plenty of leisure time in between meetings and meals. Good, good — but then I see the plans for Saturday night.

"A medieval ball?" I look up. "But I didn't know anything about this. Shouldn't we have arranged costumes?"

He leans back in his chair, waving a dismissive hand. "All taken care of."

I frown. "By whom?"

"Miss Willoughby." He pauses. "Now don't look at me like that. I specifically asked her to make you a beautiful medieval princess, so that a handsome knight...moi," he says, pressing a hand to his chest, "Can compete for your hand in marriage."

I try to smile but only manage to grimace.

"But she doesn't even know my dress size," I say, thinking more along the lines of how much Miss Willoughby hates me and wondering what the hell I'm going to be dressed in.

"She and the typists had a little debate, and finally agreed on your size. Don't worry. You're going to look stunning."

Miss Willoughby and the typists? Good God, kill me now.

He glances at his watch. "Right, drink up, I'm sure we can squeeze in another glass before we make our way to the conference room, don't you?"

Half an hour later we are entering the hotel's Oak Suite. It is a huge room with a circular table in the centre and other tables lined along two of the walls. One is laden with canapés and dainty, crust-free sandwiches and the other with flutes of champagne, orange juice and water. Mr. Baxter steers me toward the drinks.

"Let's grab ourselves another glass of bubbly, shall we?"

After a few minutes, men and women dressed in no-nonsense business suits come toward Mr. Baxter, their hands outstretched and their smiles wide. Very quickly, I am informed by not one, but several people from different companies, of Mr. Baxter's extraordinary achievements for both his clients and for Callahan's. Yep, the little man beside me is a big, big player in this ensemble. After forty-five minutes, I am standing tall and proud beside my boss, feeling that the next five days are going to be something to really look forward to.

Mr. Baxter clears his throat. "If you'll excuse me everyone, I just need the little boys' room. Hannah, will you be all right on your own for a while?"

"Of course."

He beams. "I'll be straight back."

I shake my head as I watch him amble from the room. He really is the sweetest guy. I look across at the food table. It would be a good idea for me to eat something after consuming so much alcohol. I weave through the throng of people to the table and reach rather unsteadily for a plate.

But just as I do, another hand reaches for it at the same time.

"Oh, I'm sorry."

But then my throat closes over as I look into a pair of eyes that I never, ever thought I would look into again. My own eyes begin to burn.

"Shit! Jamie?" I manage to splutter before slapping my hand over my mouth.

My heart lodges in my throat and I start to choke. And then I watch in slow-motion horror as he leaps towards me and proceeds to clap me on the back. No matter how hard I try, I can't catch my breath and I expel spittle over his suit, hacking like a forty-a-day smoker.

Someone pushes a glass of water into my hand and once I find a scrap of air between coughs, I gulp down the liquid. And even though my breathing finally regulates, I cannot find the strength of character to look at him. Not Jamie. Not now. Not here.

"Hannah?" Mr. Baxter is pushing his way toward me. "Are you all right? My goodness, come and sit down."

I feel the weight of Jamie's hand lift from my shoulder as Mr. Baxter leads me away from twenty pairs of staring eyes to the relative privacy of a vacant corner. I drop into a chair.

"What happened? Did you choke on a satay stick?" he asks.

"I'm fine, really. Something took me by surprise and I started to choke, that's all."

"Something took you by surprise?"

"Or someone."

I snap my head up at the sound of Jamie's rich, velvety voice. Good God, he is something else. My heart threatens to cut off my air supply once more, but I manage to swallow it back down to my chest where it belongs.

The Sharp Points of a Triangle

"Jamie," I whisper.

"Hello, Hannah."

He smiles down at me from his incredible six feet two inch height and I feel trapped. His smile reflects his amusement and I notice that the dimple in his left cheek is still there. Only now it's shadowed amongst the faint grey of his stubble and fifty times as sexy. I quickly turn to Mr. Baxter.

"Mr. Baxter, this is…"

But Mr. Baxter swats my hand away. "No need for introductions, my dear. I know who this extraordinary gentleman is, just like everyone else in the room." He thrusts his hand toward Jamie. "I'm very pleased to finally meet you, Mr. Young. Very pleased indeed. How do you know my Hannah, then?"

Jamie arches an eyebrow, the smile still playing at his sinful lips. He is looking at me as though I'm naked. "Your Hannah?"

Heat flares on my face as Mr. Baxter continues to talk and Jamie languidly runs his gaze over my hair, my eyes, and my lips. I silently count to twenty to keep from freaking out.

"Well, no, not my Hannah, per se," laughs Mr. Baxter. "She was once my PA, but has since become an extremely skilled Financial Adviser. It would be a huge loss to Callahan's if she were ever to escape."

Jamie smiles. "I'm sure it would."

I push myself to my feet, hoping that if I'm upright his unwavering gaze will feel a little less disarming. I meet his eyes.

"Mr. Baxter is being too kind. My new role only came into force a little over a week ago. I'm sure I still have lots to learn" I say, smiling far too brightly. "Right, well if you gentlemen will excuse me, I think I'll go back to my room for a little while before dinner."

"Of course, my dear," Mr. Baxter says. "We'll be finished here soon and I'll be up to have a shower and get changed myself. I'll see you back in the bar at around seven, okay?"

"Great. See you then." I nod at Jamie. "Jamie."

He returns my nod and I turn, but not before I catch his wink which gives me that stomach dropping feeling of going over a bump in the road too fast.

****

Somehow I manage to get from the conference suite to my room. Once inside, I close the door behind me and lean my back against it. My heart is slamming painfully against my chest, and my legs are trembling, but the rush, the adrenaline rush racing through my veins is fantastic.

Letting out a shriek, I push myself away from the door and do a little dance around my room. Correction—suite... I freeze. Wow, wow, wow!

It is huge. The deep burgundy walls are a sumptuous background for numerous gilt-framed oil paintings dotted all around the room. The carpet is the colour of clotted cream and as soft as duck feathers. My eyes lock on the four-poster bed and Jamie shoots to the forefront of my mind. Oh, yes, baby. Come to mama.

I leap onto a mattress that has got to be at least a metre thick and bounce up and down like a prize trampolinist. Fabulous, absolutely fabulous. Mid-jump I look out the window and then I'm racing from the bed to see the picture-perfect countryside laid out in front of me. The grounds below are landscaped to perfection. Flowers bloom in every colour and moss-covered angels guard the water of the enormous pond. Am I really here to work?

Turning away from the window, I exhale a long breath. Jamie. Jamie Young. How can he be here? The shock of seeing the boy who took my virginity in the back of his canary-yellow Mini, is slowly giving way to outright panic. He'd left Bristol without as much as a goodbye kiss, leaving eighteen-year-old me heartbroken and changed forever.

But then, seeing him again now, gives me the chance to show him that very little of the woman he left behind exists today. I can show him how I've changed, how strong, and focused and sexy I am.

I lower myself onto the cushioned window seat and swallow hard. The chemistry between us in the Oak Suite had been crackling so loudly, it had been on the tip of my tongue to ask Mr. Baxter if he'd heard it too. Am I really strong enough to resist acting on it? With a quick, clearing shake of my head, I pick up my bag and take out my mobile.

Punching in my best friend's number, I wait for her to answer.

"Hello?"

"Sam, it's me."

"Hey, you! How's it going? Baxter tried to seduce you yet?"

"Will you stop that? It wasn't funny the first time and it isn't funny now."

"Sorry, couldn't resist," she giggles. "How's it going then?"

I close my eyes and press the phone to my ear. "Okay."

"That's it, just okay?"

I take a deep breath. "No, I mean, okay, as in here goes."

"Oooh, sounds exciting. What is it? Have you seen someone famous?"

"Nope. Listen. Who is the one person I always say I never want to see again as long as I live?"

"Male or female?"

"Male." My teeth are clamped together and my eyes screwed into slits.

There's a long pause. "Jamie?"

My breath comes out in a rush. "The one and only."

"But what's Jamie got to do…? He's there?"

"Uh-huh."

"Wow, you haven't seen him in…"

"Six years!" I finish for her. "I don't know what to do."

I hear her draw in a breath. "I'll tell you what you do, you make sure you look bloody fantastic and then you make him beg."

"But I'm not sure I can," I say, pressing a hand to the wave of queasiness gliding through my intestines. "He looks so…"

"Yes, you can. When he pissed off to make his fucking fortune in Edinburgh or wherever it was, you were a desperate, spotty, love-sick…"

"God, keep going, why don't you?" I say, miserably.

"But now look at you," she exclaims. "You're gorgeous, single, fancy-free and just happen to be the youngest IFA in the country."

"The South West."

"Yeah, yeah, whatever. The point is you are going to drive him insane with the desire to have you."

Despite the nervous tremors taking over my body, I find myself grinning. Sam is the best friend any girl could ask for. "Do you really think I can?"

"What? Make him want to bend you over a hay bale? Hell, yes!"

"Sam!"

She laughs. "You'll have him begging for mercy in no time."

"But who says I want him?"

"Has he lost his looks then? Is he all hairy and fat and built like Homer Simpson?"

I close my eyes and bring Jamie's face to my mind's eye. Six foot two with sandy-blonde hair, eyes of the deepest green which either dance with humour or seduce with attentive admiration. Shoulders broad and strong, hands that could steady a girl with a mere press to the small of her back.

"Hannah? Are you still there?"

I sit bolt upright. What the hell am I doing? Jamie Young told me he loved me and then as soon as the opportunity came to leave, he took it. The man has been obsessed with money since I was fifteen and he was seventeen. Well, by the look of him now, he's got exactly what he wants. His entire demeanour screams of success.

Well, he can piss off because all I'm interested in now is my own success, and I don't need him distracting me from that goal. In fact, he can keep those damn bedroom eyes and shoulders as wide as a tow truck far away from me and my career.

"Hello? Earth calling Hannah."

"I've got to go," I say.

"What? We were talking about Jamie. Is he…"

"Look, there's someone at the door," I lie. "I'll ring you tomorrow."

I turn off the phone and throw it on to the bed as though it's scalding me. Reel yourself in, Hannah. Reel yourself in right now. You, my girl, have got a job to do.

The Sharp Points of a Triangle

Chapter Three

I plaster a smile on my face and begin the descent down the staircase. The four-inch stilettos I am wearing have made the staircase I admired so much when I arrived here, suddenly feel like an endless downhill path of potential catastrophe. But with God's good grace, I reach the bottom unscathed and release my held breath.

The hotel watering hole is heaving and I'm grateful for the concealment of bodies as I make my way toward the bar—even though there is a distinct disadvantage not knowing whether Jamie is already in the room. If he saw me come in, it could mean he's making his way over to me right now. I surreptitiously look around me. How am I supposed to locate one particular man among the forty or fifty other people milling around?

Taking a deep breath, I lift a hand to get the barman's attention but he either doesn't see me or ignores me, and instead serves a blonde with a chest bigger than Pamela Anderson's. I drum my fingers on the glossy marble bar as my thoughts return to Jamie. The truth is I've compared every boyfriend I've had for the last six years to him. And even though he was the selfish bastard who disappeared on me, the others have never lived up to those vivid memories of the first boy I loved. Sad but true. And yes, I'd die before I let Jamie get even a whiff of that fact.

But it isn't our romantic memories of us together that are now jamming up my brain or making me wish I'd packed my vibrator. It is pure and simple lust doing that. He looks so bloody sexy. I squeeze my thighs together. It's no good, I'll just have to make sure Jamie and I are never alone, that's all. But then again a woman has needs and...

There's a tap on my shoulder and I cry out...

And then so does Mr. Baxter. Again, and again, and again. Until I take him by the shoulders and shake him.

"Mr. Baxter, stop it. I'm sorry...you made me jump, that's all," I yell above his feminine wailing. "Mr. Baxter!"

And then he stops. "Oh, Hannah. Oh, goodness me. Help me onto a seat, will you?"

I slowly lift my head. We have a small gathering of people around us. Some are sniggering behind their hands, others are laughing into their glasses and the rest just look petrified, as if either of us might attack them at any given moment. Thankfully, Jamie is nowhere to be seen.

"Hannah? Please, I need to sit down."

"What?" I look at Mr. Baxter. "Oh, right."

I place a supportive hand at his elbow and together we try to heave his considerable bulk onto a stool. But it appears the gods are no longer with us. And once again I underestimate the humiliation that is fast becoming my regular ordeal. The only way I'm able to pole-vault Mr. Baxter onto the stool is to physically lift him onto it. So I sensibly bend my knees, slap my hands together in preparation...and then there is another tap on my shoulder.

"Allow me."

And yes, my humiliation is complete.

Jamie steps in front of me and picks Mr. Baxter up from beneath his armpits and plonks him on the stool. Mr. Baxter grins up at him like the demented moron I now believe he is.

"Oh, thank you, Mr. Young. Thank you. Hannah here gave me the fright of my life."

"Really?" Jamie's eyes lock onto mine. "What did you do?"

"Nothing. I was miles away and when Mr. Baxter approached me from behind, I may have cried out that's all."

Jamie arches an eyebrow. "From behind? Like this?"

And then he slides behind me in one smooth movement. His hands touch my hips and his breath is warm against the exposed nape of my neck. I shiver involuntarily.

"Stop it, Jamie," I hiss between clenched teeth.

He leans closer and there's an urgent twitch between my legs.

"You look stunning," he whispers.

I force a smile and focus on Mr. Baxter who is watching us with intrigued curiosity. Taking a quick step forward, I place my trembling hands on the bar.

"Well, I don't know about anyone else but I could really do with a drink," I say, smiling widely. "Mr. Baxter? Jamie?"

"A vodka tonic, please," sighs Mr. Baxter.

"Scotch with plenty of ice, thanks," Jamie says, before turning to Mr. Baxter. "Oh, and please, call me Jamie. I don't go much on formality. How about you?"

"Well, normally I like to keep things a little formal but as we are no longer at the office, why not?" he says, flinging his hands in the air. "Call me Reginald."

I turn to the bar and roll my eyes. I feel like I'm watching a very bad movie, where I'm the heroine who secretly wants to be alone with the hero, but knows she shouldn't. Not that it matters, because in every scene there's an annoying, bald, squelched up creature that refuses to disappear.

We each take our glasses from the bar and Mr. Baxter clears his throat. "Shall we toast to a successful conference?"

"Why not?" agrees Jamie.

We all clink glasses. I take a hefty gulp of rum and coke. "So, are you staying for the entire conference?" I ask, looking Jamie directly in the eye and drawing on every ounce of self-confidence I can muster.

He nods. "Yep, I'm here for the same reason as everyone else."

"Which is?" I ask.

"To drum up business, spread the name of Young's Financial Services, take advantage of the insurance company perks…" He lets the sentence drift off. "After all, that's what these seminars are about, isn't it?"

"I…"

"This is Hannah's very first seminar, Mr. Young. Sorry…Jamie," smiles Mr. Baxter. "And she's as excited as a kitten nibbling on a fish stick."

Jamie raises his eyebrows as he smiles into his glass. "Is she really?"

I face Mr. Baxter, narrow my eyes and mentally remove his tongue and hurl it across the room.

"Yes, yes it is," I say before Mr. Baxter has a chance to add anything else to the demise of my professional reputation. "But as of last week I became the youngest female IFA in the South West, so I'm pretty sure it won't be my last."

Jamie looks suitably impressed. "Congratulations. Not that I'm surprised."

The comment strikes at something deep in my chest. "Really? And why not? After all you don't know me from Adam anymore. The last time you saw me I was a completely different person."

"Were you? I don't think you've really changed very much at all."

His eyes no longer look sexy to me, his voice no longer soft and comforting. I feel my hackles rise. "And why's that?"

"You're still as beautiful and intelligent as you were when I last saw you. Why wouldn't you be successful?"

Nice shot, but I'm not buying it, Mister. Not this time. "Intelligence and looks are one thing," I say, slowly. "But mostly people change in the places you can't see. Surely even someone as self-involved as you knows that."

Colour stains his cheeks and his green eyes darken. "Someone as self-involved as me?"

I open my mouth to speak but Mr. Baxter gets there first.

"Hannah, dear, there's someone over there I would love you to meet," he says, firmly. "Mr. Young, Jamie, will you excuse us?"

Jamie nods but his eyes don't leave mine. "Of course."

And then I have no choice but to break eye contact as my boss propels me away.

"Do you want to tell me what that was all about?" Mr. Baxter urgently whispers, once we are cocooned in a corner of the bar. "The atmosphere is positively rife between you."

I shake my head. "It's nothing."

"I assume you and Mr. Young share more than a professional history?" he presses.

I nod.

He softens his voice as he touches a hand to my elbow. "What happened? You can tell me."

I meet his kindly gaze and blow out a breath. "I was barely eighteen when we split up," I say, swallowing hard. "It's ancient history. I'm a bit shocked to see him here, that's all. But I'm fine with it now."

"Honestly?"

I force a smile. "Honestly."

And then somewhere out in the lobby, a gong is sounded. I can't quite believe I let my resentment of Jamie show so quickly, or so easily. If he didn't before, Jamie will certainly be thinking he had a lucky escape six years ago, rather than wishing he'd come back begging my forgiveness. Mr. Baxter offers me his arm.

"Shall we?"

I inhale a deep breath, link my arm through his and step over the threshold into the dining room with a confident smile fixed into place. But once inside, I am once again unashamedly gawking at everything around me as though I've never been out of Bristol before. The Laurels is just what it claims to be in the brochure, 'truly the embodiment of extravagant splendour'.

The ceiling is domed, with oak beams arching over to meet in the middle. Eight circles of candles hang suspended from the beams to complement the soft and subtle table lighting. To my left are three archways where I can see the bar nestled along the back of the wall. To my right the stone wall is covered with a replica threadbare tapestry, depicting a gory battle between armoured knights, peasants and princes. A smile plays at my lips. I feel transported back in time. I am walking in on the arm of a knight, my hair flows thick and long down my back as I gaze up at my hero. I am unaware of having clasped Mr. Baxter's hand in mine until he squeezes my fingers.

"Quite a place, isn't it?" He smiles up at me with the look of a doting grandfather taking his young granddaughter out for her first day trip.

I carefully slide my hand from his before he thinks he's pulled. "It's beautiful, absolutely beautiful."

Despite the vast size of the room, the rich dark colours and the simple lighting shrouds the room in intimacy. The tables are covered with glossy white table cloths, and the glasses and napkins are the same deep burgundy as the elaborate silk drapes hanging at the windows. The cutlery shines beneath the flames of the candles dotted along each table.

"Let's try to find where we're sitting shall we?" asks Mr. Baxter, interrupting my romantic thoughts of fairy tales and princesses. "Or more to the point find out with whom we are sitting."

I eagerly follow him. Surely God would not be cruel enough to sit me within fifty feet of Jamie, so ahead of me is a night of getting to know new people and hopefully, ferret out some information concerning the reason I am here —Malcolm Jenkins.

We walk among the tables, looking at place cards and company logos. Nothing.

"I can't see our names anywhere," I say.

"Oh, we're sure to be here somewhere, dear," Mr. Baxter murmurs.

And then my stomach tightens and my heart thumps hard inside my chest when I see Jamie standing not five feet away from me. Yep, God must love getting a kick out of watching me squirm. Hey, maybe I rose up against the Church in the fourteenth century or something and now he's paying me back big time.

He is standing by one of the tables, his hand on the back of a chair talking to a sickeningly gorgeous blonde. Her size six figure is sheathed in a pale pink dress that glides over her body like a second skin, and falls to her ankles in soft delicate folds.

"Condom in heels," I mutter.

"Did you say something, dear?" asks Mr. Baxter.

"No, no. I'll bet twenty pounds this will be us," I say, approaching the table.

I walk closer to Jamie and his companion and peer at the name cards, purposely turning my back to them in an ardent display of disinterest. But then Mr. Baxter has no such qualms and comes bouncing up beside me like a God damn jack in the box.

"Jamie! What a coincidence you should be seated between Hannah and me," he gushes. "And who is this stunning, young lady? Your wife?"

Nausea rises bitter and unwelcome in my throat as my breath catches. Time stands still. I wait for his answer. Bastard. Why didn't I consider the fact he could be married? Bastard. Who the hell does he think he is, running his eyes over me like a bloody Casanova ready to pounce when he's got a wife who looks like that?

He gives a deep throaty laugh which immediately warms my body in places that have no right to be warm.

"No, no, I'm not married, Reginald," he says, with a laugh. "Let me introduce Andrea Kingsley. She's one of Lloyds' top performing advisers."

I sniff. Yeah, I bet. Performing is right—most likely on her back. But my relief rushes out on a breath.

I move to sit down but realise the chair on which Jamie is resting his hand is mine. Damn it. When I look up, he's watching me. In fact, all three of them are.

"Oh, I'm sorry." I extend my hand to Condom. "Hannah Boyd. Pleased to meet you."

She gives me a pinched smile and takes my hand. Her eyes linger on mine for a moment too long. "Pleased to meet you too, Hannah."

I smile back and hope it doesn't look as overdone as it feels. There's a long silence and I wonder which one of us is going to fill it. But we are all saved by the bell, literally. The Master of Ceremonies asks that we all be seated, and when I move to pull out my chair, Jamie gets there first. My eyes meet his and he winks.

My heart gives a hard kick, but I merely nod my thanks and gracefully sit down. Opening my menu, I promptly hide behind it. How did this happen? How could I work so damn hard to pass exams and prove myself competent as an adviser, only to find myself sitting next to the one person I was always so bloody hot for. I'd even had to demand he shove his respectful restraint up his arse, in order to lose my virginity with him, for crying out loud!

This is bad, really bad—I can feel an eruption of volcanic proportions brewing.

"You okay?" Jamie asks.

I slowly put the menu on the table and smile. "Sure."

"You were watching Andrea just now with that glint in your eye," he says, smiling.

"What glint?" I ask, my smile wavering...knowing full well my eyes were probably shooting sparks of rancour.

He leans closer and the masculine, spicy scent of his aftershave hits my nostrils and I have to fight the urge not to inhale long and deep.

"The same glint that used to come into your eye, every time I chose to play with Natasha Williams instead of you," he whispers.

My smile traitorously widens. "Well, Natasha was nowhere near as good at football as me, that's why I objected to it." I pause. "And I do not have a glint."

"Yes, you do."

"No, I don't."

"Yes, you do."

"So..." I say, deciding to change the subject before we start wrestling on the floor like we used to. Mmm, not that that would necessarily be a bad thing. "How's life, Jamie?"

"Great. Well, at least now it is," he says, leaning back in his seat and allowing my breathing to return to normal. "I've been dreading this conference but now I've got to say, I'm pretty glad I came."

"Oh?"

He nods and his gaze drifts over my subtly revealed cleavage. "Yes, and don't pretend you don't know why."

Even though I should be thoroughly disgusted at his lewd leering, satisfaction spreads through my abdomen.

"Interesting," I say, calmly. "Whereas I'm here to secure my very first client, a client who is currently so sought after I am going to bring grown men to their knees, weeping tears of failure when they see little old me walk away with him."

"Oh yes, that's right, Malcolm Jenkins is your target, isn't he?"

"How do you know that?" I snap. My nonchalant demeanour well and truly scuppered.

"Mr. Baxter mentioned it to me when you went to your room this afternoon."

I bristle. "Well, I'm not sure he should've done that."

He smiles. "There's no need to play your cards so close to your chest, Hannah. This could work out as a wonderful business opportunity for both of us."

"What do you mean?" I ask, fiddling with the stem of my wine glass and wishing someone would fill it.

"Well, Mr. Jenkins would be a pretty valuable asset to my company database too. Maybe it would be more strategic to join forces?"

"Me and you? Work together?" I ask, my eyes widening.

He shrugs. "Why not?"

"No chance, Jamie. No chance in hell."

Chapter Four

"Is everything all right between you two?"

I drag my eyes away from Jamie to face Condom. "I'm sorry?"

Her laughter tinkles. "It's just the way both of you were sizing each other up just now...Reginald and I are not sure whether to dive under the table for cover, or book you into a double room."

My smile is probably making me look as though I'm straining to push out the biggest poo in history, but at least I'm making an effort. "Ha, ha. No, you're quite safe, Andrea. Jamie and I were talking business, that's all."

"Really? Anything you'd like to share with Reginald and me?"

I look at Mr. Baxter who is staring up at Condom's flawless profile like she's the blow-up doll of his dreams, instead of a living, breathing woman who has every chance of obtaining her fair share of cellulite and droopy tits as I do. Well, maybe not, but still…

"It was nothing. Honestly," I say.

She moves her cat-like eyes from me to Jamie. "Jamie?"

I narrow my eyes. How dare she dismiss me like that! I clear my throat. "I just said it was nothing, Andrea."

She doesn't break her gaze from Jamie. "I know you did. I just wanted to hear Jamie say the same, that's all. There is so much competition at these seminars, it would be very astute of a newly qualified IFA such as yourself to keep any noteworthy tid-bits under your belt."

Jamie meets my eyes and I swear his are sparkling with amusement. Bastard. He grins. "We were discussing nothing of any interest to either you or Reginald, Andrea. I promise."

She leans closer to him and I feel a ball of something fiery ignite in my chest.

"Okay, I'll believe you this time," she purrs against his ear. "But I've got my eye on you."

Oh, Pleeease! I promptly raise my hand and snap at the waiter to bring some wine to our table. Immediately.

The meal progresses without further incident. Well, except for my struggling resolve not to eat every last bit of each delicious course. I manage to leave a morsel (approximately a square inch) of the stilton and leek brulee, one piece of Feta cheese and seventeen crumbs (yes, I counted) of the sticky toffee pudding. Predictably, Condom doesn't even get past the main course before feigning a full stomach.

So with dinner complete, the Master of Ceremonies asks us to make our way to the ballroom where there will be an evening of dancing. As we stand, Jamie is ushered away by some big shot director and I am left alone with only Mr. Baxter and Andrea for company. Mr. Baxter offers us each an arm.

"May I escort you beautiful ladies through to the ballroom?"

Andrea and I shoot glances at each other before simultaneously forcing gracious smiles, and linking our arms through his. If I thought the dining room and lobby were impressive, they are nothing compared to the ballroom. Let's just say as soon as I walk in, the idea of the medieval ball becomes an exciting prospect.

The thick stone walls are swathed in deep purple and amethyst velvet, candles are burning everywhere and at the very back of the room is a beautiful ornate alcove where empty instruments lay dormant, waiting to be played and fill the room with music.

The space is big enough to comfortably accommodate two hundred people, without seeming too enclosed or too vast. Gold candelabras hang from the beams running along the ceiling and each and every one of them glint and shine in royal splendour. In short, it is magnificent and has me longing to wear a pointy hat with a gossamer veil flowing like a shimmering waterfall down my back.

I inhale a shaky breath. The setting could not be more perfect and I begin to feel a little more positive about my costume. Maybe, just maybe, Miss Willoughby chose it with Callahan's reputation in mind, rather than her personal dislike for me.

Mr. Baxter leads us to four vacant chairs and claps his hands together.

"Right. What would we like to drink, ladies? Wine, champagne?"

I ask for a rum and coke knowing another glass of wine will result in me either saying something I regret to Condom, or worse (and yes, you can judge me all you like), shoving my tongue into the mouth of a man I haven't seen in six years. The truth is Jamie may have broken my heart and proved what a money-hungry, selfish son of a bitch he can be, but the hum of sexual attraction between us is ridiculous. He makes me want to strip my clothes off, throw him on the floor and ride him like a God damn rodeo queen.

"Rum and coke for you, Hannah," Mr. Baxter says, "And Andrea?"

"Oh, just a slim line tonic for me, Reginald," she smiles.

Oh, what a surprise. Well, you just sip on your little tonic water, darlin' because I intend having a good ol' time tonight.

Once we're alone, the silence hangs heavy between Condom and I. I purposely turn my head in the opposite direction, indicating idle chit-chat is not an option, but it appears Condom is as thick as she is thin.

"So...I understand you and Jamie used to be childhood sweethearts," she says. "How funny."

I slowly turn to face her. "Funny?"

"Yes, I can picture you all chubby with pigtails and Jamie, all skinny and pigeon-chested. What a hoot!"

"Well, it was a long time ago and for your information it was Jamie who was the chubby one and I the skinny one."

Her smile dissolves. "Oh, I didn't mean to offend you, Hannah. That's the last thing I want to do."

I smile and grit my teeth. "You didn't."

"Good, because I'm hoping we can be friends at least for the duration of the conference. I hate attending these things without having someone else to gossip with."

"I bet you do," I mutter. "So...tell me, Con...I mean, Andrea what do you really think of Jamie? It's been so long since I've seen him, I'd love the low-down from an independent source."

"Oh, he's a darling, an absolute darling. Don't get me wrong, you don't get to where Jamie is without being a cutthroat businessman, but from what I've seen and heard, he treats his staff with the same consideration and care he does his clients. And that is something you don't come across very often, is it?"

Somehow I am not in the least bit surprised, but had hoped

Andrea would be the one to provide some snippet of information that would put Jamie in a more negative light. You know, some incident where he'd screamed at a member of staff and sent her crying from the office. Or a time when he'd been caught with his dick in his hand pleasuring himself in the gents. Something, anything to douse the dangerous fire smouldering deep in my belly.

I turn to watch the musicians walk onstage, but the next question I ask takes me as much by surprise as it does Andrea.

"You're not sleeping with him then?"

She gazes at me from beneath long, black lashes before tipping her head back and laughing. "Oh, Hannah, you really are a breath of fresh air after all the wealthy clients I have to see. All the concern over the proper manners and decorum. You have no such consideration, do you?"

My face is burning hot but I don't care. I want an answer. "Well? Are you?"

She gaze is direct. "No, no, I'm not. At least, not anymore."

"But you have?"

"Yes, yes I have," she sighs. "But if you take my advice you won't waste time trying to recapture the adolescent lust you quite obviously had for him."

"Oh, and why's that?"

"I'm only warning you. I'm not trying to stand in your way or anything."

"So tell me why Jamie is so dangerous then?"

"Simple. He'll break your heart."

There is not an ounce of malice in her gaze and her lips are pursed with genuine concern. I force a laugh but my stomach suddenly feels incredibly heavy.

"Hey, who's to say it won't be me doing the heartbreaking?" I say, breezily. "He doesn't know who I am anymore. I could knock him off his feet if I felt like it."

I pause, waiting for her response, but she remains frustratingly silent. I laugh.

"Anyway, I don't know why we're even talking about this. I'm here to work and nothing else. I only recently managed to get rid of one man who adds nothing to my life, except dirty socks and premature ejaculation. Who needs more of the same?"

She shakes her head. "You and I both know it would be

impossible for Jamie to be guilty of either of those things, Hannah."

I swallow. Jamie? Premature ejaculation? Jesus, my vagina tightens just thinking about my sex life before he left. Phenomenal, absolutely phenomenal. I wave a dismissive hand. "Well, whatever. I don't want to get involved right now and that's the end of it."

"But will Jamie feel the same way? That's the question," she says quietly, before turning to greet Mr. Baxter who has returned from the bar.

I smile my thanks at him and take a hefty gulp of my drink. There's something so wistful in the way Andrea says that last sentence, I am tempted to slide an arm around her shoulders and tell her everything will be okay. I swallow. But it is more than her sadness making my heart beat a little faster, it's the way her eyes momentarily shone with unshed tears that has me wondering what the bloody hell Jamie did to her.

****

Three drinks later and Jamie has still not come back, from wherever it is he disappeared to. But it matters not one dot to me, I am having a fantastic time. The band is beyond excellent. They are stupendous. The four strapping young lads can cover anything from Duran Duran (my personal favourite) to Aerosmith. It turns out that Andrea doesn't dance any more than she eats or drinks, so I am pretty much left to my own devices.

Approximately half an hour ago I took to the dance floor on my lonesome, unable to resist the thump, thump, thump of The Reflex. And much to the satisfaction of my now drunken, goggle-eyed brain, I have loads of new friends to share the night with. I fling my leg high in the air so one of the five lads who are dancing with me can catch it. He does, and proceeds to run his hand up and down my bared leg, while I press and jiggle my body provocatively against his rather hard torso. The people standing in a circle around us absolutely love it. I'm encouraged by the wolf-whistles and clapping, knowing I'm the Goddess of Duran Heaven tonight.

He lowers my leg and I am about to drop to the floor, to demonstrate my flexibility and competence at a forward roll into the splits when a strong hand grips my elbow.

I turn and find myself looking into Jamie's angry eyes. They are no longer emerald green jewels, but more the threatening vivid green of Kryptonite. "Do you fancy another drink, Hannah?" he asks. His mouth curves into a smile but I'm so close to him that I can see the angry tremor at his bottom lip.

Yanking my arm from his grip, I put my hands on my hips. "No thanks."

"Are you sure? There's another drink at the bar with your name on it."

"Really? By the look on your face, I thought you were about to make the huge mistake of telling me I'd had enough."

"Of course not. I want to spend some time with you, that's all. This lot has monopolized you for far too long."

"Well, why didn't you say?"

I brush past him and head for the bar. People clear a path for me as I walk. Goddess, absolute Goddess. I collapse my weight against the bar and wave a hand in the air.

"Yoo-hoo, sexy barman! Over here, sweetheart," I call, laughing at my own bravado.

The scent of Jamie's aftershave hits my nostrils, as his arm presses up against mine when he leans his elbows on the top of the bar. I know I'm swaying but I try to at least keep up with the tempo of the music in an effort to disguise it. I watch his jaw clench and unclench a few times before he wipes a hand over his face and turns to look at me.

"What?" I laugh. "You're looking at me the same way my Dad did when I was seventeen and you brought me home an hour late."

"Did you notice the way people were jumping out of your way just now?" he asks. "You were wobbling from side to side like a bloody Weeble."

"So? Don't even think about judging me," I say, waving a finger in his face. "What I get up to hasn't bothered you for the last six years, so why should it now?"

"Hannah..."

"What? You want a piece of me now, is that it?" I ask, running my hands provocatively down the sides of my dress. "You want a piece of mama?"

Shaking his head, Jamie raises his hand. The barman shoots in front of him like a bullet from a gun. I roll my eyes. God, what is it with everyone brown nosing Jamie Young like he's some kind of king? He's just Jamie. Jamie with hair like the sand of the Sahara, and eyes the colour of freshly-cut grass glistening in the moonlight. Christ, I'm pissed.

"What do you want to drink?" he asks.

"Wine."

He blows out a breath. "Are you sure?"

I reach up, put a hand on the back of his neck and pull him forward so I can press my lips hard to his forehead. I proceed to mash my lips back and forth for awhile and then with a resounding smacking noise, I step back. "Yes, I'm sure."

He stares at me for a second before turning back to the bar. "A dry white wine, please."

I smile triumphantly. But then he holds out the glass to me and I take it even though my stomach gives an unexpected, out of nowhere tell-tale lurch. No, no, no. Not now. Please God, not now. He touches a hand to my elbow.

"Shall we sit outside for a bit?" he says, steering me gently away from the bar.

"Uh-huh."

We weave our way through the guests standing in the corridors and at the front porch. At this point, I can't feel my feet touching the tiled floor and realise Jamie is 'lifting' me along.

We go through a set of French doors and out into the darkness. He leads me along a veranda and I helplessly follow, because now I can't feel anything from the waist down. Eventually, he manoeuvres me on to a bench and we sit down. For a long moment neither of us says anything. We are sitting above the river that runs along the side of the gardens. In silence, we watch the water as it bubbles and cascades over a short waterfall.

I sigh. "Isn't it lovely? How did they build a hotel around a waterfall, I wonder. Do you think they built the walls to keep the water out or built the hotel and then the waterfall?" When no answer materializes, I turn to face him. "Jamie?"

He's watching me, his eyes shining with laughter and his mouth twitching. "You are incredibly drunk, Miss Boyd."

I grin. "Oh, good, you've cheered up! You were a real misery back there. Acting all macho and disproving. What was the matter with you?"

He runs a finger up my arm and I shiver.

"You were getting a bit too excited on the dance floor. I had to stop you before you ended up on your back. I didn't think you'd want to flash your knickers to everybody watching."

I poke him in the chest. "Ah, well, that's where you're wrong, Mister. I'm not wearing any knickers, so that wasn't going to happen, was it?"

He arches an eyebrow. "You're commando? In that dress?"

I smile teasingly. "Uh-huh, rather that than a Visible Panty Line."

"What? Oh, yes, right."

"So, Mr. Jamie Young, tell me about yourself. What have you been doing for the last six years apart from work? Or is that all you've been doing?"

He lifts a hand and brushes the hair from my eyes. "You always did have me spot on, didn't you? I haven't done much other than work since I hit twenty to be honest."

I look up at the blurry stars above us. "You left me when you were twenty."

"Hannah..."

"No, no. It doesn't matter, I'm just saying, that's all. So come on then. Tell me all about your sexual prowess, your relationships. We're bound to go there sooner or later."

"Are we?"

I drop my head to look at him. "Sure we are. Don't act so bloody coy. You want to know who I've slept with you, don't you?"

"Not particularly..."

I let out a wry laugh. "Yeah, right."

He raises his eyebrows. "What does that mean?"

I push his arm. "You're telling me you don't want to know who took over where you left off? Gimme a break."

As he watches me, somewhere at the back of my mind I hear a faint warning bell pinging against the inside of my skull. What-are-you-doing? Ding dong. What-are-you-doing? Ding dong. But instead of heeding it, I throw an arm out and he flinches.

"Come on, Jamie. Don't tell me there hasn't been the odd woman who's managed to get her rocks off with you. Look at you for God's sake."

"What about me?"

"Well, you know, you're all eyes and hair and shoulders."

He grins and my heart swells and presses hard against my

ribcage. And then he inches closer and I have no choice but to look directly into those God forsaken eyes.

"There have been others," he says, slowly. "But you and I know there's only ever going to be one girl for me."

I look at him for a second before tipping my head back and laughing. "God, that is cheesy!"

He laughs. "Hey, can't blame a guy for trying."

"Well, if you're going to flirt with me, at least do it with some kind of style."

"Fine."

And despite my current state of inebriation, I know he's going to kiss me and I've got zero intention of stopping him. His face is half-illuminated by the lights shining from behind the waterfall and he has never looked so handsome. And when he slowly leans in toward me, I don't move back, I move forward. And when his mouth covers mine, I slowly ease my tongue to his and sigh with satisfaction to finally feel back where I belong.

The Sharp Points of a Triangle

Chapter Five

My head hurts. No, not just hurts, pains with such intensity that my left eye refuses to fully open and I'm finding it hard to separate the bite of my teeth. I slowly reach a hand out from beneath the covers and look at my watch. Ten-forty two. I let my hand drop. I have two hours before the lunch meeting begins in the Oak Suite.

I shuffle deeper into the mammoth marshmallow mattress. Another hour's sleep and I'll be right there, feeling on top of the world. But then my eyes snap open and I sit bolt upright as though someone has stuck a rod up my arse.

Jamie. Oh, God. Then the kiss comes back to my memory with alarming clarity. And then so does the subsequent slapping of my hand to my mouth. But the hand had done nothing to halt my spectacular throwing up into the roots of a privet hedge, delicately shaped into a mother squirrel and her young. I flop back against the pillows and groan. Visions of Jamie mopping at the front of my dress with hurriedly gathered grass and leaves, floats in and out of my mind as I sink deeper and deeper into despair.

I squeeze my eyes tightly shut, trying to obliterate the memory of me laughing uproariously as I fall into the lift and flash my boobs at myself in the mirrored wall, as Jamie struggles to pull my top closed. Or had he been trying to get it off?

I lie very still and wait to die, but God isn't playing ball. God knows in his infinite wisdom that I must be punished and He will make me get up, get dressed and walk downstairs to face the one hundred and fifty other financial experts who are staying here. I slam my head from side to side. At least a third of them undoubtedly witnessed my show of unrestrained partying at some point during the evening.

I push myself out of bed. As I walk around to the other side, I freeze. I stare wide-eyed at the shallow indentation on the pillow next to mine. My brain backtracks at forty miles per hour but I can't remember a thing, since the second throwing up incident in the room's toilet. Jamie was definitely there then—did he stay? Did I pass out? I cover my face with hands. This is what living in hell must be like.

Oh, God, oh, God. My eyes dart around the room trying to locate a piece of his clothing, a wallet, anything to confirm that he had indeed spent the night here. But there's nothing. I reach for the phone and then snatch my hand back. What is the use in ringing him? I don't even know what bloody room he's in. I cover my face with my hands. Never in my life have I had a one-night stand. How could I do this? I've finally reached a fantastic place in my career and then I go back to craving Jamie Young, like I did when I was sixteen.

Shit, shit, shit. Well, I'm not having it. If he thinks for one minute I'm going to sit in the background and die of shame, he's got another thing coming. The fact is the sex couldn't have been that good because I've got zero recollection of it. It was probably over before it began.

I shower and wash my hair, rinse out my badly soiled dress (that I find soaking in the bathroom sink), and begin to feel a little better. Well, at least physically, but the mental side is still excruciatingly bad. I walk to the wardrobe and dress in a white blouse and black suit that screams professionalism. I swirl my hair up into a twist and secure it with a subtle silver clip. Taking extra care with my make-up, I paint my lips with a last sweep of colour and hope it will be enough to wipe every trace of last night into the recesses of everyone's memory.

I inhale a long breath, pull back my shoulders and tilt my chin; everything is going to be fine. But then the knock at the door has me swaying on my feet and my breath catching in my throat.

"Hannah? Are you in there? It's me."

I swallow. Hard.

"Hannah? It's Jamie."

Nausea swirls like an eddy in the pit of my stomach and I press a hand there in an attempt to still it. Slowly, I walk to the door.

"Hannah?"

I open the door and we're standing face to face, looking into each other's eyes, gauging what has already happened in such a small amount of time—and just like that I know. I know this is just the beginning and potentially Condom was right. Jamie Young may end up breaking my heart—again. And that tiny piece of knowledge has me wanting to throw up all over again.

"How are you feeling?" he asks.

I smile weakly. "Like crap. But hopefully the make-up has disguised the worst of it. What do you think?"

His gaze runs languidly over my face. "You look fine to me." I arch an eyebrow and he laughs. "Honestly, you do."

"Thanks." I turn back into the room and I hear the door click shut behind me. My nerves immediately charge to high alert. We're here, alone again in my bedroom. I make a big show of picking up my handbag, phone, pen and notepad.

I'm aware of him watching me as I walk around the room. I wish he would say something. Anything to break the silence and his continuous stare. After several endless seconds, my show of cool self-assurance collapses and I whip around to face him. He's leaning against one of the posts of the bed looking gorgeously James Bondish, in his black suit and open neck shirt. I squeeze my eyes shut so as not to become distracted from what needs to be said.

"Look, about last night..."

"I had a great time."

"That's beside the point."

"Oh. Then what is the point?"

I snap my eyes open. "Well, for one we need to be honest about this."

"I am being. I enjoyed every minute of it."

"This is not funny, Jamie. I threw up for God's sake! I was so drunk I can't even remember what happened when we got back here."

"You threw up again."

Heat sears my cheeks. "I know."

"And?"

"Well. What happened after that? Did we...?" I let the question hang in the air.

He smiles and my stomach flips over. "No, Hannah, we didn't. I might be a lot of things but I'm not the type of bloke who does that. I want you to be completely aware of what we're doing when we have sex."

My eyes widen. "When we have sex?" I laugh and cross my arms. "That will not be happening, Jamie."

"Why not?"

The question should seem arrogant, egotistical but it doesn't. The way he's looking at me and the way my own body is resisting the invisible thread between us, makes the whole notion of us tumbling around in bed a very real one. But this is impossible. I'm hardly the same person I was six years ago and I'm not stupid enough to think Jamie is either.

"Look, I've already told you the only thing I'm interested in is bagging Malcolm Jenkins for Callahan's," I say. "I've got a lot to prove at this seminar. Unlike you."

"Meaning?"

"Meaning you're already at the top of your game. You walk around in suits tailored to fit you, people literally bow when you enter a room..."

He laughs. "No, they do not. And if they did, I'd bloody hate it and you know it."

"Why? Why do I know it? I haven't got a clue who you are now, anymore than you have a clue who I am."

He takes a step forward and I raise a hand, warning him off. "Stay there. I mean it. Stay right there."

I want to slap the sexy, gorgeous smile playing at his lips right off, but that would be a huge indication of my current state of weakness. "I've worked hard for this, Jamie. That might not mean a lot to someone who owned his own IFA business by the age of twenty-five. Or to someone who now ranks high in the countries top fifty..."

"How do you know all this? Have you been keeping tabs on me?"

"Of course not! You can wipe that sanctimonious grin off your face. Mr. Baxter has been singing your praises like a God damn groupie, ever since he realised we knew each other. Believe me, I lost interest in you the minute you walked away from the four years we spent together like they never existed."

Our eyes lock for a long moment before he looks away and up to the ceiling. "I left for the opportunity of a lifetime, you know that.

And if I'm honest, it was still the best decision at that time."

"Oh, really."

"Yes, really."

I know deep-down he's probably right. We were kids. Far too young to pursue the marital dreams I had mapped out in my favourite Spice Girls ring binder. I shake my head.

"Look, none of that matters now anyway. The important thing is that you understand I did not come here to get embroiled in some kind of sex fest with an ex-boyfriend. I'm here to work, okay?"

"But you are single?

"Jamie..."

"It's a question, Hannah. That's all."

"Yes, I'm single. Just."

"Just?"

"Yes, just."

He does not need to know how newly single I am. That is none of his business. I brush past him toward the door. "Are we going?"

He lifts his shoulders. "I still think we could make a great team."

I tilt my chin. "Professionally or personally?"

His eyes lock with mine and I feel that damn quivering in the pit of my belly again. "Well?"

"Professionally. For now."

I flash one long, lingering glare at him before turning on my heel, leaving him to shut the door.

****

During the elevator journey downstairs, Jamie tells me he is one of the principal speakers at the meeting. This serves as a blessed relief to my overwrought nerves. At least I know I won't have to spend the next two hours sitting beside him, fighting the urge to either straddle him or strangle him. He heads into a preparation room next door to the main conference hall and I bid him good riddance—for now.

But ho-hum, as I reach the door to the conference hall, I find Andrea is right there by the door waiting to greet me. The Condom has now become Business Woman of the Year but she isn't wearing the requisite skirt suit of every other female in the room. Oh no, Andrea has somehow managed to look twice the professional, although, how she does this when dressed in a sleek black cat suit and heels, reminiscent of Michelle Pfeiffer in Batman Returns, I have no idea.

"Hannah! Good, you're here," she gushes, taking me by the elbow and propelling me towards a table laden with tea, coffee and water. "I was getting worried I wouldn't have anybody decent on side, for the team-building exercise."

I actually feel the blood leave my face as a huge, unexpected tidal wave of nausea whooshes across my insides. "Team-building exercise?"

She nods. "Are you all right? You've turned very white. There's nothing to worry about, you know."

I look into her shining, bloodshot free eyes. "And what exactly does this 'team-building exercise' entail?"

"Well, I don't know what exactly," she giggles. "It's something Lloyds have organized, but these things are usually a major hoot."

I force a smile. "Great."

She links her arm through mine. "From what I can gather it involves costumes, a broom and one of those old-fashioned boxes we used to jump over in gym," she whispers. "I'm so glad I didn't wear a skirt today. You'll have to tuck yours in your knickers I suppose."

I snap my head round to look at her. "I am not..."

She roars with laughter. "You should see your face! Oh, it's priceless, Hannah. I'm pulling your leg, you ninny."

And right then, I know a bad day is about to get a whole lot worse. Andrea had obviously decided to become my new best friend since last night. With her manicured nails still clinging to my forearm, I pull her in the direction of the drinks table.

I manage to lift the coffee pot and pour myself a nice strong cup, before we are asked to take our seat. Reluctantly, I follow Andrea to the two front seats she has thoughtfully reserved for us. I sit down and take a sip from my steaming mug before I feel a tap on my shoulder. I turn around to face two grinning men sitting so close together, the smaller of the two may as well have been sitting on the other's lap. They begin to nudge each other.

"You say it."

"No, you say it."

Oh, great. Here we go. The obligatory Tweedle-Dum and Tweedle-Dee. Why is it every work do, whether it be conference or

Christmas party, there is always two nerdy guys like these two morons? They always walk into a get-together thinking they look like Steve McQueen and Robert Redford, but actually look like a lot more like Danny DeVito and Borat.

"Look, guys," I say, sighing. "Will one of you just say it?"

The taller one's grin spreads even wider. "How's the head?"

And they both burst into hysterical laughter.

"That's it?" I ask. "You've had all night to think of something to take the piss out of me with and that's it? Jesus."

I turn back around to find Andrea watching me with a sympathetic tilt to her head. "Don't take any notice of them. They're just being spiteful. Anyone with an iota of decency would know you do not need to be reminded of last night. It was shameful enough as it is without people enjoying the aftermath."

I'm confused. "Aftermath?"

Colour stains her cheeks. "Well, you know. Everyone saw you on the dance floor, Hannah."

"So?"

"And quite a few of us were chatting in the lobby when Jamie helped you back to your room."

I pull back my shoulders. "For your information last night was nothing. If I'd been out with the girls I most probably would've danced naked on the stage while using Mr. Baxter's head as a swivel ball."

Nothing could be further from the truth, but to see Andrea's mouth tighten into a disapproving line and hear the low whistles of approval from my two new admirers behind me, it was worth the probable onslaught of gossip about me later. Smiling to myself, I lift my cup to my lips as the room descends into silence and the big toffs take their seats at the front.

I watch over the rim of my cup as Mr. Baxter slowly takes the steps onto the stage with careful precision. He slumps into the plastic chair with all the enthusiasm of an exhausted slug. His eyelids are heavy and his pallor is a dodgy shade of algae green. What's wrong with him?

But then my eyes widen and I squirm a little deeper into my chair, as I remember encouraging him to mix a glass of brandy with his whisky. I clench my teeth together. Yes, Your Honour. Guilty as charged. It was I who'd urged the surrounding circle of spectators to clap their hands and shout, 'Down in one, down in one.'

Jamie takes his place behind the podium. How can someone look that good after the night we've just had?

"Good afternoon, ladies and gentlemen and welcome to an hour or two of discussion and healthy debate. Once the boring bit is over we'll be going outside and attempt to demonstrate the efficiency of dedicated team work."

He continues to outline the afternoon and then a discussion opens on the recent changes in various investment funds and their fund managers. I take the opportunity to look around the room. Surely my target client is in here somewhere? I glance over the heads of my fellow IFA's to the back of the room. There is a row of seats set against the back wall.

A man very close to Mr. Baxter's description of Malcolm Jenkins is concentrating on every word being said, while jotting down notes on an A4 pad. With my expert eye to quality clothing, I take in the navy Savile Row suit and Italian leather brogues. Mmm, not short of a penny or two. I narrow my eyes as I study the other two men sitting either side of him. One is too old, the other too young. Nope, the guy in the navy suit has got to be Malcolm Jenkins.

I turn around at the feel of someone's bony elbow hitting my ribs.

"Ow." I hiss, scowling at Andrea. "What was that for?"

She nods toward the podium and I look up. Jamie is looking at me expectantly, a hint of a smile lifting the corner of his lips. He has obviously asked me a question and is waiting for an answer.

"I'm...um...sorry, could you repeat the question?"

"I didn't ask a question, Miss Boyd," he says.

Bastard. "Then why everyone is looking at me? Am I really that interesting?"

He grins. "Oh, yes. And beautiful."

Bastard. Heat flares hot in my cheeks. How dare he undermine me in front of all these people? Didn't I tell him how important this seminar is to my career? Well, fine. If that's the way he wants to play it.

"Why, thank you, Mr. Young."

"My pleasure."

I give an exaggerated grimace. "But don't you think you're overstepping the mark of professionalism a little?"

He clears his throat, his eyes darting quickly over the audience.

"In what way?"

"By talking to me like that."

"It was merely a compliment, Miss Boyd."

"Maybe so, but an inappropriate one. I know men like you never allow anyone to come above your career, but do you really need to stoop so low as to compliment women in full view of your admiring public, just because you can never spare the time to be with one alone?"

The room lapses into silence, except for the shifting of bums on seats and the odd forced cough. I wait for his reply. He stares at me, his emerald eyes are almost black, his jaw tight. I tilt my head to the side.

"Well?"

He blinks and his face instantly changes. Once more the sexy smile is in place and his shoulders relax. "I apologise, Miss Boyd. It won't happen again."

I nod my approval. "Good."

He throws his arms out. "Well, as I was saying, please will you all join me in congratulating Miss Boyd for the fine achievement of becoming the youngest female IFA in the South West? Please, Miss Boyd, won't you stand up and take a bow?"

Tentative clapping turns to full-blown applause.

I meet Jamie's eyes. I watch for a speck of irony there, a flash of piss taking, but there is truly nothing except genuine pride. I nod my thanks before standing up and turning to face the audience. I bow deeply and when I do, I give Mr. Jenkins full eye contact and am more than a little pleased to see him clapping and smiling along with everyone else.

I need to speak to him. And the sooner, the better. I sit back down and Jamie announces there is time for a quick cup of coffee before we go outside. The management makes their way from the platform to mingle with everyone else, and I purposely turn away from Jamie. But I am still so conscious of him that when he brushes past me to speak to someone else, it's as though a surge of electricity shoots up my backside and violently shudders my heart.

"So," says Andrea, holding out a hand. "Congratulations. You must be so proud."

"I am. Very."

She looks at me for a hesitant moment and I feel sure she's about

The Sharp Points of a Triangle

to say more when I feel a tap on my arm.

"Hannah? May I speak with you, dear?"

I turn to face Mr. Baxter. "Of course. Sorry, Andrea."

She smiles gently. "No problem. I'll catch up with you outside."

I watch her retreating back. So sad. I don't know where the thought comes from but it's there, crystal clear in my mind. She seems so heartbreakingly sad.

"Hannah?"

I quickly look down at Mr. Baxter. "How are you feeling this morning?"

He lifts a handkerchief to his perspiring head. "I've got to talk to you. As much as I enjoyed last night it must never be spoken of in the office or anywhere else," he whispers. "I have never acted so raucously in my life. If Mrs. Baxter were to hear of it, she would be insanely jealous and as for Miss Willoughby? Well, suffice to say she would resign purely out of principal."

"My lips are sealed," I say, secretly thinking Miss Willoughby's resignation would be pretty fantastic. "I wasn't proud of myself either when I woke up this morning." I leave out the fact that my behaviour wasn't exactly a one-off as he claims his to be.

He looks relieved. "Well, good, good. I'm glad we understand each other. But I'm must say, you and Mr. Young seem to be getting along splendidly."

Is the man insane? I glance across the room. Jamie's eyes meet mine and I quickly turn away.

"Um, yes, we're fine."

"Was he as handsome as he is now when he was younger?"

A very strange question for a heterosexual man to ask about another man, I know but there you are. I smile softly, "Yes, he was Mr. Baxter. Every girl in the playground wanted Jamie Young to catch them when we played kiss chase."

"And what about you? Did you want Mr. Young to kiss you?"

But before I can answer, there is a tap of silver against china and Jamie is once more standing at the podium.

"Okay, everyone. It is nearing four o'clock so it's time for some fun and games before we change for this evening. Tonight is yours to do as you please. The town centre is a fifteen minute taxi ride away and Reception are more than happy to book any cabs if you should want one."

He flashes a smile around his assembled audience. "Right then, on to the team-building exercise. Put together by Lloyds, this exercise will illustrate both physical strength as well as helping to identify the importance of motivation, delegation and reward. I have split you into teams and when I call your names and group title, can you please come and stand at the front of the room?"

The Sharp Points of a Triangle

Chapter Six

I am livid. No, pissed off. No, fucking furious. I am dressed from high neck to toe in a medieval gown the colour of baby puke and it stinks of moth balls and old men. On my head is not the pointed, veiled hat of a princess but a tea towel, secured in place with a tasselled tie-back from a pair of the hotel's fucking curtains.

The idea of this 'exercise' is for the management to dole out our various team jobs and leave us to get on with it while they swan off and are nowhere to be seen. One team disappeared around the back of The Laurels about half an hour ago, and all we have heard since is a lot of hammering and banging. My job as delegated by Jamie (and when I see him, I'm going to kill him) is to help all the other girls get into their beautiful, jewel coloured costumes like I'm a bloody woman's maid or something.

Mr. Baxter is hurrying along dressed in tights and a quarter-sectioned tunic, which makes him look like an oversized and rather rotund playing card. He comes waddling towards me, excitement evident in the attractive beetroot red of his face.

"Oh, Hannah, you look wonderful. Absolutely wonderful! Isn't this fun?"

I cannot think of one single thing to say that will not result in my instant dismissal. So I manically thread my lace handkerchief through my fingers in a bid to pass the time.

"Hannah, Hannah, yoo-hoo."

Ah-ha. Saved. I turn toward Andrea's voice, hoping and praying she is dressed in the same frigging costume as me. But no, of course she isn't. She's wearing a dress of crushed silk in the soft hue of pale pink rose petals dappled with morning dew. The pointed hat, cascades its ethereal veil over her mane of golden hair, making me want to lunge forward and scratch her eyes out. But I don't. I smile widely and press my hand to my chest in awe.

"Wow, Andrea. You look wonderful."

She opens her eyes wide as she lifts the edges of the skirt with an expression of 'what this old thing?' and yes, I want to slap her across the lush green grass and into oblivion. She rolls her eyes.

"Believe me, I would much rather be wearing what Jamie's in. I am so much more of a tomboy than people realize."

A jolt of the unexpected possessiveness adds to my already volatile state of mind. "You've seen Jamie's costume?" I ask.

"Oh, yes...we...um...let's say he needed a bit of a hand getting into it," she giggles.

"Really?" I smile although my lips are trembling with the effort. "Is he nearly ready?"

She claps her hands together excitedly. "He and Mr. Lawson of Lloyds will be the last two out into the arena, I'm afraid. So, you'll just have to wait a little longer."

"Arena?" Both Mr. Baxter and I ask in unison.

She grins. "You won't believe it when you see it. We're going to have an absolute hoot!"

We and the rest of the entire conference are standing on the impressive driveway of The Laurels waiting for further instructions from a member of Lloyds. Apparently the pinnacle of this afternoon's delights is out of sight behind the hotel. And with each passing second, I'm feeling more and more apprehensive.

Eventually a female member of Lloyd's staff, also dressed in a gorgeous gown of the deepest ruby red and matching pointed hat, comes onto the terrace and directs us around to the back lawns. When I see what has been made from the limited resources of MDF and white banqueting roll, I want to cry. My earlier suspicions are confirmed—we are about to witness a medieval jousting session. I look down at my dress, what the hell is my role going to be in this farce?

Two old-fashioned gym 'horses' have been set up nose to nose, over which two medieval crested blankets have been thrown. To the side of each horse is a broom with the brushes removed and replaced with massive pieces of foam, secured with duct tape. I sigh loudly. It's not as though things could get any worse, is it?

But then Mr. Baxter is once more beside me and I'm reminded that it can. He gives me a hearty nudge in the ribs. "Do you know, Hannah, you are the only lady not dressed in any finery. I wonder if you're supposed to be a young whore, who's going to be locked in the stocks for giving her virtue to all and sundry."

I turn my head slowly. "Thank you, Mr. Baxter, now I feel ten times better than I did a few seconds ago."

"Oh, my dear, I didn't mean anything derogatory by it. I think it's exciting to be different, don't you?"

I look him up and down. "Obviously."

A sudden screech of a badly executed trumpet fanfare causes the entire audience to fall into abrupt silence. The girl from Lloyds takes centre stage.

"If all the ladies would like to go the area circled to the right of me, and all the gentlemen form a line to the left, we can begin."

I follow on behind the beautiful, enthusiastic princesses feeling like a thorn, among a myriad of multi-coloured roses. I am literally the only woman out of twenty dressed in the most hideous dress known to man. What is this? Am I going to be a further object of ridicule? Did they not see me last night? Didn't I give them all a big enough laugh already? Despite my purposeful efforts to sit as far away from Andrea as possible, she tracks me down like the blood hound she is.

"Hannah, you're sitting in the wrong place," she says, tugging on my hand. "You and I have to sit in the very centre of all the ladies."

I narrow my eyes. "Why? And how is it you know more about this little performance than anyone else?"

She gives my hand another tug but I stay where I am. She lets go of my hand and fists her hands at her hips. "Look, I don't know any more than where you and I are supposed to be sitting. Now, Jamie says..."

"Oh, Jamie again. I might have guessed."

She raises her eyebrows. "Is something wrong?"

I sniff rather inelegantly. "It just seems to me that you don't give him a lot of breathing space, do you?"

She smiles and leans forward. "I'm not encroaching on your territory, Hannah. I've told you, he's all yours if you want him."

I laugh. "Want him? Whatever gave you that idea?"

"There's nothing between Jamie and I now."

"But I don't..."

She smiles. "I've told you before. It's about what Jamie wants, that's the problem. Surely you know him well enough to know that."

"I don't know him at all," I say, looking away from her loaded gaze.

"Ah. He left you without as much as a backward glance, didn't he?" she asks.

I feel my eyes widen. "He told you about that?"

"Once. Briefly."

I swallow back the nausea in my throat. "Well, what does it matter? It's ancient history."

"Uh-huh. Well, history has a nasty habit of repeating itself as far as Jamie's concerned. I should know. He did the same to me."

A heavy stone of disappointment drops low into my belly. Part of me wanted him to have changed—to have more in his soul than money and work. But it seems Jamie Young is still the selfish, uncaring man who left all those years ago. That's what I'll keep reminding myself. Focus on the day he left and the pain I felt, not the other one-thousand, four-hundred and sixty-two days where he cared, brought me flowers, made me laugh until I thought I would pee my pants or, the nights when he made love to me until I had to beg him to stop for fear I'd never walk again.

"Did you love him?" The question is out of my mouth before my brain has time to register the inappropriateness of it.

Her eyes lock with mine and they're suddenly shining just a little brighter than a few seconds before. She takes my hand. "Hannah, I..."

"Excuse me, ladies? Can you kindly take your seats?"

We both turn to the see the Lloyds girl gesturing toward two empty places among the others. With a final look at each other, Andrea and I sit down and any chance of continuing our conversation is destroyed by another blast of the trumpet. The girl from Lloyds stands up.

"Ladies and gentlemen, Lord Young and Lord Lawson have come here on this fine July afternoon to battle for the hand of the beautiful Princess Kingsley..."

I turn my head to look at Andrea. Bloody Princess Kingsley. Any ounce of sympathy I have brewing for her slowly disintegrates. Whatever immaterial crush Jamie did or didn't reciprocate, could not have been as bad as the love he so callously threw back in my face. She's beautiful and I'm...well, me. There are plenty of other fish in the sea for someone who looks like a long-lashed, cutsie Condom. She sits a little straighter in her seat and her grin stretches so bloody wide, I'm convinced her face will split in half as her hand flutters delicately above her bulging bosom.

"Oh, please," I mutter.

I am about to get up and leave when the voice of the Lloyds girl comes filtering back.

"But is it really Princess Kingsley who has captured the Lords' attention? Has the duel been arranged as a ploy for one of the Lord's to take the hand of another?"

I swallow. Me? Is she talking about me? Why else would Andrea and I have to sit centre stage? Excitement takes flight in my stomach and when Andrea turns to look at me, her eyes are flashing dangerously. I tip her a wink.

When Jamie walks out, I am ashamed to say that I actually gasp. He looks every inch the knight in shining armour. Jamie is a few inches taller than his opponent and when he walks towards us with his helmet tucked into the crook of his arm, my hands and other parts if I'm honest, moisten.

Andrea shifts in her seat and I wonder whether she's getting the same throbbing between her legs as I am. He lifts the hair that has flopped across his forehead with a sweep of his fingers and then he smiles directly at me. And my heart literally turns over.

Both Jamie and Mr. Lawson bow deeply at the waist and all of us ladies give a discreet nod, acknowledging their intentions. I give a subtle glance to either side of me and there is not one female looking at poor, pock-faced Lawson.

Both men put on their helmets and take up their positions on the 'horses'—well, eventually they do. There are several minutes of hysterical laughter when Jamie misjudges his pivot onto the horse and flings himself all the way over. The entire enactment comes to a momentary halt, so Jamie can get his breath back and try to stop laughing.

But then they're off. Cheers and hoots come from all directions, the women waving their laced-edge handkerchiefs while the male spectators hold their wooden swords aloft. Jamie and Lawson lunge with their foam-covered lances for all they're worth. My conversation with Andrea is completely forgotten. I'm thoroughly enjoying myself, tears of laughter run down my face as I scream wildly for Jamie to knock Lawson off his stead. Andrea tuts and huffs beside me while shooting me glares of disapproval.

"What?" I shout. "Loosen up, will you?"

"Hannah, we are supposed to be in the fourteenth century and you're acting like a fishwife at a soccer match."

"So? This is the best fun I've had in ages. Hey, if Jamie wins your hand, he'll expect you to be a little less tight in the old sack, you know."

"The old sack? What do you...? Oh, for goodness sake!"

I grin as she snaps her head away from me. This isn't turning out to be such a bad day after all. Jamie continues his battle and the excitement mounts, as Lawson holds his lance aloft and slams it to into the side of Jamie's head. There's a huge 'oooohhhh' as we wait with bated breath. Jamie teeters in his saddle.

But then he re-aligns himself and we all explode into great whooping cheers, as he comes back fighting stronger and harder than ever. He knocks Lawson from his 'horse' with one almighty lunge. Yeeessssss! I punch my fist out to the side, completely forgetting about Andrea until I hear her scream and I feel the skin of her cheek against my knuckles.

"Oh, God! Andrea, sorry," I say and I really mean it. An angry red patch is already rising on her face.

She lifts a hand to it and closes her eyes. "What is wrong with you?" she hisses through clenched teeth. "Are you some sort of animal?"

"Andrea, sorry, I really am," I say. "I was just excited..."

"We all were, Hannah, but there are better ways for ladies to conduct themselves."

"I know, I know, but still..."

"No. You are a danger to others, inelegant and crass. I thought we could be friends, but now..."

I stare at her, pull back my shoulders. "Are you kidding me? I said I'm sorry, but if you're going to sit on your tiny size two arse and start preaching at me, I take it back."

"How dare you!"

But then the knights are standing in front of us and we are ordered to stand. We rise. Andrea quickly manages to pull herself together, once she realises Jamie is about to ask for her hand in marriage. Mr. Baxter emerges from the crowd and steps between Jamie and Lawson. He loudly clears his throat and unrolls a fake parchment.

"Ladies and gentlemen, today you have been witness to a show of great courage and honour. The two knights have fought for the hand of one lady and that lady is Princess...wait, wait a minute. Is this correct?"

Mr. Baxter creases his brow in dramatic confusion, waving the parchment in the air as though it has suddenly become incredibly hot. He looks from Jamie to Lawson and back again.

"Am I to believe that it is not the hand of Princess Kingsley that you gentlemen have come here today to claim?"

Both Jamie and Lawson solemnly nod their heads. Mr. Baxter's face suddenly breaks into a grin.

"Well, well, well, today is a day of great surprises. A day of revelation and testimony that we should go through life with our minds wide open, be prepared to accept things are there to be changed, rules are to be challenged and ideas to be explored..."

I try and fail not to roll my eyes. So there's the corporate message. Okay, the teachings have been delivered and understood. Come on, come on, let Jamie claim his bride, for crying out loud.

"...and so may I ask that the victorious knight step forward and claim his lady love," finishes Mr. Baxter.

My heart thumps against my rib cage as Jamie removes his helmet and steps towards me. He drops to his knee and bows his head. I swallow the painfully hard lump in my throat.

He lifts his head and his eyes are glistening emeralds. "Mistress Hannah Boyd, will you please accept this ring as a token of our betrothal to be married?"

My cheeks burn, my eyes water but when I look down at his fingers, my breath stops.

"Oh, Jamie," I whisper, so quietly that only he, I and maybe Andrea can possibly hear.

Between his thumb and forefinger he holds a cheap, metal ring with a glass sapphire set in its centre. A ring that to anyone else would be grotesque, but to me? I lift a hand to my grinning mouth. He won it at the Easter fair when he was nineteen and I was seventeen. He'd said he would keep it until he could buy me something as real and as precious as me.

I blink and one solitary, traitorous tear slips from beneath my lashes. "How did you...? Did you know I would be here?"

He nods.

And then I'm grinning.

"Yes, Lord Young," I breathe. "I gladly accept your proposal of marriage."

And as the rest of the conference and I suspect this doesn't include Andrea, erupt into cheers of congratulation, I breath in Jamie's comforting scent as he presses a kiss to my forehead.

Chapter Seven

But my elation lasts about as long as the metal on this ring will without turning my finger green. I step back. "Wait a minute. How did you know I would be here?" I silently curse the stinging in my eyes. "Did you plan this?"

"Come out with me tonight, Hannah," he whispers. "Please."

"Answer me," I hiss. "Did you plan to do this to me all along?"

"Do what?"

I squeezed my eyes tightly shut for a second before opening them. "To…to….."

His eyes are pleading. "Please. Don't read into this. Come out with me and I'll explain everything."

He holds tight to my trembling hand and I'm aware of Andrea curiously watching us along with Mr. Baxter, Mr. Lawson…and what feels like the entire conference. They have no idea what we are saying and no idea how my heart is unexpectedly aching. I meet his eyes.

"How did you know I'd be here?"

His Adam's apple shifts beneath his stubbled throat. "Your name was on the attendance list."

The attendance list? I stare at him. "There was an attendance list? And why wasn't I given one of those?"

"I don't know. What does it matter…?"

"It matters because if I'd known…"

"What? You wouldn't have come?" he says, gripping my fingers a little tighter. "That's exactly what I was afraid of. I had to see you."

Heat burns my cheeks and I sharply look left and right. "You can't do this, Jamie. You can't carry on as though we still..." I purse my lips together. "As though we..."

"Still like each other?" he suggests.

I snap my head around. "I didn't like you," I snap..."I loved you. There's a huge difference."

His jaw tightens. "Then come out with me."

"No."

"Why not?"

"Because it's too bloody dangerous, that's why."

His eyes continue to bore into mine but the waiting crowd are still watching us. I turn away from him and force a wide smile onto my face. I give them a regal wave and there is a low rumble of laughter. My smile dissolves as I turn back to Jamie.

"Look, let go of my hand. Can't you see we are keeping our adoring court waiting?"

He blinks and looks around him as though remembering where he is. He immediately smiles and pushes to his feet. He grips my hand even tighter. Side by side, we bow deeply. There is another round of applause and the girl from Lloyds steps forward.

"Bravo! Bravo!" she says, clapping her hands. "Well, that went spectacularly well, better than we could've hoped for. A big thank you to Jamie and Hannah. And of course, let's not forget Lord Lawson, Princess Kingsley and well, everyone!" More applause ensues. "Okay, well, thank you for all your hard work. You are now free to do as you please. The Laurel's restaurant will be open from seven-thirty but as Jamie said earlier, please feel free to venture into the town centre where there are plenty of restaurants, bars and clubs."

Slowly people begin to filter off left and right. Jamie stays standing beside me, his fingers intertwined with mine. I can not deny how perfectly our hands fit, or the wave of physical awareness sweeping back and forth between us. Slowly, I extricate my hand.

"I'm...um...going to my room to get changed," I mumble.

"Hannah..." Jamie begins but then Andrea leaps to his side. I'd completely forgotten she was still there.

"Okay, Hannah," she smiles. "We'll see you in the morning. I'm assuming you have plans of your own this evening?"

She moves another step closer to Jamie but he still doesn't look at her. Unfortunately, his eyes are still on me.

"Actually, I do," I say. "I'm going to stay in my room, order room service, watch TV and sleep. Last night was fun but my hangovers seem to take a lot longer to get over these days."

"I'm sure they do. Well then," she says, turning to Jamie and linking her arm through his. "How about me and you hit the town? We could find a nice little restaurant somewhere. What do you think?"

My heart picks up speed.

But then he finally breaks his gaze from the side of my face and turns it on her. "No thanks, Andrea. I've got plans of my own."

"Oh?"

He clears his throat. "Malcolm Jenkins will be accompanying me to a recommended restaurant in town," he says, shifting his helmet from one hand to the other. "I was hoping Hannah would be interested in joining us, but it seems she's not really up to it."

I narrow my gaze. What the bloody hell is he playing at? "Malcolm Jenkins is going out with you tonight? But why didn't you...?"

"It's business, Hannah. What did you think tonight was about? I want to seal the deal with Jenkins as much as you do and if that means forking out the cost of a slap-up meal, so be it."

Liar! I saw what was in your eyes Jamie Young. I saw it and if you think this is a game, you've just taken on the opponent of your life. I slowly shake my head from side to side. "Don't you dare patronize me! Why weren't you honest about Jenkins coming out with you this evening?" I ask, trying not to spit venom on his armour. "Why insinuate we would be alone when you know being alone with you is the last thing I want?"

He smiles and I want to slap him. "Because being alone with you is exactly the thing I want, and I know that irritates the hell out of you."

I can't resist flicking a triumphant glance at Andrea. A girl's got to take her kicks where she can. Yep, she looks as though she's chewing a rabbit's poo pellet. I lock eyes with Jamie again. "Really? Well, I'm sorry but you can keep dreaming about that little scenario ever happening. But as for a meal with you and Mr. Jenkins? Count me in."

He grins. "Good. That's settled then. You've finally seen the advantage of working for Young's instead of a runner-up like

Callahan's."

"What?"

"Jenkins is coming out with me tonight to learn about Young's and what we can do for him and his money. If you come with us, you'll be there as a representative."

I cross my arms. "Yes. Of Callahan's."

He lets out a dry laugh. "He won't want that, Hannah."

"Crap. I think a man of Jenkins' stature will appreciate a bit of good old-fashioned competition, don't you? Why don't we ask him? Let him decide whether he would like to eat with both Young's and Callahan's tonight? That way, he can decide for himself where he wants to put his hard earned cash."

Jamie shook his head. "He won't go for it."

"We'll ask him. Unless of course, you're scared he might actually prefer little old me, rather than an arrogant hot-shot adviser like you."

My reward comes in the flash of colour bursting from the neckband of his metal chest plate. He forces a laugh. "Fine. I'll ask him."

I shake my head. "No, we'll ask him. I'm sure I saw him walking inside. Why don't we see if we can catch him before he goes to his room?"

He stares at me for a long moment before throwing his hands up in surrender. "Fine."

"Fine."

I turn to theatrically march toward the hotel but instead bash straight into Andrea. "Oops, sorry, Andrea," I say. "Are you coming in?"

Her scowl instantly turns into a forced sunshine explosion of happiness. "Oh, no, thank you, Hannah. I think I'll join my colleagues for a nice glass of Perrier before I go upstairs for a long, hot bubble bath."

I smile. "Great. Okay.....well, see you."

And then Jamie and I scramble, half-run toward the hotel, rivalry like a fortress between us. I don't look at him, I don't speak to him. This is war. I will have a seat at that table tonight if it's the last thing I do. We push open the double doors of the hotel with such force that the people standing in the lobby stop what they are doing and turn to stare at us. Neither of us apologises.

I frantically look left and right for a glimpse of Mr. Jenkins' salt and pepper hair and goatee beard. I spot him ordering a drink at the bar. I turn on my heel and sprint toward him. I hear Jamie mutter "Shit!" and know he's right behind me. My mind is racing. No matter what, I've got to get to Jenkins first. I have to charm him with my knowledgeable know-how and impressive pushed-up bosom. But then Jamie's overtaking me on the right hand side and instinct takes over. I stick out my foot.

He tips, and then he tips some more. It's like watching a movie in slow motion. But then the metal of his armour hits the polished stone floor and he's off like a bullet shot from a gun. Careening along at the most incredible speed. I bite down on my bottom lip as I watch a gorgeous six feet two man, screaming wildly, his hands outstretched in front of him as he grasps feverishly at thin air.

"Oops." I say, with a grimace.

"For fuck's sake!" Jamie comes to a stop by way of a china plant pot against his forehead.

I hurry past him. Mr. Jenkins has quite obviously witnessed the entire thing because he's now watching Jamie with his eyes wide, and a glass of red wine hovering at his lips. I smack on a smile and approach Jenkins with my hand outstretched.

"Mr. Jenkins, I am so pleased to finally meet you," I say. "Hannah Boyd. Callahan's Insurance."

"I...um...pleased to meet you," he says, his gaze still at the floor and I know I have approximately two seconds before Jamie's beside me. Shit, too late.

"Mr. Jenkins," pants Jamie. "So glad I found you. Would you like a drink? Ah, you already have one."

I turn and shoot him a glare while keeping a careful smile of wistful content on my lips. But then Mr. Jenkins leans forward with his gaze firmly focused on Jamie's forehead.

"Are you all right, Mr. Young?" he asks. "That was quite a fall."

Jamie lifts a hand to the protruding, egg-shaped lump on his head and a fleeting moment of remorse passes through my conscience, but it's quashed with Jamie's next words.

"Yes, yes, I did. Miss Boyd here was in such a desperate bid to grab your attention, she felt the need to deliberately handicap one of her rivals."

I suck in a breath. "I did no such thing. I..."

But the words catch in my throat as Mr. Jenkins' eyes shift to me. A tremor of fear shudders across my small intestine as his razor sharp gaze meets mine. Malcolm Jenkins is a man in total control, a man whose entire life is input and saved, on the micro-chip of a Blackberry. God knows what he will make of such childish displays of opposition.

"Is this right, Miss Boyd?"

My swallow is audible. "No, not at all. I was merely hurrying to make your acquaintance as I have not had the pleasure of speaking to you yet. Mr. Young happened to trip over my foot as he walked past me."

There's a long tortuous silence and then he draws in a breath. "And how do you know who I am?"

Think, think. Don't mention his money. It's not about his money. Um...shit, ahh...oh, fuck it. "Because you have enough money to buy this place, and I would be a pretty smug financial adviser if you were to pick me out of this lot of amateurs who don't know their equity funds from their cash funds."

I keep my eyes locked with his. I don't move. I wait. Second by excruciating second, I wait for an indication of whether or not I'm going to be burned at the stake or pressed with welcome enthusiasm to his rather distinct man boobs. And then...Yes! His face breaks into a grin and his laughter booms out around the bar.

"Ha, ha! What a diamond in the rough, you are!" he cries, clasping a hand to my forearm. "Let's get you a drink."

Hallelujah!!!!

"A diet coke would be lovely. Thank you."

He chuckles. "Coming right up."

I tip a victorious wink to Jamie when Jenkins turns to the bar, but my gloating disintegrates when I see the huge, whacking great grin on his face. He actually looks proud, as if I'm his bloody girlfriend or something.

"What?" I demand, failing to wipe off my own grin.

"You're bloody fantastic, that's what," he says, leaning so close to my ear I feel the whispering heat of his breath.

"Am I? Even though you've got a rather attractive lump on your head, right now?" I ask, shivering right down to the tips of my toes.

"Yep, even though."

"God, you're sad."

I turn back to Mr. Jenkins and take my drink from his hand. "Thank you."

"You're welcome. So you already know Mr. Young then?" he asks.

"Yes, we're...old friends."

He beams. "Well, in that case I have the most fabulous idea."

"Oh?" I ask innocently.

"Yes. If Mr. Young has no objections, I would love you to join us for dinner tonight, Hannah. What do you say, Mr. Young?"

Jamie nods. "That's absolutely fine by me."

****

When I let myself into my room an hour later, a heavy exhaustion falls onto my shoulders. I walk to the bed, unbuttoning my hideous costume as I go. I throw the tea-towel in the general direction of the bin and the dress is left in a pile on the floor. I collapse onto the mattress. Images of Jamie, past and present swirl around inside my head until I feel dizzy.

I haven't felt this much sexual excitement since I discovered The Rabbit. But deep inside I know it is madness. For one, he's my main rival at the conference, two, he's obviously still the type of man who can walk away from a relationship without a care in the world, a la Andrea and three, I have always made it my personal rule never to reinstate a finished relationship. Why go back? It will never work out.

So why am I so excited to be going out with him tonight? Why does the thought of fighting it out with him to secure Mr. Jenkins' business fill me with so much sexual arousal, that it is weirdly freakish? I cover my face with my hands. And I just know he will be feeling the exact same way. I drop my hands from my face. Maybe I need the voice of reason to interject. That will get me back on track and focusing on my career. Yes, that's it. That's what I need to do.

I reach for my phone and inhaling a shaky breath, dial Sam's number.

"Hannah! Hey, how are you lovie?" she cries.

"Great, how are you?"

"Fine, fine. So, are you having a good time?"

The question stumps me. Am I? "I don't know."

"You don't know?"

Unexpected tears blur my vision. "I honestly don't know."

"Hey, babe, what's happened? Are you crying?"

I nod. "It's...it's Jamie."

"Jamie? What's he done?"

"He hasn't really done anything," I say, covering my eyes with my arm. "It's me. I think....I think I want him, Sam."

There's a long, long silence. I say nothing, just wait for Sam to gather her senses and tell me that yes, as I suspected all along, I have lost my freaking mind! I hear her take a long, deep breath.

"You want him?" she asks slowly.

I swallow. "Yes."

Another silence. "Does he want you?" she asks.

"I don't know. One minute he's sidling up to me like a dog on heat, the next he's talking about business meetings and sealing deals. As far as I know he could be playing one massive game and I'm the main pawn."

"What's your gut telling you?"

"I don't know."

"Have you thought about Mark?"

I fling my free arm up in the air. Now this, I am not expecting. "Mark? What's Mark got to do with anything? You can't stand him."

"I know. That hasn't changed. The trouble is, now you've been away from home for more than forty-eight hours, Mark's decided he's going to start following me around like a God damn sniper."

"He's following you?"

"Yep."

"Oh, God, I'm so sorry."

She blows out a breath. "Hey, if he wants to hang around outside my work pretending to be reading Salmon Fishing in the Yemen by Paul Torday, when the last thing he read was Dr Seuss, let him carry on."

I grin. "He's really doing that?"

"Uh-huh. Now forget sad Mark, Mr No Life. Do you want my honest opinion about Jamie?"

"Yes."

"You're not going to like it."

"Just tell me."

She inhales a breath. "I think you should go for it."

"Go for it?"

She sighs. "I'm not talking about some big romance of the decade thing. I'm talking good old-fashioned banging of the uglies, that's all. You've been tied up with Mark for so bloody long you've forgotten how to enjoy yourself. Don't think about the consequences for once in your orderly, studious life. Just enjoy the fact that after six years, Jamie's still got the hots for you."

I sit up. "But I can't just...."

"Look, it's not as if you want to marry Jamie, is it? What you really want to do is jump his delicious bones." She pauses. "I'm assuming his bones are still delicious?"

I swallow as red-hot heat flares between my legs and tweezers of acid scorch my nipples. "Yes, he's still bloody delicious."

She snorts. "Well, get it on then, girlfriend!"

I squeeze my eyes shut. "But if I jump into bed with him, it could mean the end of my career before it's even started."

Sam sighs. "And how do you figure that?"

"I want to be taken seriously, Sam. I've worked hard for this. Mark never believed I could do it, but Baxter did. He's trusted me to go after one of the biggest accounts Callahan's could possibly ever have on their books. How can I throw all that away by getting the reputation of being some sort of pathetic bunny boiler, who still fancies a guy who walked away from her years ago?"

"Can you hear yourself? Stop analyzing it and just go for it. You're a big girl. You can control this situation. Go out tonight, thank him for a lovely evening and close your bedroom door if that's what you want. I'm not asking you to do anything you don't want to."

Excitement gathers momentum in my stomach. "You really think I should?"

"Yes. This is Jamie. You have to know one way or the other, babe."

I press a hand to my belly and take a deep breath.

"Okay. Okay, you're right. I'll go with the sole intention of taking this account right from under his nose and then see what happens next."

"There you go. Simple."

"And if needs be, I can come upstairs and get into bed alone."

"Of course you bloody well can. Now put this phone down and

The Sharp Points of a Triangle

go make yourself look like a one-thousand-pound a night hooker."
"Sam!"

Chapter Eight

Jamie gives a low whistle as I enter the bar and I whip my hair back over my shoulders, as though this is an automatic response every time I walk into a room. I'm awarded with one of his smiles and immediately feel like the sexiest woman in the room. Despite Sam's advice, I disregarded the hooker route and instead carefully dressed in a slinky satin, midnight blue dress that accentuates my thirty-six C rack and nips in at my waist with the help of a two-inch black belt. The skirt falls in soft folds to just below the knee, leaving my bargain eBay® purchase of the year on full display. Black, four-inch heeled Manolo Blahnik sling-backs.

"Drink?" he asks, lifting his glass of red wine.

I smile. "Sure. Dry and white, please."

He steps forward and touches a hand to my waist which feels deliciously small within the span of his hand. "You look amazing, Hannah."

"Thank you."

And I still look professional. Once I launch my attack on Mr. Jenkins, neither he nor Jamie is going to know what's hit them. As long as I can keep the invisible sexual chemistry between Jamie and me to a humming vibration, rather than an all out fanfare with fireworks and marching band, everything should be okay.

"No sign of Mr. Jenkins yet?" I ask, accepting an ice-cold glass of Chablis.

He shakes his head. "Not yet. We'll give him another ten minutes or so and then I'll ask reception to buzz his room."

I sip my wine. "So...where are we actually going tonight? I hope I'm not over-dressed."

"You're dressed perfectly."

I smile. "As are you."

"Why, thank you, ma'am."

Our eyes locked over the rim of our glasses and my fanny whirrs into overdrive. To put it bluntly. Jamie looks like he should be eaten. His crisp white shirt is open at the collar, the shoulders of his jacket filled with broad, muscular shoulders and his formal trousers are tailored beneath and around a subtly protruding bulge of pleasure...

I bite my lip as I raise my eyes from his groin to his face. He smiles softly and leans close enough for his aftershave to hit my nostrils like an airborne aphrodisiac.

"You're a naughty, naughty girl," he mutters.

I smile impishly, no shame at being caught looking in a place I have no right to be looking. "I know."

"You're going to make me beg, aren't you?"

I take a step back and clear my throat. "So...is this a restaurant you've been to before?" I say, changing the subject in the hope I can get my nipples under control, before they poke straight through the material of my dress.

He watches me for a moment longer. "Nope, recommended by the hotel. It's called The Net."

"Seafood by any chance?"

"I hope that's okay....."

I lift a hand. "It's fine. I love seafood."

He slowly exhales. "Good. That's good."

I pull my eyes away from his unrelenting gaze, in order to catch my breath. He suddenly sounds nervous. Almost as though he's booked the restaurant for a date, rather than a three-way business meeting. Heat warms my cheeks. I cannot allow anything Jamie says or does to trick me into trusting him he wants Jenkins as much as I do, and you don't get to Jamie's heady height of success without some ruthlessness along the way.

Neither of us speaks for a few loaded seconds and then the hotel concierge approaches Jamie.

"I'm so sorry, Mr. Young," he says. "I have a message for you from Mr. Jenkins. He is feeling a little under the weather and has asked whether it's possible to postpone your dinner this evening until tomorrow night?"

Disappointment lands heavy in my belly. Damn it. Now, I'll have to endure another twenty-four hours of tip-toeing around waiting for my chance to strike Jenkins unexpectedly in the gullet. I watch Jamie from the corner of my eye. His jaw has tightened and if I'm not mistaken, he looks a little unsure what to do next. Something I thought I'd never see.

"That's fine," he says to the concierge. "Could you kindly tell him both I and Miss Boyd hope he is feeling better soon and we'll meet up sometime tomorrow?"

"Of course, sir."

We simultaneously take generous gulps of our drinks while watching the concierge walk away. But as soon as my glass is away from my mouth, words spill out before my brain can catch up.

"Well, there's no point in wasting the table is there?" I say, happily. "Why don't you get us a cab?" What is the matter with you? For once in your life, can't you keep your mouth shut?!

He turns to face me. "Are you serious?"

I lift my shoulders. "Sure, why not?"

A smile tugs sexily at his lips as he places his empty glass on the bar. "Wow."

I swallow. "What?"

His eyes sparkle with an invisible boost of life, making my stomach turn over and my toes curl.

"I just didn't think you'd even consider coming out with me alone," he says. "Not after everything you said today."

My heart is racing. Beneath the soft light of the bar and with his eyes and mouth so full of sudden happiness, I remember the way he used to look, standing outside my bedroom window waiting to take me on our first grown up trip to the theatre. I match his smile.

"I've had a little talk with myself," I say, finishing off my wine and placing the glass next to his.

"And?"

"And, I'm going to enjoy my time here. And if that means tolerating your company every now and then, so be it."

"That doesn't sound very complimentary."

"It wasn't meant to be."

He tips his head back and laughs before offering me his arm. I take it and together we head to reception to book a taxi.

****

The sun is going down when we pull up outside the restaurant. He offers me his hand as I get out of the cab and I take a long deep breath, before taking it and stepping onto the cobblestone street. It is one of those sultry summer evenings the British desperately yearn for. The sky is slowly turning pink out across the huge lake ahead of us, as the restaurant lights flicker and dance on its surface. It could not have been built in a more strategic location, high above the lake's banks.

Tall Victorian lamps flicker in each corner of the huge wooden veranda, stretching out upon the water. The tables are dressed in soft lemon table cloths, the chairs painted gleaming white. The kitchen and inside seating area are set back from the outside tables giving the diners plenty of privacy and space. I jump when Jamie places his hand at the base of my spine.

"Shall we?"

I nod, unable to trust myself not to turn and grin up at him like a girl of seventeen wearing rose-tinted glasses. We are shown to a table in the far corner of the veranda and when we sit down it feels as though we are in the middle of the water. Alone. And despite my reservations, it feels wonderful. I watch his profile as he glances around the restaurant. Alone with Jamie. Something I thought would never happen again. He's the only man I have ever loved before and since that fateful day six years ago.

He turns and I have to blink to sharpen my blurred vision. I force a relaxed smile. "This is lovely, Jamie. Really lovely. Thank you."

"I'm not sure why you're thanking me," he smiles softly, "but you're welcome anyway."

I tread carefully. He cannot know what I've been thinking. I pull my shoulders back and place my business head firmly in place. "It's just nice to get away from the conference for awhile, that's all." I pause. "Even though I have absolutely no intention of leaving without Jenkins' commitment to Callahan's."

He watches me carefully for a long moment before leaning back in his seat. "We're back to business then?"

I nod. "Always."

"I see." He blows out a breath, looks past me toward the lake. "And does that mean you'll do whatever it takes to get Jenkins in your pocket?"

I narrow my eyes. "To a certain extent. Yes."

He turns, meets my eyes. "But that doesn't include working for me?"

"No."

"Why not?"

"It's a ridiculous idea."

"You won't even think about it?"

I put my hands into my lap to hide the trembling. "Why would you want me to work for you, Jamie? You have no idea of my work ethic, my capabilities. It makes no sense, and I do not believe for one minute you do anything nonsensical."

He leans forward, his gaze intensifying until my heart is pounding. "I want you, Hannah."

The saliva leaves my mouth but I refuse to look away. I swallow. "Why? Because you know how good I am at my job? Because you know how far I've come in the last twelve months and now you want to poach me from Callahan's? If you knew me at all, you'd know how much loyalty I have to Mr. Baxter and Callahan's."

"I know that. But I, on the other hand, always do whatever I have to, to get what I want."

The way he's looking at me, the way my body is traitorously heating beneath his gaze, confuses me. I no longer know what we're talking about—business or me? The only sound is the swishing of the water against the wooden pillars beneath us, and the odd burst of subdued laughter somewhere in the distance. I look at him and the answer suddenly looks clear in the softness of his eyes. I shake my head.

"Jamie, don't do this."

"Can I take your drinks order? Sir? Madam?"

We both jump at the sound of the waiter's voice. Jamie clears his throat and picks up the wine list, neither of us have even looked at since we sat down.

"Red or white wine?" he asks.

"White."

He slaps the menu shut and holds it out to the waiter. "A bottle of the Sauvignon Blanc, please."

"Of course, sir," says the waiter, making a note on his pad. "I will be back shortly to take your food order."

Once we are alone again, Jamie leans forward on his elbows. "Why don't we take this chance to talk?"

"About what?" I say, busily shaking out my linen napkin.

"Hannah. Please. Look at me." I don't but he continues anyway. "I want to talk about why I left."

I meet his eyes and every single ounce of pain he inflicted bites at my skin, my heart, my soul. "There's no need," I say. "You left for London so you could pursue your dream of making an absolute fortune by the age of twenty-five. I stayed behind, eventually healing a heart smashed into so many pieces I thought I might die. Now here we are, a few years on sharing a meal together like two mature adults. What else is there to say?"

He opens his mouth to speak but then Jon Bon Jovi fills the warm summer air, and I dive-bomb into my bag like a kamikaze pilot and punch the talk button on my mobile.

"Hello?"

"Hiya babe, it's me."

My tongue curls back into my suddenly dry mouth. And conveniently sticks to the roof of my mouth. "Maarkk?"

I glance at Jamie. He leans back in his chair, his face a sombre mask of interest as he plucks and proceeds to tear apart a bread roll from the basket the waiter has placed on the table. I peel down my tongue. "Why are you ringing me?"

"'Cause I'm pissed out of my brain, why else?"

I smile my thanks at the waiter as he fills my glass with the most welcome golden liquid I could ever ask for. I take a hefty gulp and squeeze my eyes shut.

"Mark, I'm going to put the phone down now."

"Hannah. Babe. No, listen to me. I just called to say I love you. Hey, that's a song!"

My face turns to a burning hot plate of fire as Mark bursts into a Stevie Wonder rendition. "Very nice. Well, bye bye then. Do not call me again!"

I snap the phone shut and switch it off. I turn to the waiter and order scallops to start and baked cod for my main meal. He moves away and I take another gulp of wine before having the guts to lift my eyes to meet Jamie's.

"Who's Mark?" he asks.

I pick up my knife and start hacking at my bread roll as though it is Mark's head. "My ex. Conversation closed."

"Ex? Why is he still ringing you?"

I attack the butter with the same verve as the roll. "What can I say? Just because you couldn't see how fantastic I am, he obviously can."

The silence that follows rolls out a sea of accusation and hurt. I'm slowly slipping lower and lower into the depths of the undignified rejected ex syndrome.

"How long?" he asks.

I snap my head up and look him directly in the eyes. "A lot longer than yours."

"Hannah..." He laughs. "For God's sake."

And then my own laughter bubbles at the base of my throat.

"Oh, shut up!" I say, picking up the remainder of my roll and hurling it at him.

When our laughter finally subsides, we sit for a long moment just looking at each other. And as I watch the breeze lift the soft hair at his forehead, and see the reflection of the candle burning against the dark green of his eyes, I know there is no going back.

"Did you love him?" Jamie asks, breaking the silence.

I shake my head. "No."

"Did you think you did?"

I swallow. "Yes."

"Was he good to you?"

"He did the best he could."

There's another long silence as we both contemplate this. And deep down I know it's the truth, Mark did the best he could. It just wasn't enough, not for me.

"What made you call things off?" Jamie asked.

Because he was just another one who wasn't you. "Because I want more in my life than I could ever have with him."

He slowly nods and I can tell he is digesting what little I have told him. My turn.

"What about you? Did you love Andrea?"

Shock registers for a second before being wiped from his face. "She told you?"

"Uh-huh. Thirteen months, wasn't it?"

"Yes. And no, I didn't love her."

"She loved you."

"Yes."

"Did you break her heart?"

"Yes."

Nausea swirls around in my stomach, rises bitter in my throat. What did I expect? I am saved from saying more when the waiter reappears with our starters. The scallops do nothing to calm my stomach.

"Hannah?"

"Yes?"

"I can't bear the thought of you hating me."

I blow out a breath. "I don't hate you, Jamie. How could I? I haven't even seen you for six years."

"I see it in your eyes."

I pick up my fork. "Well, let's eat and see if you can't make it disappear."

Chapter Nine

The meal is delicious, the wine exquisite, the company excruciatingly tempting. An unspoken agreement passes between us and we both know, mentioning either Mark or Andrea again will spoil this one special night. Sometime over the last two hours, darkness has fallen, cocooning us in a star-spangled blanket of obscurity. No-one here knows us or our history. And as we finish off the second bottle of Sauvignon Blanc, I can see he is feeling as foolishly happy as I am.

"How about a walk?" he suggests, looking out across the lake. "There's a man-made beach not far from here. We could pretend we're in the Caribbean."

I grin. "Sounds like a plan."

He gestures to the waiter for the bill and that's when I notice we are the only ones left in the restaurant. I stand up and feel the soft blush of attraction heat my body in the dropping temperature. I know I'm letting myself believe this one night won't lead to disaster but for now, I truly don't care. I am a twenty-four year old, single woman, on the brink of a career that could take me wherever I want it to. I am no longer a girl of eighteen without a clue and I 'm not in love with Jamie.

We leave the restaurant and take a slow stroll to the beach and then I let him take my hand when I bend down to take off my Manolo Blahniks. And I let him stay holding it as we step onto the deserted beach. It is nearing eleven o'clock and the moon is casting long shadows across sand that feels warm between my toes. We walk in silence farther and farther along the beach until we come to a spot sheltered from the breeze. He turns to face me.

"Are you glad you came out with me tonight?" he asks.

I inhale a deep breath and put a finger to the corner of my mouth as though pondering his question. "Well, the meal was fantastic, but the company? Mmmm...not so sure."

He smiles. "Good, 'cause this place is too nice to enjoy alone, so I don't want you bailing on me, okay?"

The tone of his voice implies he is referring to more than tonight. We carry on walking. "Do you want to know who convinced me that coming out with you wasn't such a bad idea, after all?" I ask.

"Who?"

"Sam Winslow."

"Sam Winslow...Sam Winslow...hey, not your friend who was never away from your side? Blonde hair, blue eyes..."

"The one and only. And she's still pretty much at my side twenty-four seven now."

"Wow, well I can't say I'm surprised," Jamie says, bending down to pick up a shell. "You were never one to abandon one friend for another. If there's one thing you are, Hannah Boyd, it's loyal."

My stomach twists uncomfortably. "Can I ask you a question?"

"Sure." He launches the shell into the water ahead of us.

"When you saw my name on the attendees list, what were your intentions?"

He turns to face me. "You really think I had some big plan in mind when I came here, don't you?"

"Didn't you?"

"No. I saw your name and if I'm honest, it was like a kick in the gut. I had to see you. Just to see if you'd...I don't know, changed."

"And have I?"

"I didn't think so at first. But yes, you have."

"In a good way?"

He steps closer and touches a finger lightly to my jaw. "I thought it would be impossible to better what you were before, but now? Now you're even more confident, sexy and fascinating."

I give a nervous laugh to cover the burning beneath his finger. "God, I must've been pretty bloody boring before then."

He smiles and tips his head forward. He's going to kiss me. Do something. Say something. Move yourself.

"Fancy a swim?" he whispers.

"What?" I ask, taken completely off guard.

"I said, do you fancy a swim?" He takes a couple of steps back and shrugs off his jacket. "Come on, it'll be fun."

And then he pulls his shirt over his head and I lose the basic human ability to speak. To see him fully clothed is one thing but to have a chest and a stomach like his revealed to my poor, protruding eyes with no prior warning, is just plain mean. I watch my hand slowly stretch out and cannot do a damn thing to stop it. My fingers brush over his skin, his nipples, lower and lower.

"Now this I wasn't expecting," he murmurs.

"What?"

I look down at my fingers lingering above the waist band of his jeans. Have I lost my mind? I whip my arm back so quickly I hear a crick in my shoulder.

"Sorry, sorry, I don't know..."

But then his lips are pressing down hard against mine. I feel his arm come round and support my back which I am bloody grateful for, because although swooning women are a thing of the past, I'm not sure my legs will hold me. He pushes his tongue tentatively into my mouth and I lift mine to meet his, his lips linger somewhere between soft and firm, and for a long moment my mind is whirling. There is a red hot stirring between my legs and I kiss him back with everything I've got.

I lift my hands to his face and pull him closer. A gasp escapes my lips when he gently nudges my feet apart and presses a thigh firmly between my legs. He begins to tug at the hem of my dress and with our lips still connected, I lift my arms. The silky material glides up my back and our mouths separate for a brief moment as he lifts it over my head, before joining once more.

"Hannah."

He breathes my name into my mouth and I feel a solitary tear slide slowly down my cheek. This is all so wrong, but I can't stop. I don't want to stop. Eventually, I have to pull away for fear of drowning.

"Let's swim."

We quickly discard the remainder of our clothes and sprint towards the water. I cannot believe what I'm doing, and I'm secretly hoping the moonlight isn't bouncing too savagely off my lily white ass. My breath catches as I leap head first into the waves and when I re-surface, Jamie snatches me close.

I can feel the length of his erection pressing up against my belly. I smile as I reach up to push the hair from his eyes. "Now that's just showing off," I say.

"What is?" he murmurs, his eyes lingering over my breasts as they bob above the water.

"There aren't many men who could dive into cold water like this and maintain an erection of that size."

He raises an eyebrow. "That size, huh? The lady is impressed."

I reach my arms around his neck. "Nah, not really."

He throws his head back and laughs. The sound penetrates my skin and fills my heart. And I know in that moment, I want to hear him laugh forever. I look into his eyes and purposefully, push the notion of regret to the back of my mind. I lean closer and his smile slowly dissolves as my lips find his. I taste salt, feel heat and hear my own blood rushing through my veins as he lifts me. My legs easily encircle his waist. The world drifts farther and farther away from us. It's Jamie and I, alone, happy, re-discovering each other.

"Hey you, Mr. and Mrs. Naked Lovers! Yoo-hoo!"

We break apart and turn to the shore. I slap one hand over each tit. "Oh, good God. Nooooooo!"

But it's too late. The three teenagers have taken our clothes and they're running, screaming and laughing up the beach like the little shits they are. I turn to Jamie who is staring at them as though hypnotized. I shake him.

"Jamie! Quick, do something." Silence. "Jamie, for Christ's sake!"

He slowly shakes his head. "The little bastards."

****

If my humiliation wasn't complete before, it is now. I walk up the steps into the hotel and hang my head in shame. At this point I must give Jamie credit for his valiant attempt at retrieving our clothes. After I had gently nudged him in the region of his abruptly flaccid penis, he took to the shore like a man possessed. I watched in hopeful wonder as he ran down the beach, his arms waving above his head with as much ferocity as the swinging member between his legs.

Of course, with all his yelling and my screaming, it wasn't long before this beautiful performance was witnessed by the newly assembled crowd of spectators cheering from the promenade.

But that was then, this is now. It is ten minutes past midnight, our freezing cold bodies are draped in the dirty plastic fabric of the two abandoned windbreaks Jamie found on the beach. My dried up, salt-covered hair resembles the nest of a large golden eagle and I am shivering, crying and laughing all at the same time. And to top it all, I can't wipe the trail of snot running from beneath my nose without exposing myself to the elderly couple to my right who, up until twenty seconds ago, were enjoying a quiet night cap.

I shuffle to the reception desk behind Jamie.

"Um, keys to rooms 401 and 412, please," he says, smiling politely.

The receptionist peers around him, looks me up and down before turning back to Jamie with a rather loud sniff.

"I see," she says.

I pull myself up to my full five feet seven inches, ready to launch an indignant attack when I feel Jamie's heel dig into my toes.

"Ow! What are you doing?"

He moves his foot and slowly turns from the receptionist to me, the polite smile still firmly fixed in place. "Don't even think about it."

"What?" I protest, innocently.

"I think it best if we apologise for our current state of undress and hope this kind lady, will still let us spend the next two nights in this beautiful establishment, don't you?"

I open my mouth to say more but then drop my shoulders in defeat. He's right. I look like a lunatic escaped from an asylum for crying out loud. Do I really want to be thrown out of The Laurels looking like this? I force a smile and we both turn back to the receptionist.

"I'm sorry," I say.

The corners of her mouth turn up in a smug smile and she lets out a long, melodramatic sigh. "Oh, very well. Here are your keys."

She drops them into Jamie's outstretched hand. The sudden lack of his two hand hold on the windbreak results in a three inch gap at the back. I consider telling him that his beautiful tight arse is on show when I glance to my right and see the elderly woman having a good old ogle. I clamp my lips tightly together. The woman must be eighty-two if she's a day, how many more moments like this is she going to enjoy?

Jamie turns and together, we walk silently into the lift and travel to the fourth floor. The doors part and we carry on walking past the staring eyes of the fellow conference attendees who are saying their goodnights in the corridor. Jamie stops outside my door, inserts the key and lets the door swing open. Unable to extend an arm to gesture me inside, he tilts his head in the general direction instead. I bite back the urge to laugh.

"Thanks," I manage.

"You're welcome," he says, rolling backwards and forwards on the balls of his feet.

"You look adorable," I smile.

"You don't."

I open my mouth wide, "Why, you..."

But he cuts me off. "It's a joke."

We exchange mischievous smiles but after a moment, Jamie's slowly dissolves as his gaze wanders over my face. For a few seconds, neither of us speaks and then he leans close and I smell the salt water upon his skin. His breath grazes softly against my ear.

"See you in the morning. Sleep tight," he whispers.

My heart thumps hard against my ribcage. "You too."

We step apart just as Mr. Baxter gets out of the elevator and comes hurrying towards us. His face is flushed and his hands are balled into fists as they swing at his sides. He clearly does not come bearing good news.

"Hannah? What on earth do you think you're doing?" he says. "Now, I am not one to poo-poo on young people's fun, but this? Walking around a hotel of this calibre in nothing but a...what is that?"

"A windbreak," I mumble, staring at the carpet. "We found it on the beach."

"The beach? What were you doing...?" He stops as understanding hits him between the eyes. He slowly tilts his head back to look at Jamie. "Mr. Young, I am disappointed you would take advantage of Miss Boyd's naivety. She is a young girl who has great career aspirations with Callahan's. I wouldn't have thought it would have been you trying to ruin such a path for her."

I feel my heart swell for the little man in front of me who is defending my honour with such vigour. I look pointedly at Jamie who clears his throat.

"Believe me, Reginald. It was not my intention to ruin Hannah's career. In fact, I care very much about her career."

"You do?"

I and Mr. Baxter ask the question in unison. The expression on Jamie's face is as though he's trying to convey some secret message to me. I watch him and then the reason for everything that happened tonight becomes clear. Jamie still wants me to consider joining him at Young's. How could I have been so bloody stupid?

My fingers tightened around the edge of the windbreak as Jamie continues to speak. I want to punch him.

He nods. "You have the makings of a fine financial adviser," he says, looking straight into my eyes. "And whether you work for Callahan's or..." He pauses. "Anyone else in the future, I'm sure you'll be a valuable asset to their team."

Mr. Baxter looks from me to Jamie twice before aiming a steely gaze up at Jamie. "Well, yes, good. As long as you understand that, we'll say no more about tonight's unfortunate events." He turns to me. "But as for you, Hannah..."

I drag my gaze away from Jamie. "Mr. Baxter, I..."

He holds up a hand to silence me. "What am I supposed to do about this show of complete disrespect? Last night got a little out of control for us all, but this act of tomfoolery is just too much."

"I'm sorry, really I am," I say. "Believe me, tonight has turned out to be one of the worst in my life."

From the corner of my eye, I see Jamie turn to look at me. "What?" he says.

I continue to look at Mr. Baxter. "Tonight has been full of incidents that I didn't expect and didn't ask for," I continue. "Everything that has happened...or been said tonight, is now making me feel sick to my stomach."

Mr. Baxter stands between us, his eyes narrowing into slits in an attempt to figure out whether my apology is genuine.

"Right, good. Well, I accept your apology and I think it best if we all say good night. Tomorrow is another day."

"I agree," says Jamie, stiffly. "Goodnight."

And with that, he turns and walks down the corridor toward his own room. A leaden weight descends on my heart and I suddenly find it hard to breathe. I turn to Mr. Baxter.

"I'll be on my best behaviour from now on, I promise."

But instead of the final admonishment I am expecting, he looks up at me with sympathy in his eyes and a wobbly smile at his lips. "Mr. Young is a handsome man, is he not?"

I curse the burning at the back of my eyes. "It's not what you think."

"I'm not thinking anything, Hannah. You know as well as I do that Callahan's has a reputation of hard work, family, love and lasting relationships, not one of one night stands and failing at the first difficult hurdle."

He raises one eyebrow and gives me a look to see if I understand, and I do. He's warning me off Jamie, but there's no need. Jamie is doing a pretty good job of that all by himself.

Chapter Ten

The next day breaks with beautiful sunshine and a cloudless sky. I fling wide the doors opening onto the balcony outside my room and inhale the fresh air. Having slept badly, every bone in my body is aching as much as my stupid, blind heart. The look in Jamie's eyes last night had reflected nothing but disappointment. I still don't understand what he expects from me. Did he really think he could just poach me from Callahan's like that? I'm not dumb enough to even be flattered by his insistence.

But one thing is certain, there is more to his wanting me to work for Young's than he is letting on. And if my gut instinct is right, Jamie is as money-hungry now as he's always been. He must have seen the interest Mr. Jenkins had in me as I did, when we spent that hour chatting in the bar. Oh yes, Jamie is genuinely scared of the competition.

I watch the guests taking breakfast on the lawn below me. They seem so carefree whereas Jamie and I are turning this seminar into a two-man war. My motivation makes complete sense, but his?

Why the hell would someone as successful as Jamie feel threatened by a first-timer like me? And would he really stoop so low as to snatch a quick fumble in a moonlit lake in an attempt to seduce me into his corner? When I look back over the last forty-eight hours, everything Jamie has done, said or implied, could be misconstrued as flirting but could just as easily have been poaching.

Well, I ain't no chicken, and Jamie had better prepare himself for the cock-fight of his life.

Turning back into the room, I remember I haven't turned my phone on since last night for fear of Mark ringing again. I switch it on and wait. Yep, twelve missed calls, all from Mark. Feeling exhaustion fall heavy on my shoulders just at the mere thought of talking to him, I toss the phone onto the bed and take a shower instead.

Thirty minutes later, I am showered, made-up and dressed. There is another meeting this morning and early this afternoon, and then we are free to prepare for the Medieval Ball. As I blow dry my hair, I contemplate tonight. I am yet to see the costume Miss Willoughby selected for me, plus Mr. Baxter is watching my every move. In short, tonight has got to be about Callahan's and my career, nothing else. I will be on my very best behaviour. So far I'm lucky I haven't lost my job.

I make my way downstairs and feel I deserve at least a brownie point for actually showing my face at breakfast for the first time since I arrived. The tables are laid out with seats for four or six people. I quickly scan the room looking for Mr. Baxter but can't see him anywhere, not that it matters because this is a perfect opportunity for some networking with the other guests. Pulling back my shoulders, I head for a table with two women in their thirties who look friendly and chatty and my sort of people as they munch their way through the pain au chocolate sitting on their plates.

"Do you mind if I sit here?" I ask.

They both turn to me and smile. "Of course not. Sit down."

The waitress comes over and I order a full English, with orange juice and tea. As I settle back in my seat, I notice both of them are looking at me, their eyes twinkling with amusement.

I take a deep breath. "Okay," I say, waving my white napkin in the air like a flag. "I surrender, yes it was me on Thursday night dancing to Duran Duran, and yes, it was me last night who came into reception dressed in a windbreak."

Their smiles widen to grins.

"You're fabulous!"

"Never laughed so much in my life!"

"Yep, that's me. Hannah Boyd. You can always rely on me for a laugh," I say, and it surprises me that I actually mean it. I'm a good-time girl and as long as I work hard too, what's the problem?

Mr. Baxter enters the dining room. He looks around, spots me and his expression changes from concern, to that of an adoring Granddad. He's a kind and caring boss even if he is the tiniest bit weird and misunderstood. I owe it to him to secure Jenkins' business and make him proud.

"Do you mind if my boss joins us?" I whisper to my two companions.

They both turn to see Mr. Baxter approaching and exchange a look of 'let's get out of here.' "Um...we were just off anyway," one of them says. "We'll...um...leave you to it."

They hurry off and I pat the seat beside me as Mr. Baxter comes closer. He's dressed in a three-piece suit, his head shining to perfection and a huge, self-satisfied grin on his face.

"Hannah! Good morning, my dear," he exclaims. "You look absolutely wonderful! What a beautiful suit."

I smile. It is clear last night is forgotten and for that I am grateful. "Thank you. You're looking very dapper yourself."

"Well, today is the day we battle out the recommendations for the upcoming financial year," he says, shaking out his napkin and tucking it neatly into his collar. "I always love these meetings. Although they can get quite volatile from time to time, you know."

I raise an eyebrow. "Really? Over investment funds?"

"Ohh, yes. Passionate stuff," he says earnestly.

My breakfast arrives and Mr. Baxter orders pancakes with maple syrup and black coffee. I pick up my knife and fork and I'm just about to take a mouthful of bacon and egg when Jamie walks into the room. His eyes immediately lock with mine.

Please, don't let him come over here. I wait with bated breath to see what he's going to do. But after a moment, he abruptly turns and joins Andrea at another table. I hadn't even noticed her. I am no longer hungry. I put down my knife and fork and reach for my glass of orange juice instead.

"So, are you looking forward to seeing your costume, my dear?" Mr. Baxter asks, oblivious to my distinct change in mood. "I promise you, you are going to love it."

I drag my eyes away from the back of Jamie's head and force a smile. "Yes, yes, I am. It should be fun."

"Yes, but not too much fun, eh?" he warns.

I nod. "Absolutely."

His breakfast arrives and I manage to clear a third of my plate, within the time it takes him to finish his and order seconds.

I put down my knife and fork. "Um...I think I'll take a quick walk around the gardens before the meeting starts."

"Well, of course, my dear. Are you not feeling well?"

I stand up. "I'm fine, honestly. I'll see you at the meeting."

I hurry from the dining room through the reception area and out into the morning sunshine. Inhaling huge gulps of air, I walk around to the back of the hotel and its beautifully landscaped gardens. The gravel crunches beneath my feet as I walk along the pathway, my heart racing with mixed emotions. Despite knowing this whole time has been nothing but one big corporate endeavour to Jamie, when he'd entered the restaurant and looked at me so coldly, it had been ten times worse than him not looking at me at all.

The truth is, every part of me is still drawn to him like a sexually-charged magnet. Even in the very beginning of my relationship with Mark, when you're supposed to be humping in bar toilets and apartment elevators, I'd never once felt an instant tornado of excitement swirling around in my stomach whenever I laid eyes on him like I do with Jamie.

My phone vibrates in my pocket. I pull it out and groan. Mark. Again.

Squeezing my eyes shut, I press talk. "What do you want, Mark?" I sigh.

"Hey, you!"

His unwavering enthusiasm and obvious indifference about ringing me pissed out of his head last night, kick-starts a flicker of anger. Why couldn't I see him for what he was two years ago?

"Why the hell do you keep ringing me, Mark?" I say. "Didn't I make myself perfectly clear how I feel about you when I threw you out of the house?"

He yawns loudly. "Do you want to know what I'm doing?"

I sigh. "No."

"I'm lying in bed, nursing an almighty hangover and thinking of you."

My shoulders slump. "Look, will you just say what you have to say and leave me alone. I'm here to work, Mark. This seminar is important to me."

"Yeah, Sam told me you'd gone away."

"Oh, yes, about that. Leave Sam alone, do you hear me? Whatever's happened between us, she does not deserve to be dragged into it."

"She never liked me, did she?" he asks, sulkily.

"Exactly, so leave her alone or I won't be held responsible for what she does to you when she's had enough."

"Okay, okay... But I'm not accepting we're over, Hannah. I never will."

"Yes, Mark, you will."

"You'll be regretting your decision once you come home."

"I don't think so."

"You will. Especially when you see what's going on next door. Woo-hoo, have they been busy."

"My new neighbours?"

"Yep."

I sit up a little straighter. "What do you mean? And how the hell do you know what they've been doing?"

"I've still got a key, haven't I?"

"Well, push it through the front door. Today! You shouldn't be..."

"You're not going to believe it when you see it."

"See what? Mark, what are you talking about?"

"They've had a huge hot-tub installed!"

"A hot-tub? Oh, god, please tell me they're close to our age and not knocking ninety-two or something?"

"Well...they're both in their sixties. But honestly, babe, they are such a laugh!"

"Sixties? Oh, God." I pause. "Hang on a minute. How do you know they're a laugh? Have you been over there?"

"Not yet, but I've chatted over the fence with them and they seem pretty wild."

I slowly shake my head. "At least tell me the hot-tub's covered by a parasol or something and I don't have to risk seeing them in there naked?"

He erupts into high-pitched laughter not unlike a hyena. "Nope, it's all open-air and when the Mrs spotted me with my binoculars..."

"Binoculars! You've been watching them through your binoculars?"

"What? It was fine, she beckoned me over but I didn't have the guts to go without you."

Queasiness rolls through my stomach. "Me?"

"Yeah, well, I've told them when you get back, we'll pop over for a drink with them."

"You are seriously deluded. Do you know that?"

"Hannah, I love you. We can make this work."

"No, Mark, we can't. I don't even want to."

There's a long moment of silence. "Is there someone else, is that it?" he sneers, all joviality gone from his voice.

I cover my eyes with my hand. Oh, what the hell. At least it will get him off my back for good. "Yes, Mark, there is someone else."

"Shit, I knew it! You don't like sex so all's not lost. I bet you haven't even shagged him yet, have you?"

I don't believe this. "Actually, Mark, I love sex, I just never discovered that little fact when I was with you!"

I drop my hand and shut my phone with a satisfying snap. And then I look up to see Jamie carefully watching me. Great.

I shove the phone back in my bag and leap to my feet.

"How long have you been standing there?" I demand, wondering how he managed to walk over the gravel without me hearing him.

"A few seconds," he says. "So you love sex? That's good to know."

I cross my arms. "Will you just stop it. I've seriously had enough."

"Stop what?"

"Stop with the stupid loaded questions. Stop with the sexy smiling and twinkling eyes."

He smiles sexily. "Twinkling eyes?"

"Oh, for God's sake!"

I move to walk past him when he grips my elbow. "Where are you going?"

I glance pointedly down at his fingers and slowly he lifts them away and fists them through his soft, sandy hair instead. "Please, Hannah. Last night ended in disaster."

"This is all a big joke to you, isn't it?" I say, quietly.

"All what?"

"This messing around. The flirting, the innuendo. But to me, Jamie, to me, my being here is bloody important so why don't you stop pissing about and tell me what it is you really want?" I say, ever so slightly panting. "Because to be honest I've had a gut-full and all I want is to get out there and be the best IFA I can."

His eyes bore into mine. As time stretches on, I struggle not to take a few steps back. I can feel the heat from his body. Or maybe it's the heat from mine? Either way, there should definitely be more space between us.

"Well?" I say.

He finally looks away from me and glances toward the hotel. "Andrea thought it would be a good idea if we clear the air before the meeting."

I blow out a breath. "Andrea thought it was a good idea, did she?"

He turns back to face me, his gaze indecipherable. "Yes."

"And how the bloody hell does Andrea know what happened last night, Jamie?"

His neck turns the tell-tale pink of his childhood. The same flash of coloured guilt that used to give him away to his mum, every time he'd been caught doing something he knew was wrong. My eyes widen. How could I be so naïve?

"Did you go to her room after you stormed off last night?"

"I didn't storm off."

Hurt and disbelief, anger and pain whirl around in my stomach, forcing acidic bile to burn my throat. "But you did go to her room?"

The pink turns scarlet. "You made it pretty damn clear how you felt about what happened at the lake, Hannah," he says, angrily. "Was there really any reason for me to hang around to hear more?"

I ignore his question. "Did you go to Andrea's room, Jamie?" My voice is dangerously close to breaking.

He glares at me. "Yes. Happy now?"

I open my mouth and close it again. I lift my hand and let it drop. And then second by painful second, I feel hot tears spring into my eyes and my feet move faster than they have for a very long time. I sprint along the path toward the hotel, ignoring Jamie's shouts for me to stop. He slept with her? He actually slept with her?

I'm going to be sick. I slap a hand over my mouth and run for the lobby toilets. Thankfully no-one else is in there and I rush into the nearest cubicle. I slam the bolt into place and bring up what little breakfast I'd managed to eat. Beads of sweat merge with my tears as I pull the flush and lower the toilet lid. I sit down heavily, covering my face with my hands. How could he? The Jamie I thought I knew would never have done a thing like that. Ever. I close my eyes. That's the point, isn't it? How the hell do I know who he is?

I groan with real physical pain. I can't delete the image of Jamie touching Andrea's bloody perfect body, kissing her with those beautiful lips and whispering empty promises into her ear. One thing is for certain; none of this is her fault. It isn't malice I see in Andrea's eyes when she speaks about Jamie, its heartbreak. Why wouldn't she sleep with him if he offered it to her on an extremely handsome plate?

I snap my head up at the sound of the main bathroom door creaking open. The tip-tap of high heels comes to a stop outside my cubicle and I clamp a hand to my chest.

"Hello? Miss Boyd?"

I recognize the voice of the Lloyd's girl. "Yes?"

"Are you all right? The meeting's already started and Mr. Baxter's worried about you. Is there anything I can get you?"

"No, no, I'm fine. I'll be right there."

"Are you sure?"

"Yes, I'll be there in two minutes."

Chapter Eleven

When I walk from the conference room two hours later, I have a headache bad enough to split my skull open. The discussions were intense, bordering on frightening. Have you ever seen a fund manager take on an actuary? Ugly, I tell you, ugly. Someone, in their infinite wisdom, had seated me in between Jamie and Mr. Baxter. So I had Jamie's thigh pressed up against mine as though welded there by super-strength super glue, the entire duration. If I tried to move away, he subtly followed. We sat through the whole meeting without speaking or looking at one another.

Which suited me fine. He'd slept with Andrea and now the bastard was trying to sidle up to me. Who the hell does he think he is?

"Hannah?"

I turn to find Mr. Baxter looking up at me. His bald head is wrinkled and he's throwing glances over his right shoulder at such a rate I'm sure he's going to crick his neck.

"Yes?"

"Jamie Young has managed to arrange an impromptu lunch meeting with Malcolm Jenkins," he says, urgently gripping my elbow. "As he promised you a seat at yesterday's dinner, he expects you to be at the lunch. We have a few minutes alone while he goes off to order the buffet."

Well, well, well. At least Jamie has a miniscule of moral obligation somewhere in the recesses of his being. I slap on a smile.

"That's great news. I'll quickly go upstairs and grab some documentation. Where are we meeting?"

He throws another anxious glance over his shoulder. "Are you sure you don't want me to sit in for you, dear?"

Disappointment drops like a stone into my abdomen. "Why? Don't you trust me to do this anymore?"

He shifts uncomfortably. "Well, after yesterday, I'm a little concerned..."

I cover his hand that is still at my elbow. "Look, I know I've messed up but believe it or not, I have spent a decent amount of time preparing an outstanding portfolio for Mr. Jenkins," I say, my voice pitching higher and higher with each word. "I want to prove to you I can do this. I know it may look as though I've lost my mind since being here but..."

"Sshh, dear. People are looking," he says, patting my hand. "Okay. You go in there and give Mr. Jenkins such a fantastic presentation he'll not be the slightest bit interested in what either Young's or Lloyds have to say."

"Lloyds?"

"Oh, yes, Lloyds have managed to worm their way into the meeting too. The competition has doubled, I'm afraid."

"And who's going to be representing Lloyds?" I ask.

"Andrea Kingsley, I believe."

Bugger. "Well, that's good news."

"You're meeting in the Sycamore Room so go grab your things and hurry down there," he says, pushing me toward the elevator. "And good luck."

Fifteen minutes later, I'm armed and ready for battle. My briefcase is filled with insurance company literature, past performance charts and presentation notes. I know exactly what I want to say and how I'm going to say it. Inhaling a long deep breath, I push open the door of the Sycamore Room.

A smile plays on my lips when I discover I'm the first to arrive. There's a trestle table set up at the back of the room, with a cling-film covered buffet and a square table set for four in the centre.

Quickly dumping my briefcase on a chair, I hurry over to the table to check the name cards and move Jamie's so he's sitting next to me rather than opposite me. I don't want the distraction of him watching me while I nail Jenkins — yes, I'll have to share his body heat, but that's still preferable to those bloody eyes of his.

I quickly snatch my hand away from the card as the door opens. Jamie walks in. His gaze briefly meets mine before he turns to hold the door open, allowing Mr. Jenkins and then Andrea to step through. I come forward with my hand outstretched.

"Mr. Jenkins. How are you? I hope you're feeling better today?"

I'm encouraged by his wide smile. "Very well, thank you, Miss Boyd. I'm so sorry about last night. I suffer from the occasional migraine and was struck down yesterday afternoon."

"Oh, I am sorry."

"No, no. I'm quite all right now. In fact, I think it would be a good idea to eat first and thrash out negotiations afterwards, don't you? I barely ate a thing yesterday. Mr. Young, Miss Kingsley, is that okay with you?"

"Of course."

"Lovely."

He gives us each a smile before heading for the buffet table. Turning quickly on my heel, I follow straight on behind, desperate not to have to embark on any small talk with the new Laurels Lovers. But obviously Andrea has other ideas and sidles up beside me at the table. I begin to tremble with the effort it takes not to dig one of my stiletto heels into her bare toes, left exposed and vulnerable by her strappy sandals.

"Hi, Hannah."

I pretend her voice makes me jump. "Oh, Andrea, sorry I was miles away."

Her eyes flash with renewed vitality and spirit. You'd take one look at her and think, now there's a woman completely and utterly in love. My green-eyed monster doesn't just materialise, she thrusts herself forward like a God damn ogre. My grin is so wide that to an outside witness I probably look a tad insane. Bitch. I suppose she's going to fill me in on her night of sex with Jamie now.

"Wow, did you win the lottery or something?" I ask. "You're positively glowing."

She giggles. "Am I?"

"Come on, tell all. What's happened?" I ask, my cheekbones aching.

She waves a dismissive hand. "Oh, you know. This and that."

"Really? Nothing you want to share with me? You know, us being friends and everything," I say, glancing at Jamie who is now deep in conversation with Mr. Jenkins.

I should really be over there courting Jenkins, not listening to

Andrea but God help me, I want details!

And then she gives a little squeal and digs her three inch nails into my forearm. "Oh, I'm so glad you said that, Hannah. Because I really would like us to get on. All girls together and all that."

Yeah, right. That doesn't mean you can sneak around and fuck my ex-boyfriend at the earliest opportunity, you skinny, jumped-up mare. I smile even wider. "Absolutely. So, what has left you looking like the cat that got the cream, huh?"

She looks left and right before leaning closer towards me. "I could tell you but then I'd have to shoot you."

I join in with her hysterical burst of laughter. "Ha ha!" My smile dissolves. "Seriously, tell me."

She flicks a glance in Jamie's direction. "But I promised I wouldn't."

I turn and follow her gaze. "You promised Jamie?"

"Uh-huh," she nods.

I wave a dismissive hand. "Oh, he won't mind if you tell me."

But then the smell of him attacks my nostrils. An avalanche of scent particles lining up to disarm me. "Come on, girls," he says, cheerfully standing between us. "Grab some food and come and sit down. Mr. Jenkins is keen to get started. Unless, of course, you've come to your senses and decided to throw in the towel and give me the account. That way we can all go and get ready for the ball a little earlier than anticipated."

I pick up a plate and lean over the table to show off the curve of my arse in the most provocative way possible. "I don't think so, Jamie. You're dead meat, sunshine."

He laughs. "Dead meat?"

I turn to face him and casually slide a cocktail sausage in and out of my puckered lips a couple of times. His eyes stay glued to my mouth. "I mean it. Dead meat."

He steps to the side allowing me to glide past him and join Mr. Jenkins at the table. My heart races inside my chest and my hands are clammy with nerves. But to Jamie and Andrea, who I can feel staring at me in stunned shock, I'm cool personified.

Careful conversation ensues over lunch, no business matters, just casual talk of holidays, the weather and current events. It's as obvious to me as the nose on my face that Jamie and Andrea don't intend to give away anything about their plan of attack any more than I do. The magnitude of the task before me has become clearer and clearer over the course of the last twenty minutes. If the truth be known, I am feeling a little out of my depth and my stomach is churning with nerves, but I'm determined to see this through to the bitter end.

Finally, the last sandwich is eaten, the final cup of water drunk — it's crunch time. I stand up and offer to clear everyone's plates. Once my back is turned at the buffet table, I take a moment to inhale a few deep breaths.

"Okay," I say, turning and clapping my hands together. "Who's first?"

****

Two hours later, we follow Mr. Jenkins from the room and he turns. His face is an inscrutable mask.

"Right. Well, thank you very much, ladies and gentleman," he says, with a theatrical bow. "I've listened carefully to your presentations and have each suggested portfolio tucked into my briefcase. I will take everything you've said into consideration, as well as deciding who I would most like to sleep with. Ha ha!"

There's a moment when no-one moves and then we all burst into a chorus of forced laughter. Once he's calmed down at his own hilarity, Jenkins' face sobers. "Ahem, on a more serious note, I will take all things into account and tell you who I would like to be my financial adviser in the morning. Is that acceptable to everyone?"

"Of course."

"Take your time."

"No hurry."

Jamie, Andrea and I mumble like a trio of arse-kissing brown-nosers. This is obviously an aspect of the job I'm going to have to get used to pretty damn quick. But the fact is, I hate any sort of arse-kissing including the sexual kind, so this is coating my tongue like day old garlic.

"Good. Well, I'll see you all later at the medieval ball then."

He walks away with a nod and all three of us let our shoulders drop simultaneously.

I turn to Andrea and Jamie. "See you later."

But as I move away, Andrea being Andrea isn't going to allow me the dignity of escaping unscathed. "Do you mind if I have a private word, Hannah?" She winks. "I've got something to tell you, remember?"

Heat sears my cheeks. "Look, I know what happened..."

"Please. Can we talk?" she interrupts. "In the ladies?"

I look at Jamie and he stares straight back at me for what feels like an hour, before blowing out a breath. "Right then, I'll leave you to it," he says. "See you later."

Andrea and I watch his retreating back in silence before walking across the tiled floor of the lobby. Once inside the ladies toilets, we awkwardly wait for the two women already in there to wash and dry their hands. The door swings shut behind them and then we're alone. And in a snap of time the sexy, come hither Andrea turns into Andrea Amazon Woman.

"Right, I've had enough of your crap, Hannah," she says, waving a finger at me. "Do you think I'm a fucking idiot?"

I stare at her wide-eyed. Now this is an Andrea the rest of the conference has no idea exists.

"Of course not," I stutter. "What are you talking...?"

"The way you keep dismissing everything I'm saying, glaring at me as though you want to smack me in the face."

"I don't glare."

She steps closer and I automatically step back until I feel the cold porcelain of the sink against my spine. But she keeps coming. In fact, she keeps coming until her face is barely inches from mine and I can smell the coleslaw she had at lunch on her breath.

"Yes, Hannah, you do," she says, quietly. "And I want to know why."

I swallow. The blue of her eyes darkens as they flicker dangerously. Okay, now I'm scared. I now see the girly-feminine act is all a show and Andrea is really a black belt in Tae Kwon Do and is about to happily snap my bloody head off. I slide to the side and slowly manoeuvre around her, managing to put a more comfortable distance between us. Just in case.

"Andrea, listen to me," I begin. "The thing is..."

"What? Come on, Hannah. I'm all ears," she says crossing her arms.

And then it hits me. What right do I have to question her relationship with Jamie? What he does or rather who he does, has got absolutely nothing to do with me. She's single, he's single. They can do whatever the hell they want. I turn away from her scrutinizing gaze.

"I have no idea why I'm doing it," I mumble.

She leans forward, places a hand behind her ear. "I'm sorry, I didn't quite catch that."

I snap my head up. Okay, maybe I've been treating her like a prize bitch when she's done nothing to deserve it, but she isn't going to stand there patronising me.

"Don't speak to me like that, Andrea. I said I don't know why I did it, there's no need to get all..."

She laughs. "Crap! I know exactly why you did it. God, Hannah. Do you think I'm the sort of person who will put up with your jibes and silly school-girl jealousy? I'm twenty-nine years old and ridiculously successful. I didn't have to come in here to talk to you, you know."

I pull back my shoulders and fist my hands at my hips. "I didn't ask you to, did I?"

We lock eyes for a long moment before she flings her body around and walks to the mirror. She pulls a brush from her bag and I watch in silence as she unclips her hair from a neat chignon and it tumbles down her back in one golden sheet, reminiscent of the Timotei adverts.

My shoulders slump, all the fight suddenly gone. I'll let her say her piece and then get out of here. Survival is the name of the game. Two more nights and I'll be back home. Normal life resumed.

I meet her eyes in the mirror. "My school-girl jealousy?"

"Yes. I told you I had a secret. Now do you want to hear it or not?"

I sigh heavily. "No, I don't think I do."

"Yes, you do. This is all down to Jamie, isn't it? You think he and I slept together last night."

I swallow. "No, I don't."

"Yes, you do."

"Look, I couldn't care less if you did or didn't..."

"We didn't."

"You're both free to have sex whenever and wherever you like. It's got nothing..."

"Hannah, I did not have sex with Jamie last night."

I stop. "You didn't?"

My dismissive hand halts mid-air and my heart picks up speed. Despite my bravado, I can't ignore the surge of relief that sweeps through me, turning my small intestine into a mess of knots and tangles. "But he said he came to your room last night."

She puts the brush back in her bag and extracts a lipstick. "He did."

I laugh, press a hand harder to my belly. "And what? You talked?"

She paints her lips, smacks them together on a tissue. "Exactly."

Her eyes meet mine in the reflection. Shit, she's telling the truth. "Oh."

Her mouth curves into a soft smile as she watches me. There's no malice, no ridicule, no enjoyment. She looks decidedly happy for me. She drops her eyes, throws the lippy back in her bag and zips it shut.

"Well, I say we talked. It was more a case of Jamie talked and I listened."

I still say nothing.

Drawing in a shaky breath, she turns. "He quickly made his way through an entire bottle of Cabernet Sauvignon whilst telling me about the moment he saw your name on the attendance list and felt as though he'd been given a second chance. A second chance to grab you with both hands and never let go."

"He said that?"

She laughs softly. "Yes, Hannah. He did. And I really believe he means it. I never wanted to believe it possible, but it seems to me that Jamie Young is more than capable of true love and you are the girl who has taken his heart."

"But..."

"But what? Isn't this what you want? Isn't this what everything has been about since you got here?"

I look at her. "No. This is crazy. We haven't seen each other for six years. I'm different, he's different."

She shrugs. "He said at first he was looking forward to seeing you again, sharing old times as well as satisfying his curiosity. But when he saw you?"

She trails off and I feel fit to explode. "Yes?"

She sighs, clears her throat. "I quote, 'as soon as I saw her, I knew I had made a terrible mistake by leaving. She's the one, Andrea.

Unquote."

The floor shifts beneath my feet. "He was drunk when he said this?"

Andrea lifts her shoulders. "Yes, but..."

I stand up straighter, waved my hand about. "He didn't mean it. He probably had no idea what he was saying."

She smiles in what I can only describe as sympathy. "Think what you want, Hannah, but I know Jamie and he meant every word. He wants you and if Jamie wants you, he will not quit until he has you."

I swallow. "And what about you?"

"What about me?" she asks, her perfect brow creasing.

"I know you still love him, Andrea."

She tips her head back and looks to the ceiling. "I don't love him, Hannah. I was pregnant by him."

Shock catapults through me with the force of a demolition ball. It slams into my gut, pushing my heart up to the roof of my mouth. "You were pregnant? Does he know?"

When her eyes meet mine, they are swimming with tears. She shakes her head. I step forward and put my arms around her. "Oh, Andrea."

"I'm fine, I don't know why I'm crying. It's daft."

"But Jamie wouldn't have walked away from you..."

She steps out of my arms. "He finished with me two days before I found out. I could see no good in telling him so I went ahead and had an abortion."

"Oh, Andrea," I say again.

Her eyes frantically search mine. "Promise me whatever happens, you won't tell him. I couldn't bear having him confront me about it. I had the abortion a year ago and it still hurts every time I see him, but I know it was the right decision." She pauses. "And now, I have proof."

"What? Me? That's silly. Of course I won't tell him but maybe you should. He wouldn't have deserted you. Jamie would never do that."

She gives a gentle laugh. "Listen to you. Still defending him. He deserted you, didn't he?"

"But I wasn't pregnant."

"No, you weren't, were you?" Pulling herself from my arms, she picks up her bag and hitches it onto her shoulder. "But I was and the decision was mine. Please, don't look at me like that, Hannah. I wasn't ready for a baby any more than Jamie was."

"But still..."

"No. It was the right thing to do. Please. Give me the respect of keeping this to yourself, okay?"

I open my mouth to say more but then clamp it tightly shut. What do I know? I mutely nod. And she walks from the toilets. Once the door swishes closed behind her, I stand at the mirror and look at my reflection. How can I face Jamie knowing what I know? He could've been a father by now. I drop my head and stare at the sink. Surely nothing else can happen at this conference?

Chapter Twelve

I shut the hotel bedroom door behind me and throw the key card onto a side-table. I feel so emotionally and physically drained, I want nothing more than to sink into a bath of bubbles and drown. Just knowing Andrea was once pregnant with Jamie's baby and he has no idea, makes me feel as though I'm betraying him when in reality I don't owe him any loyalty at all.

I slump onto the bed and my mobile vibrates along the bedside table. I look at the display. One missed call from Mark and two from Sam. Well, Mark can forget it. I punch in Sam's number and drop back onto the bed.

"Hiya, it's me."

"Hannah! How did it go?"

"How did what go?" I sigh.

"The meal with Jamie! You didn't even ring me back to let me know what happened."

I cradle the phone between my ear and shoulder so I can unbutton my blouse. "You wouldn't believe the things that have happened since I spoke to you yesterday."

"Then hit me with it."

I draw in a long breath. "Well, first of all, me and Jamie ended up eating alone."

"Oooh, and?"

"And somehow we managed to end up skinny-dipping in a lake, having a mind-blowing snog, before some kids stole our clothes and we had to come back to the hotel dressed in multi-coloured windbreaks." Silence. "Sam? Did you hear me?"

Her scream of hysterical laughter is so loud I have to hold the phone away from my eardrum for fear of it exploding. "You're joking! Please, tell me you're joking?"

"Nope, and it gets worse."

"Worse? What happened? You trapped his penis in a snorkel tube?"

"Ha ha, very funny."

"I'm sorry," Sam says, drawing in several long controlled breaths.

"Well, Jamie left me standing outside my room in the windbreak and went to his ex-girlfriend's room..."

"Wait. His ex-girlfriend's there? Why didn't you tell me? This is of paramount importance."

"Yeah, well, she is. And I came away thinking they'd slept together and so about thirty minutes ago, I was in the ladies toilets having a slanging match with her."

"Did you win?"

"It ended up turning into something infinitely worse." I pause. "She aborted Jamie's baby, Sam."

Silence.

I wait.

"Does he know?"

I shake my head. "No and she made me promise not to tell him. How can I look him in the face knowing that?"

"Hannah, listen to me. I know you, and you'll let this become a major factor in your life, which I refuse to let happen. Ultimately, this is about his ex and Jamie. Not you. All right?"

"I know, I know but..."

"No. If she chose to have an abortion, that's her business."

"But Jamie might have stayed with her if he'd known."

"But he didn't, did he? So let it go."

"Shouldn't I tell him?"

"What good would it do? There's absolutely nothing he can do to change what's been done. My advice is to stay out of it."

"Okay." But deep down inside, despite what Sam says I know I'm involved right up to my neck. This isn't some snippet of insignificant information I have picked up from an ex, this is huge. Even the thought that Andrea could abort the baby without even giving Jamie a choice, makes my stomach swirl with nausea.

"Hannah?"

I blow out a breath. "I'm here."

"Are you okay?"

"I'm fine."

"So what happens next?"

"I've got this stupid medieval ball to go to tonight," I say, pushing myself off the bed to unzip my skirt. "So no doubt I'll be seated right in between Jamie and Andrea."

"Who's Andrea? The ex?"

"Uh-huh."

"So is a chance of a shag with Jamie off the agenda then? He didn't sleep with her last night, did he?"

"No. Apparently he got pissed and told Andrea that he'd made a mistake by running off to London and wants to make it up to me."

"Sounds good to me." She pauses. "But make the bugger beg."

"Sam, I have no idea what he means by that," I protest. "And nor does he most probably. He'd made his way through a bottle of wine by the time he'd said it."

"So? Don't most of us say what we really mean when we're pissed?"

I stand up and let my skirt fall down around my ankles, before stepping out of it and throwing it onto the bed. "I suppose. There's still this...this thing between us. There always has been and now I'm wondering if there always will be."

"What thing? A love thing? Are you saying you still love him?" Sam asks, incredulously.

I think about his face, his smile, his hands, his voice and I squeeze my eyes tightly shut. "I don't know. But what I do know is every time I've been near him over the last two days, even when I wanted to slap him, he makes me feel better about myself than Mark ever did. I can't ignore that."

I hear her draw in a shaky breath and wait.

"Then why not take this time to figure out what it is you want?" she asks, quietly.

Tears burn my eyes and slip over my cheeks. I swipe at them. "What are you saying? I should sleep with him?"

Sam softly laughs... "Good God, girl. Can you really not think about anything but your vagina?"

A wobbly grin spreads across my face. "Shut up."

"I'm not sure this is about love at all," she continues. "You just want to jump Jamie's rock hard bones."

"Maybe I do, maybe I don't."

"Ha ha! This is physical, girl. Pure and simple."

My stomach twists and turns inside me. If only that were true. But excitement ripples through me causing the hairs on my neck and arms to stand up, when I think of Jamie's hands on my skin again. I inhale a deep, long breath.

"I don't know if I can."

"Of course you can."

"I'm supposed to be working, not sorting out my sex life."

"Hey, you'll get the client and the man. Two for the price of one. Come on, Hannah, women are multi-taskers."

I'm saved from saying more by a sharp knock on the door. We say a quick goodbye and I snap the phone shut.

"Just a minute," I call out in the general direction of the door before rushing into the bathroom.

I pull on the thick complementary bathrobe over my bra and knickers before hurrying to the door. I pull it open to find Mr. Baxter standing there with a cellophane wrapped costume draped over his arm.

"Hi, Mr. Baxter. Is that my costume?"

"It is, my dear, it is," he cries. "May I come in?"

"Sure." I step back and gesture him inside.

He walks to the bed and lays out the costume with a flourish. "Ta-da!"

"Hey, I get a pointy hat!" I say, rushing to pick it up.

"Yes, you do, dear. Didn't I tell you Miss Willoughby wouldn't let you down?"

"I should have had more trust in her," I say, as I finger the soft fabric of the dress through its plastic covering. I quickly come to the conclusion that maybe Miss Willoughby doesn't resent me as much as I thought. "So, I'm guessing you're looking forward to the ball?"

He claps his hands together. "I only wish Mrs. Baxter were here to share in it with me. We like nothing more than dressing up and transporting ourselves to another world, another time."

"That must keep your marriage fresh," I say, politely.

"Oh, and exciting my dear. Exciting!" he says, his eyes suddenly alight with erotic flair.

I quickly clap my hands together in a succinct bid to end the conversation right there. "Okay, then. Well thanks for dropping off my costume. I can't wait to try it on."

"Oh, you're going to look a vision, Hannah. A vision, I tell you."

I smile encouragingly while steering him toward the open door. "I'll see you in just over an hour then."

"Yes, yes, you will." And with that, he turns on his heel and heads back toward his room.

I shake my head in bemusement and then sniff the air as I close the door. Something stinks. I sniff a little deeper. I don't believe it. Mr. Baxter has just inadvertently dropped a bloody great fart in his current state of excited elation. I close my eyes and shut the door.

Less than an hour later, I get out of the bath and guiltily put my razor back in my toilet bag. I have shaved every part of my body known to man and a few that aren't. I've cut and shaped my toenails, even plucked my eyebrows. I can no longer kid myself that tonight is just a work thing. Tonight is about Jamie and whether or not I take my clothes off. My belly is trembling with anticipation and I keep cupping my breasts trying to decide whether or not Jamie will still be impressed.

I walk to the dressing table and look critically at my dark brown hair. It falls to my shoulder blades in a wavy mass of nothingness. I tilt my head to the side and wonder if I should curl it. Picking up my pointed hat, I plonk it on my head. Yep, big, bouncing curls falling sexily to my shoulders should do it.

Taking out my curling irons, I set to work. Forty minutes later, I am standing in front of the full-length mirror with a huge self-satisfied smile on my face. I look fantastic. I am never one to brag because I've often very little to brag about, but tonight I look magnificent. Regardless of whether anything happens between Jamie and me, heads will turn.

I send up a silent thank-you to Miss Willoughby. The dress is the richest sapphire blue with a low cut neckline that actually makes my breasts look closer to the double D that men so avidly lust after. Silver piping runs in intricate patterns over the bodice, which is sewn to a full and beautiful floor length skirt. Carefully, I lift the hat onto my head and let the flimsy silver gauze attached to its tip fall down my back. Still grinning like an idiot, I carefully arrange my curls so they brush along my newly-pushed up tits.

I glance at my watch. The ball officially begins in five minutes so I throw my phone, brush and lippy into the little drawstring bag that conveniently comes with the costume. And then I reach for one last thing. My trembling hand hovers over the foil packet. Am I really going to do this? Me? Hannah Boyd, voice of morality extraordinaire? I quickly stuff the condom I got from the hotel toilet, into the bag and pull it tightly shut before I can change my mind. I have no idea how tonight will pan out but whatever happens, I'm prepared.

At exactly eight o'clock, Mr. Baxter knocks on my door. I pull it open and my smile freezes. No, no, no, no! No!!!!!!!!!!

Despite the excruciating pain, I can't stop my gaze wandering from the soft velvet beret perched at an angle on his head, down and down until sharp, stinging tears burn like hot needles behind my eyes.

"Wow," I manage to croak.

He gives a twirl. "You like?"

Not trusting myself to speak, I merely nod. What am I supposed to say? He is barely five feet tall, rotund, fifty-four years of age, and has quite obviously somewhere along the line lost his mind.

He is dressed in pea-green tights and a matching tunic that is far, far, far too short. And it is from the area just beneath its hem, that I am unable to drag my eyes, even though it is what I want to do more than anything else in the world. For there, in all its glory is an elephant-sized bulge protruding grotesquely from between the V of his tiny, weeny legs.

I swallow and force my eyes to meet his.

He grins. "I know what you're thinking, my dear. And yes, it is indeed all mine."

Okay..... Kill me. Kill me now. I continue to smile because my desert-dry tongue is now welded to the roof of my mouth. He offers me his arm and I take it like a programmed robot and let him lead me in traumatized silence to the ballroom.

****

The double doors are flung wide open and once we enter, we are catapulted back to the fourteenth century. Rich, sumptuous colours of deep burgundy, gold and claret decorate the huge rectangular room. People are standing around chatting and laughing, dressed in full medieval costume. They are knights, and princes, kings and queens. The walls are swathed in burgundy and silver velvet, iron candelabra hang from the ceilings and either side of the bar. The bar! Excellent.

"I'll get us both a drink," I say, snatching my arm from Mr. Baxter's grasp and heading for the bar like my life depends on it. I cannot, will not, stand next to him again for the rest of the evening. I worship the ground the man walks on but what is he thinking? There is every chance three or four people have already mistakenly thought I am his partner for the night, there will be no more. I race forward and I'm actually panting for breath as the young girl serving smiles at me.

"What can I get you, Miss?" she asks.

"Vodka. Lots of it and a tiny drop of coke," I say, narrowing my thumb and forefinger together to make sure she understands.

She smiles and pours the drink. I hold it aloft in a toast before taking a nice hefty gulp. It burns my throat. Yep, that's the stuff. I quickly finish that one and once I have another fresh glass in my hand I feel strong enough to turn around.

I inhale deeply. The air is filled with the subtle aroma of rose petals and the soft music of a lute serenades the guests through camouflaged speakers. I tip my head back, close my eyes and breathe it all in. But the smile on my lips falters when rose petals are suddenly replaced with the distinctively masculine scent of sandalwood and musk. It wafts beneath my nostrils like an invisible drug. My heart thumps wildly behind my ribcage as I struggle to remain undaunted. But then he's pressing himself up close behind me. It seems Jamie is as keen to forget our last argument as I am.

I refuse to turn around.

"Evening, Jamie," I say, my voice so under control I can barely believe it's mine.

His lips graze my ear. "Sir Young, if you don't mind."

It's no use. My smile stretches to a grin and my clitoris contracts. "Surely a knight would not be so presumptuous as to assume that he can stand so close to a lady without causing offence," I say.

"But how can he resist such beauty?"

"I have no idea, but it is a problem for which I suggest you find a hasty solution."

I move to walk away but he catches me around the waist and pulls me close. I gasp.

"I cannot let you walk away from me without at least one dance," he says, his voice a comical low growl. "I will die if I do not hold you in my arms for a few sacred minutes."

I'm lost for words as he loosens his grip, winks and takes me by the hand to the dance floor. I'm incapable of resisting him, so my eyes hungrily survey his costume as I follow. I lick my lips. Good enough to eat. The black and red tunic looks as though it was made for him. Belted at the waist, it accentuates the huge breadth of his shoulders. His muscular back forms a perfect triangle, tapering down to a hard, buff arse. The trousers are tucked into calf-length leather boots and he carries a deadly looking sword in his hand.

Oh, yes, my lord. Let's go find that hay bale.

I bite back a giggle. He drops my hand so he can slide the sword into his belt and lifts his eyebrows up and down several times in a bid to impress me.

"You're an idiot." I smile.

"Why, thank you, my lady. You, on the other hand, are all I've ever dreamed of."

The music starts as everyone valiantly tries to stay in character. The ladies swish and swirl their skirts and the knights and lords skip and jump about looking like a mixed bunch of extremely camp homosexuals, or painfully emasculated heterosexuals, I can't decide which. Jamie, of course, looks fantastic.

After two dances, my ribs are aching from non-stop laughter and I beg Jamie to let me get another drink. We fall towards the bar, giggling and holding each other, like we have fallen back to a time when he was barely twenty and I had just turned eighteen. But I can't ignore the constant niggle at the back of my mind, reminding me neither of us have mentioned the last time we spoke.

"Phew. We must have shifted a thousand calories between us out there," I pant. "I didn't realize how ridiculously unfit I am."

"Well, if you are, you hide it pretty well," he says, his gaze running over my body.

I'm ashamed to say I push my breasts out a little farther. "Thanks."

"You're welcome."

"So...about last night," I say tentatively. "Do you think we ought to talk about it?"

Our eyes lock. He's so handsome, it borders on the insane. He's also so hardworking, it borders on fanatical but most of all, I suddenly want to have sex with him so much, it borders on obsession.

He looks away. "Sure. Shall we take these outside?" He lifts his glass. "I'm bloody roasting in all this gear."

"Sure." But then I glance around me, remembering Mr. Baxter. "Shit. I was supposed to be getting Mr. Baxter a drink half an hour ago."

Jamie points across the room. "He doesn't look too bothered about it to me."

"What?"

I follow the direction of his outstretched finger. Mr. Baxter is executing a pirouette while holding the tails of his tunic aloft. With his massive balls swinging to and fro, he looks like a bald-headed gorilla carrying out a complicated mating dance.

"Oh, God. Please. Let's get the hell out of here."

The Sharp Points of a Triangle

Chapter Thirteen

We burst into laughter and make our way out the door. The underwater lighting of the pond and waterfall has been switched on and long pink-hued clouds drift lazily along the sky as the sun kisses the horizon. My heart turns over in my chest. With the people standing around talking and the beautiful rainbow of colours of the costumes, I feel as though I'm the star in a period drama.

"Doesn't this look amazing?" I breathe.

"You always did like dressing up."

"I did, didn't I?"

I tilt my head back and watch Jamie's Adams apple shift as he swallows.

"I had to go, you know," he says, quietly.

I look to the grass beneath my feet. "I know."

He touches a finger to my chin, forcing my eyes to meet his. "Leaving you was the hardest thing in the world but it was what I had to do."

I'm trembling. Trembling from complete self-pity and the way he's looking at me, willing me to understand. I lift my hand and gently remove his hand from my face. "It's ancient history, Jamie. But..."

"But?"

I squeeze my eyes tightly shut. "But you're making it hard to stay that way."

"So? Is that so bad?"

A solitary tear spills warm over my cheek. I need to tell him how he's making me feel. Enough of the anger and denial that I'm in control here. I'm not, I'm in love. I need to be honest with him. I draw in a long breath through my nostrils and exhale.

"Time and maturity have lessened the pain I felt when you left…" I pause. "…maybe I've even accepted how important money and ambition are to you. But to meet again after all this time and then seduce me with wine and a meal before kissing me in the lake and then expecting me to carry on as though nothing happened..."

"Seduce you? I didn't seduce..."

I squeeze my eyes tightly shut. "Jamie, please."

"What?"

I open my eyes and stare at him. "I know now it was part of your plan to get me to leave Callahan's and come work for you, please, at least have the decency to admit it."

"Hannah…." He pauses, looks to the sky and then back into my eyes. "Believe me, I didn't plan for any of this to happen."

I smile wryly. "I want to believe you, but I know you don't do anything without a reason. You never have."

"Hannah, I promise you. You just..."

"What? I just what?"

He drops his gaze. "It doesn't matter. Look, am I right or wrong that your career is your top priority right now?"

The sudden change in his mood causes yet another wave of unease to pass over me. I note the clench and release of his jaw over and over again, as my mind races to catch up to where he's going with this. But nothing gives. So I pull back my shoulders, and let my false nonchalance emanate from me like an invisible shield.

I'll show him I'm not a silly romantic, nonsensical woman but a full, career-minded ball breaker. I will... Of course I will. "Yes. And?"

"Well, Mr. Baxter told me how you went from being his PA to a qualified IFA in less than two years. He told me you weren't happy with the minimum qualifications and you went on to take several of the advanced exams."

I narrow my eyes against the stinging. "Is this going somewhere?"

"I want you to work with me because a female component to the company will encourage a lot more women investors and gain a good addition of wealthy clientele to our database."

Nausea turns over in my stomach. "I see. And what about Jenkins? I suppose you're thinking if I get him for Callahan's, he may just follow me over to Young's if I move, is that it?"

He smiles and lifts his hands in mock surrender. "You've got me."

"God, you really are a piece of work, aren't you," I say, turning away from him.

His hand is warm when it clasps tightly around mine. "What are you doing?" I demand. Yet I don't pull away.

He looks at me, his shoulders ever so slightly slumping. "I don't want to do this anymore."

"Do what? Jump from business to pleasure like a kangaroo with two meals to choose from?" Not the best analogy, but hey, I'm under pressure here.

A small smile twitches at his lips but lucky for him he manages to hold his laughter, otherwise I would have had no choice but to bite him.

"Come with me," he says, glancing over his shoulder. "I can't talk to you with all these people around us."

I stand my ground. "What more is there to say, Jamie? I think you've made everything pretty clear."

He tugs my hand. "Come on."

I meet his gaze and heat rushes to my face. His green eyes have lost their determination of a fight and now glow with desire. And I hate him for it. My heart picks up speed as I try to resist it but the' thing' between us is already charging the air around us with electricity, making my lips and arms want to connect with his. I am so bloody weak. Yet, tomorrow we go home, tomorrow I'll never see him again.

His jaw tightens. "Please, Hannah."

And then he's leading me silently away from the rest of the crowd. We keep walking farther and farther away from the hotel until we reach a small wood at the very edge of the grounds. We exchange a single brief look before ducking our heads and entering the thicket of trees.

The light inside is dappled from the canopy of leaves above us. We step over fallen branches and stones, heading deeper and deeper into the semi-darkness. I have no idea where he's taking me or what he intends to do when we get there, but all I do know is that I want to be here. Despite what he has told me, I still want to look at him with no distraction, no thought and no regret. Just for now—I'll worry about later once this, whatever this is, is over.

"Jamie?"

"What?"

"Where are we going?"

He turns, a smile playing at the corners of his mouth. "Do you really care?"

I should turn and run for my life, but instead I grin back and we carry on walking. The place where we stop looks man-made in its perfection. The trees have formed a hidden paradise where no-one will see or hear us. The foliage within the tiny circular space is dotted with a stunning purply-pink hue of blooming foxgloves. The trees are separated above us, allowing enough of the twilight to filter through and illuminate every one of Jamie's striking features as he stands before me.

Our eyes lock and all I can hear is the faint laughter of the guests far away at the house. He steps closer, the bracken snapping beneath his shoes. When he's barely inches away, he touches a hand to my cheek and it takes all my self-control not to turn my face into it.

"The only reason I kissed you last night, was because it's what I've wanted to do since I saw you the first afternoon we arrived." His eyes travel over my hair. "And I held you last night because I wanted to feel you in my arms again. I know now I shouldn't have touched you or kissed you, and if it makes you look at me the way you did just now, I promise I won't do it again. I don't want to make you unhappy, Hannah. That's the last thing I want."

"Jamie?"

"Yes?"

"Kiss me. Now."

His eyes bore into my mine and I feel my blood heat beneath his gaze. He is so handsome, so sexy. I need to feel his skin beneath my fingertips, his lips pressed forcefully against mine. If he refuses me now, I will be completely humiliated, but there is nothing I can do to stop the incessant humming between my legs that needs to be satisfied.

He takes another step closer, forcing me against the hard bark of a tree. It digs into my bared shoulders as he drops his forehead to mine. I feel his hesitation and know this is the worst idea possible — even by my catastrophic standards. But he seduced me and now I'll seduce him. That way we're equal.

I cup my hand to his jaw and he looks into my eyes. "Touch me."

And after a long, long moment, he finally nods his understanding. The breath I didn't know I'd been holding exhales in a rush. He traps me within the circle of his arms with his palms pressed against the tree. His lips are as hot as the flames of a fire against mine, and I let them burn and heat and singe. Our tongues meet and savour, tease and enjoy for a few blessed moments before he pulls away to trail hungry kisses along my jaw.

I lift my head allowing him access to the sensitive curve of my neck. My hat slips and softly thuds against the mossy ground. His tongue caresses the hollow between my collar bones before sinking lower. I can't go any longer without touching him. With my eyes closed I reach forward and unsnap the top buttons of his tunic so I can slip my hands inside. The strong hard muscles of his shoulders and chest quicken my heart and stoke the heat between us. My mind is blank; all I can think about is us and this moment. My body quivers with the need for release.

His lips rejoin mine and then he's slowly pulling the criss-cross of lace from the bodice of my dress and it slips through the holes like liquid silver. I draw in a sharp breath as the cool night air hits my hot skin. I'm not wearing a bra and when he pulls away to look at my breasts, I don't feel the habitual spark of self-consciousness I felt with Mark, but instead feel powerfully intoxicating.

"God, Hannah, you're..."

I press a finger to his lips. I don't need his compliments, I just need him. He drags his eyes from mine and I see them flutter closed as his flicks his tongue over and around my nipple. I shudder and score my fingers through his hair. My knickers are damp, impatient for his touch. As though reading my mind, his fingers move downwards, achingly slow. A moan escapes my lips and the sound seems to fan the flames of his own longing as he bends down to lift my heavy skirts. I feel so wonderfully erotic. My legs tremble when he pulls my damp knickers to the side. His fingers slide over my clitoris and I squeeze my eyes tightly shut. My breath comes in short, sharp pants.

"You're so wet," he murmurs.

"Jamie, please..."

He makes no move to take off his trousers as he strokes and rubs me closer and closer to orgasm. The first tremors begin to build and my legs threaten to subside. He pushes them further apart with his thigh and then he's sliding his fingers deep inside me. My moans are primal but I am neither embarrassed nor ashamed. I don't want him to stop. I grip his shoulders as I feel myself tighten around his fingers.

"Oh, God."

And as I come, he urgently rubs my clitoris with his thumb while his fingers stay firmly inside me. His mouth covers mine, swallowing my scream. Slowly, the sensations begin to subside and I drop my weight against him, our foreheads touching.

"Thank you," I whisper.

I feel his smile against my cheek. "You're welcome."

"You don't understand," I pant. "It's been a long, long time."

"Surely Mark...?"

"No...No, he hasn't. Not ever."

And with that admission, the world stops turning. His body freezes beneath my hands, the birds fall silent and the chattering guests disappear. I close my eyes and tip my head back. What am I doing, telling him things like that? The silence stretches out between us and with each passing second I feel my defences clicking into place.

"Say something," I mutter. "Anything. Don't just stand there."

With my heart pounding and tears burning my eyes, I brush down my skirts and fumble with the lacing on my bodice.

"You've been with the guy two years and he hasn't managed to find out what turns you on?"

I snap my head up. "Look, will you just forget I said anything?"

"But...."

Shame floods through my veins. Even Mark doesn't deserve his private life talked about like this. "Jamie, please, leave it. Don't start slagging him off." I pause, meet his eyes. "He's lazy through and through but there's nothing wrong with his heart, okay?" I swallow as I realise what I'm saying is true. "And what's more, his feelings for me are real. And God knows, I really should cut him a little slack having felt the same painful stabs of unrequited love myself."

"I don't mean to slag the guy off but bloody hell, look at you," he says. "You're so sexy, erotic. How can Mark be happy knowing you're unsatisfied?"

I glare at him. "He was happy because he didn't know, all right?"

He stares at me. "You mean....?"

"So what? I faked a few orgasms!" Shame clogs my throat and I snatch up my hat. I want to get back to the house and be surrounded by people and welcome obscurity. "Are you going to walk me back to the house, or not?"

He moves forward and takes the hat from my hand. He places it in position on my head and even tugs at my misshapen curls until they sweep along the upper curve of my now slightly pink breasts. He presses a kiss to my forehead.

"I'm sorry. I didn't mean to poke my nose into your personal business." He runs a thumb over my tender lips. "But I can promise you one thing."

I curse the fact my body immediately begins to tremble. I defiantly tilt my chin. "Oh, yeah? And what's that?"

"There will be no more faking it for awhile."

My cheeks burn and my fanny throbs. "Bloody hell, you're so incredibly full of yourself."

He grins. "I don't care. I'm going to do it to you over and over again."

For a long moment, I'm hypnotised by his eyes, his lips, his fingers...and then Andrea, Mr. Baxter and my entire fucking future slams into my conscience like a demolition ball. I vehemently shake my head to clear it and meet his gaze.

"No."

His handsome brow creases in confusion. "What?"

"I want to be taken seriously by everyone inside that conference. If I start something with you, they will assume every success I have in the future is down to you, not me."

"Don't be ridiculous."

I hold up my hand, hoping he doesn't notice it shaking. "I've made my choice, now do me a favour and leave me the hell alone, okay?"

The Sharp Points of a Triangle

Chapter Fourteen

I lift my skirts and run back through the trees. I hear his footsteps rustling through the bracken behind me but I meant everything I'd said to him. Losing my career over a fumble in the trees will be the stupidest thing I can do. I didn't break things off with Mark to fall headlong into another waste of time relationship, for crying out loud!

"Hannah, wait!"

My heart leaps into my throat. "Jamie, just leave it," I yell over my shoulder.

"No."

I break through the trees and hurriedly straighten my dress, pat a hand to my hair as I power walk toward the hotel like Charlie Chaplin on acid. Everything will be all right, I didn't have sex with him, so strictly speaking nothing happened between us. I grimace. That sentiment smacks of a certain president and his intern but hey, he got away with believing it for as long as possible too.

"Shall we?" he says quietly.

I turn and meet his eyes. "Jamie, I'm serious. This isn't going to happen."

His breath is slightly harried, his gorgeous face flushed red. "Fine. Just let me walk you inside."

"But..."

He takes my elbow and propels me toward the door before I can protest. Once inside, I manage to extract myself from his ridiculously strong grip without having to knee him in the balls. I sprint to the ladies. Rushing to the mirror, I assess the damage. It's not as bad as I'd feared. I remove a sycamore leaf from my hair and adjust my boobs until they comfortably sit below the neckline of my bodice instead of feeling like two melons forced into a boned nipple extractor, and manage to look relatively normal.

Reaching inside my bag, I sweep a coat of coral lipstick across my lips and dab powder over my shiny nose and forehead. Better. Much better. I then throw everything back into my drawstring bag and exhale a shaky breath. It's all okay. Everything's going to be fine. I leave the bathroom and make my way across the lobby. Jamie is standing with his back to me and as I wonder whether I can head him off into the ballroom, almost as though he senses me there, he turns around.

And his smile almost floors me. I look around uneasily. People are watching him. He knows they're watching him. Swallowing hard, I force a smile onto my face when he holds out his arm. Drawing on every ounce of self-preservation, I walk toward him and place my hand through the crook of his elbow and onto his muscular forearm. Needs must. And avoidance of another unseemly outburst is paramount after the stunts I've pulled already at this damn conference.

"Ready?" he murmurs.

I nod and we re-enter the ballroom. It feels strange that everything is as it was before we left. There is no evidence of my screaming, toe-curling orgasm, no-one is turning to congratulate me or chastise me, depending on their moral ground. Jamie leads me toward two vacant seats by the edge of the dance floor. My backside has barely touched the velvet upholstery when Mr. Baxter materializes in front of us.

I squeeze my eyes shut for a second. God, I'd completely forgotten about elephant nuts. And now he's standing in front of me with them practically at eye level. Nausea burns the back of my throat as my eyes are drawn to his massive genitals. Not only is the sight more than I can bear under the most challenging of circumstances, but now there is a dark sweat patch circling the area too. I swallow down bile.

"Hannah! Jamie!" he exclaims. "Where have you two been hiding yourselves? I haven't seen you all evening."

I force a smile. Can't the man learn to keep his voice down?

Jamie holds a hand out and they shake warmly. "Oh, we've been around, Reginald. I've been introducing Hannah to a few of the people outside and in the lobby."

Mr. Baxter taps a finger to the side of his nose and leans forward to whisper into Jamie's ear in what I presume is supposed to be a conspiring manner. "Ah, good thinking. Good thinking."

My eyes widen and I stiffen in my chair. The move is so abrupt I fear the forward swing of his scrotum might actually cause him to crash right into Jamie's chest. Thankfully, he remains upright and I am able to breathe again.

Jamie clears his throat. "Indeed."

With a wink Mr. Baxter turns to me. "Well, I hope you have the names noted down, my dear," he says. "I'll ensure Miss Willoughby arranges meetings with them when we return to the office. That way you can go in for the kill before they have time to forget you, eh?"

I stand up. "Absolutely. Anyone for a drink?"

"Ooh, a vodka tonic would be splendid," Mr. Baxter exclaims.

Jamie turns and gives me an encouraging wink that turns my insides over. "Just a beer, please."

Heat flares at my cheeks like he's pointed a verbal blow-torch on them. He's neither clever nor funny. I glare at him. Why is he making it so damn hard for me not to be with him? "I'll be right back, excuse me gentlemen."

I move to walk away when Mr. Baxter snatches a hand to his head. "Oh, I almost forgot. Just a moment, my dear."

I turn. "Yes?"

He reaches into his inside pocket and pulls out a mobile phone. Not any mobile phone, but my mobile phone.

"Is this yours by any chance?" he asks, smiling.

A horrible warning tremor flows through my stomach. "Yes, yes it is. Where did you find...?"

"Not me, but someone else found it outside your bedroom door. You must have dropped it when we left to make our way to the ball. They found my name on your contact list. Good thinking, eh?"

"Yes. Brilliant." But my gaze is already concentrated on the screen. "Thank you. Oh, good and I've no missed calls. Good. Great. No harm done."

"All taken into hand, my dear."

I look up. "What?"

"I told your boyfriend, Mark isn't it? That you were with Mr. Young somewhere. He was most gracious."

My smile freezes. "You spoke to Mark?"

"Yes. Quite the comedian, isn't he?" He pauses. "Are you all right, dear? You've turned a little pale."

But his tone sends shivers down my spine. The man may be a mad as hatter and twice as fat but Mr. Baxter knows how to show concern with those pale grey eyes of his—and it is not what he is showing me now. In fact if it's not contempt burning like wildfire in his gaze, I don't know what is.

I force a laugh. "No, no, I'm fine. It just you seem a little..."

"A little what, dear?"

Angry? Upset? Pissed off? "Confused," I say.

"Oh, no, not confused, Hannah," he says, his smile slipping with every passing second. "A little worried why I couldn't find you anywhere, seeing as I must have circled the gardens and lobby at least half a dozen times."

He knows. He knows I've been getting up close and personal against the bark of a bloody tree. I swallow. Didn't he warn me? Didn't he tell me in no uncertain terms what Callahan's deems important? Family, love, lasting relationships. You know, important things.

I suddenly want to wipe away the look of disappointment from Mr. Baxter's face with every fibre of my being. I want to drop to my knees and grip the hem of his tunic while begging forgiveness. Actually, figuring what hangs beneath the hem of his tunic...anyway, I want to say sorry. "Mr. Baxter, I can explain..."

He stabs a hand in the air cutting me off. "Absolutely no need, my dear. After all, all's well that ends well, eh?"

I frown. "What?"

"Well, your boyfriend of course."

"Who?"

"Mark. Quite the romantic your young man, isn't he?"

I blanch. "He is?" I steal a quick glance at Jamie. His eyes are glued to Mr. Baxter's face.

"Oh, yes," Mr. Baxter beams.

"I don't know what you mean," I say, turning back to Mr. Baxter. I meet his eyes and resist the urge to shiver. I now understand with shocking clarity, how he came to sit in the heady position of Managing Director. It is suddenly very clear, he is not always as jovial and slapstick funny as he likes people to think. Right now, his eyes are colder than Antarctica.

"Mr. Baxter?" I press.

"I can't possibly tell you what he said, dear. It will spoil the surprise."

"Surprise?" I choke.

Antarctica is instantly replaced with the sunny glory of Jamaica. His face reddens with excitement and I swear to God another fart escapes his rectum. It seems that whatever is coming next belies his earlier concern at my unexplained disappearance.

"You'll see," he chuckles.

"Mr. Baxter..." I step forward, suddenly intent on pressing my fingers around his chubby neck, and squeezing harder and harder until he explains the reason behind his manic grinning. But blessed with the knack of sixth sense as far as I'm concerned, Jamie steps forward and digs his fingers into my wrist restraining me.

"Wow, what a tease you are, Reginald," he says grinning so wide, his face is in serious danger of cracking clean in half. "Why don't you get those drinks Hannah and I'll try to wheedle some information out of him."

Mr. Baxter chortles. "Am I going to be interrogated, Mr. Young? What fun!"

Jamie tilts his head purposefully towards the bar, his eyes telling me to trust him. I open my mouth to protest and then abruptly close it again. What choice do I have? Mark has said something to whip Mr. Baxter into a frenzy, and the sooner I find out that something is the better.

I slowly turn on my heel and walk toward the bar as my hand slides up to my neck desperately trying to ward off the fingers of dread tightening there.

****

"Mark's here," Jamie says.

"What?" I stare at him.

"Mark's here."

"What?"

"Hannah," he smiled. "Focus. Mark's at the hotel. Right now."

"Noooooo!"

"Ssshhh."

He takes my hand and leads me through to the lobby. "Where are you taking me?"

"Baxter said Mark checked into a B&B down the road. Apparently, he was planning on taking you out for dinner tomorrow night as a surprise, but Baxter convinced him it would be okay to turn up unannounced at the ball instead."

"So he's really here?" I cry, grasping his arm. "In the hotel?"

"He's in the bar. You're going to have to get yourself in there."

I dig my heels into the carpet. "But I don't want to."

"You have to."

I cross my arms and scowl like a petulant child. "No, I don't. I've told you Mark and I are finished. If he's stupid enough to drive all the way here without speaking to me first, that's his own fault. I am not going in there."

He holds his hands up in surrender. "Fine, I'll go and tell him you've gone to bed," Jamie says, glancing toward the frosted glass doors of the bar.

"No, you can't do that," I snap.

"Why not? I won't say anything incriminating."

"Incriminating?" I hiss. "I haven't done anything wrong."

"Exactly. So get in there and speak to him. Even if it's to tell him to leave."

I stare at him. He's right. Why am I standing here with guilt coursing through my veins as though I've cheated on Mark? I've done nothing wrong. I am single. A free agent. I inhale a long breath and slowly exhale it.

"Okay.....I'm going in."

He smiles. "Good girl."

I take a step.

"Oh, and Hannah?"

"Mmmm?"

"Don't tell him about your orgasm. He won't like it."

I narrow my eyes. "Funny, Young. Real funny. Why don't you do me a favour and throw yourself off one of the many balconies surrounding this place?"

His tips his head back and his laugh penetrates my entire being, with its familiarity, its warmth....and then a shadow descends over us like a blanket of doom and I know Mark is standing right behind me. I turn around in slow motion horror.

And as soon as I see the look on his face, I know he heard every word Jamie said. I want to run, I want to hide. Anything but stand there and watch Mark glaring and glaring and glaring at Jamie. Now I have something to feel guilty about, now I'm in the wrong. The silence is suffocating. I feel sick. I have to do something. Anything to break his awful glaring.

"Mark, what are you doing here?" I demand, grabbing his hands and turning him to face me. "What on earth were you thinking turning up like this?"

Finally, thankfully, he turns to face me. There's a moments delay when his face resembles something very close to a Hollywood psycho before it breaks into its habitual lop-sided grin. He snatches his hands from mine, throws them out either side of me in order to run his gaze up and down the length of my body.

"Hey, babe. Wow, look at you. You look bloody fantastic! Sexy, sexy, sexy." He gives a low whistle. "Woo-hoo, we're keeping this one on all night long, baby-girl. Oh, yeah."

"What are you doing here, Mark?" I say, steadfastly refusing to even as much as glance at Jamie.

"I missed you," He leans forward with his eyes closed and his lips puckered. I step back.

"You missed me?"

"Uh-huh."

"Oh, come on, Mark, you know damn well..."

His eyes snap open and when they do, they are most certainly not full of yearning. "Let's get out of here, shall we?" he says, his tone colder than ice-water. "Get a drink in town or something."

I cross my arms. "I don't think so."

He throws a look at Jamie before turning back to face me. "Come on, Hannah. Half an hour, an hour tops."

"I'm working, Mark. You shouldn't be here."

"Of course I should. The..." He pauses to lift his fingers in the air imitating speech marks, "...seminar has finished, hasn't it?"

I am trembling with the desire to slap the condescending grin from his face. I shake my head.

"What part of we're finished, didn't you understand, Mark? I really can't believe you had the nerve to come here. What the bloody hell...?"

But he interrupts me mid-rant and thrusts an outstretched hand toward Jamie. "Apologies for Hannah's lack of introduction. I'm Mark Hardy. And you are?"

I stand on the sidelines in immobile terror. My ex-boyfriend and new, not even an hour before, lover are shaking hands. My heart beats an erratic tattoo against my ribcage.

"Pleased to meet you," Jamie says, taking his hand. "Jamie Young."

I look down at their joined hands. Mark's knuckles are showing white through almost translucent skin. Any second now this could go from two guys meeting for the first time, to my ex-boyfriend throwing a punch and then being pummelled to the ground. Mark may think he's got a fighting chance with Jamie, but he hasn't felt the size of Jamie's biceps beneath that tunic, I have.

I clear my throat and step between them, deftly breaking their hands apart. "Well, seeing as you're here, I suppose I can spare the time for one drink," I say, facing Mark with my back purposely toward Jamie. "You can say what you've come to say and then leave."

Mark's gaze finally leaves Jamie's and meets mine. The out and out fury storming in them causes my breath to catch. I have never seen Mark so astonishingly furious. His smile is wolverine.

"Why don't we go upstairs?" he says.

"Upstairs?" I whisper. "No."

"I want to talk to you, Hannah. Alone. You owe me ten minutes, surely?"

I want to shout that I owe him nothing but I can't. I'm scared if I refuse him this, my entire career will be over once he plunges his fist into Jamie's face.

I glance toward Jamie. "Mark, you're embarrassing me."

"No, I'm not. Jamie here knows all too well what it's like to be parted from the woman you love, don't you, mate?"

Burning hot heat rushes to my face as Jamie looks at me, not Mark and says, "Yes. Yes I do."

And with one swift lunge Mark pulls me into his arms and I am super-glued to his chest. He lets out a long sigh. "I'm ashamed to admit it, Jamie boy," he says against my hair. "But the truth is, I just couldn't go another minute without grabbing this fine arse of hers."

"Mark, for God's sake!" I yelp as he clasps both my buttocks in his hands and gives them a jiggle. "Get your hands off me!"

I push away from him and as I do, I look around to see the few people standing in reception smiling into their drinks. This is bad, really bad. Jamie's jaw is locked and his eyes are boring into the side of Mark's grinning face with unadulterated loathing. I've got to get Mark out of here.

"Look, why don't I introduce you to Mr. Baxter," I say, pulling on Mark's arm. "I'm sure he'd love to meet you face to face."

But Mark ignores me. "Oh, no, babe. Not a chance. I was deadly serious about going upstairs. We've got some catching up to do."

"Mark, I can't just go upstairs. I'm here to work."

"Work? Is that what you've been doing while I've been waiting for you in the bar for the last half an hour? Working?"

"Of course."

"Where, Hannah? Where have you been working exactly?"

The use of my name speaks volumes. It sounds almost alien on his lips. It's babe, it's always been babe. And that's when I see it's pain in Mark's eyes, not anger. He knows I've been with Jamie and it's hurting him like hell. I may as well have picked up a knife and stabbed him straight in the heart.

My shoulders drop, my head aches. He's right. The least I can give him is ten minutes. "Let's go upstairs, Mark," I say in defeat.

He flicks a triumphant smirk at Jamie before taking my elbow and together we walk toward the lift.

The Sharp Points of a Triangle

Chapter Fifteen

He slams the bedroom door hard enough to make me flinch. I have never known Mark to flip his lid over anything. Yes, he was a little miffed when I asked him to move out, but nothing like this. His face isn't red with rage; it's so deathly pale I am worried he'll pass out. The quicker I get him out of here, the better.

"Okay, so here we are," I say, throwing my hands in the air. "What did you want to say that couldn't be said in the bar?"

He slowly meanders around the room, taking in the four poster bed, fingering the heavy velvet drapes at the windows and then he spots the complimentary bottle of champagne and two glasses.

"This doesn't look very business like to me," he says, picking up the bottle and proceeding to rip off its gold foil.

"That was here when I arrived. Hardly saw the need to open it, being here on my own and everything."

He arches an eyebrow. "Well, you're not on your own, are you? Is Jamie Young the other bloke you were on about?"

"Other bloke? Oh, you mean what I said on the phone?" I give a nervous laugh. "I don't why I said that, Mark. There isn't anyone else. I just can't be with you anymore."

"I see."

He pops the cork with a loud 'bang'. I jump and clutch a hand to my throat before emitting a sound much akin to a chicken being strangled. He smiles at me while catching the foaming liquid in one of the crystal flutes.

His newly calm demeanour is unnerving. I have no idea what he knows, suspects or thinks. I gratefully take the glass he offers me and down its contents in one go to ease the dryness in my mouth.

"How was it?"

"How was what?" I slowly ask, swallowing a belch. Shit, here we go.

He grins around the rim of his glass. "The champagne. How was it?"

"Oh, right, yes, good. Yours?"

He tips his head back and drinks. "Yeah, not bad."

He re-fills his glass and then nods to mine. I hold it out desperately hoping the alcohol will make this situation a little easier to bear. He fills it while I concentrate on keeping my hand steady or else the whole lot is going to end up on the rug.

"Mark, listen," I say when he finishes pouring. "I really ought to go back to the ball, so if you've nothing to say to me..." I don't finish the sentence instead lift my glass casually to my lips.

"Have you slept with him?"

The bubbles explode at the back of my tongue and then defy gravity by flowing up into my nose and out through my nostrils. The golden liquid cascades through the air and pebble-dashes his face.

I slap a hand over my nose. "God. Mark. I'm so sorry."

He swipes a hand across his cheek and flicks the excess liquid across the room. My relief rushes from my mouth in a guffaw as I meet his now smiling eyes and grinning mouth. Maybe he's not so mad after all? Maybe he didn't come here to confront me in a drunken rage, or to cause a scene and wreck my chances of landing the corporate deal of the year. He just wants to say a final few words and then he'll walk out of my life forever.

I must have heard him incorrectly; he didn't ask if I'd slept with Jamie. He couldn't have. He wouldn't be smiling at me that way if he thought I did, would he?

He turns and drops heavily onto the bed. And just as a little of the tension seeps from my shoulders, his face is set once more. "You'll do anything for a diversion, won't you?"

I give a nervous laugh. "Sorry about that."

He looks at me directly. "So you did then."

My smile wavers. "Did what?"

"Sleep with him."

"Who?"

He blows out a long breath. "Don't make this more difficult than it already is, Hannah. Did you sleep with that fucking moron downstairs or not? Just tell me before I lose it completely."

I swallow hard, keep my eyes locked with his. Come on, Hannah. Deal with this. He doesn't own you. I tilt my chin.

"No, Mark, I haven't slept with him. Not that it would be any of your business if I had. We aren't together anymore, remember?"

His eyes bore into mine and the passing seconds are like the ticking of a bomb. He tips his head back and drains his glass for the second time. "Is he the Jamie from the good old days? The one who used to make you laugh until you thought you might piss yourself? The one you thought you were going to marry?"

The unease in my blood starts to pulse. "Yes. But that was a long time ago..."

"What happened?"

I frown. "When?"

He clicks his tongue against the roof of his mouth. "Here. At the seminar. With Jamie."

"Nothing." I shrug. "Nothing happened."

He jumps up from the bed and lunges forward. "Don't lie to me!"

The glass slips from my hand and shatters against the floorboards with a crash. I'm so shocked that tears leap into my eyes and my heart lodges painfully in my throat. For all the ups and downs, ins and outs Mark and I have been through in the last two years, not once have I heard him shout. He is suddenly a terrifyingly different person to me. It's as though he's peeled back an important and vital layer of his personality revealing something so secretive, so dangerous that I want to run as far away from him as I can.

I realise I don't know him at all. Don't know what he's capable of or who he is. I take a few steps back, the glass crunches beneath my feet. I hold up my hands as though warning him off.

"Mark, you have to calm down. Please," I say, my voice cracking. "This won't do either of us any good."

"I love you, Hannah. How can you turn around and fuck somebody else like that, when you know how I feel about you?" He screws his hands into his hair. "I fucking love you."

"I didn't sleep with him," I say, slowly walking backwards towards the door. "Now, I want you to go."

"No."

"Mark, please. You're scaring me. I want you to go."

"Not until you tell me what happened."

"Nothing. Please, just go..."

"Hannah, for God's sake..."

My fear is giving way to resentment. He has no right to ask me these things. I want him out. Now. "Fine. I kissed him, okay?"

"And?"

"He touched me."

"Where?"

"Everywhere."

For a long, long time he says nothing, just stares at me. And then he blows out a dismally defeated breath and drops his chin to his chest. And as I look at him, I know I have changed something inside him forever.

He lifts his head. "I wanted to marry you, you know," he says, softly. "Have children with you."

Hot tears prick the back of my eyes. I'm desperately fighting the feeling I am the biggest piece of shit in the world for doing this to him. He looks so different. Yet once again the garbled accusations have given way to hypnotic speech. It's as though I've killed his spirit.

"No-one can force themselves to love someone, Mark. I'm sorry. I really am."

He slowly walks toward me and when he stops just a foot away, I see his eyes are glassy with unshed tears too. We stand facing each other in silence. Somewhere outside the room there is a giggling female scream of delight as a male voice roars after her lion-like down the corridor.

He touches a hand to my chin. "I'd better go."

"Mark..." I shake my head. I don't know what else to say.

His hand gently slides from my face and he brushes past me to the door, stepping across the threshold with one hand gripping the hair at his crown.

****

I didn't go back to the ball and thankfully no-one came looking for me. So the next morning, I wander into the conference room with a head aching so badly, I feel as though I've slept wedged between Mr. Baxter's mammoth balls. I approach the table bearing coffee like it's a mirage in the middle of a corporate desert.

"You're alive then?"

I squeeze my eyes shut for a moment before turning around. When I open them again, Jamie's bottle green irises stare down at me.

"Yep. I'm alive. Mark didn't kill me if that's what you're trying to say." I lift the coffee pot and fill a porcelain mug.

"Are you all right?"

"No."

"Do you want to get out of here after the meeting? We could head into town, find a quiet pub somewhere and have a bit of lunch."

I blow out a breath. "I don't know. I feel so bloody tired of it all."

Pink colour stains his cheeks. "He has gone, hasn't he? He's not still in your room?"

"Of course he has!" I snap. "You haven't got a very high opinion of me if you think I'd spend the night with him, after we….we….did what we did, have you?"

"Well, you can't blame me. You didn't come back downstairs. I just thought…"

"Yeah, well you thought wrong. All I had to deal with last night was Mark scaring the life out of me and now you're..."

"What do you mean? Mark scaring the life out of you? If he as much as laid a finger on you, I'll..."

"What? Punch him? Everything's gone way past that, Jamie. Last night, Mark forced me to remember what it's like to have someone rip your heart out and stamp all over it like it's a God damn trampoline. Mark didn't deserve to find out what we did and right now I feel like fucking shit for hurting him so badly. So if you care about me at all, you'll stay well away from me for the next twenty-fours until I leave."

I storm away and find an empty seat. I sit down with my heart racing.

"I thought you wanted to win the Jenkins account?"

I roll my eyes heavenward. "You are really rubbish at taking a hint."

Jamie drops into the seat next to me. "Well?"

"What?"

"Jenkins' has come to a decision. He's going to tell us who gets his business after the meeting. I was going to treat us all, including Andrea, to lunch."

I look at him. "Andrea?"

"She has a stake in this too, remember? What's the matter?"

I turn and stare into the depths of my coffee. "Nothing."

"Hannah, look at me."

Reluctantly I turn.

"What is it? Something about Andrea? It's obvious you don't like her, but business is business."

"You're wrong. I do like her. Maybe too much."

He frowns. "So what's the problem?"

"You. You're the problem."

It's on the tip of my tongue to tell him what I know. But how can I sit and watch the concern in his eyes turn to disbelief, maybe even horror. God, it's like I've walked onto the set of 'Nightmare on Elm Street' or something.

He reaches for my hand. "Hannah…"

I lurch away from him, slopping some coffee onto my trousers. "Damn it."

"What is it?" he says. "Tell me."

I slap at my wet leg, ineffectively spreading the stain wider and wider. "Fine, I'm having a little moral dilemma with your ex if you must know."

"What do you mean?"

"Andrea."

"What about her? Why are you looking at me like you want to slam your fist in my face?"

"Because sometimes Jamie, I think you haven't got a bloody clue about the real world, that's why?"

"What have I done now?"

"You just walk around like the big I am, hurting and discarding people like they don't deserve to breathe the same air as you. For your information, Andrea was…"

"Hannah!"

I jump so high in my seat I feel air pass beneath my arse. Oh, shit. I plaster a smile on my face, stand up and fling my arms around Andrea's neck.

"Sorry, sorry," I whisper urgently into her ear. "I don't know what came over…"

"Well, goodness me Hannah. You are pleased to see me this morning, aren't you?" she laughs, slowly extricating my arms like

I'm more Boa Constrictor than human.

She glares meaningfully at me, until I purse my lips together so not one more word can escape them. She turns to Jamie, her perfect smile firmly in place.

"Did I hear an offer of lunch?"

"Yes, about one o'clock, after the meeting," says Jamie, hesitantly. "Are you two up to something?"

Andrea tips her head back and lets out a tinkle of laughter. "Women do like their secrets, Jamie. Surely you know that."

Looking from me to Andrea and back again, he shakes his head. "Okay, well, I'll see you both for lunch then."

I release my held breath. "Absolutely. Get ready to watch me take Jenkins from under your nose and walk away from this seminar a happy woman."

"Excuse me. Andrea?"

Me, Jamie and Andrea all turn to the young executive gazing up at Andrea as though she's a Victoria Secret's model—which, in fairness, she could be. "Could you spare me a minute?"

Andrea looks first at me, then at Jamie, her immense anxiety illustrated in the way she suddenly gnaws at her bottom lip. "Um, no, sorry I can't..."

I touch a hand to her arm, meet her eyes. "Go. Everything's fine."

She glares at me. "Are you sure?"

I give a firm nod. "Really. Go on, I'll save you a seat."

She walks away, throwing a final warning look at me over her shoulder before following her new found friend. I turn to Jamie. I am now, albeit belatedly, in full professional mode. Nothing is going to distract or turn my head from the matter in hand. Securing Jenkins as a Callahan's client.

"So..." I take a sip of my coffee; watch him over the rim of my cup. "...you still think you have a pretty good shot at Jenkins, do you?"

"You know I do."

"I know the man wasn't gazing out the window for the best part of my presentation like he was during yours."

He laughs. "Yeah, right."

"It's the truth and you know it."

For a long moment our eyes hold and my heart stops. It's these moments when we're staring into each others eyes, laughter between us like adhesive that I can't resist. They glue me to him like a necessary and vital part of my entire being, almost as though if the moment as much as cracks, so will I.

I quickly snatch my gaze away and pointedly look at my watch. "What time is this thing supposed to start?"

"Come work for me, Hannah. Please."

I look at him. "Jamie..."

"We have some of the highest net worth customers in the South West. How can you not at least consider it? Just think about it, please."

"No."

"Why? I need a female adviser and I seriously believe you are going to be the best. Whatever Baxter's paying you, I'll beat it."

I let out a dry laugh. "Surprise, surprise. It always comes back to money, doesn't it?"

"So?"

Shaking my head, I put my empty coffee cup down on the chair next to me. "News flash Jamie, money is not the most important thing in the world to most of us."

"Bullshit. Everyone loves money and so will you if I offer you a £30,000 basic plus all the commission you can earn."

I fight to maintain my calm exterior when inside I am pooping kittens. Thirty-thousand-pounds basic? Oh. My. God! "I could never leave Callahan's," I say, coolly. "Mr. Baxter has been so good to me. I owe him my loyalty."

"Thirty-five thousand then."

"Can everyone please make their way to their seats, please?" The girl from Lloyds stands at the front. "We are ready to start."

We sit back in our seats and I look eagerly around for Andrea. I spot her sitting at the front next to Mr. Baxter who's mopping his brow like he's in the Amazon Rain Forest. He obviously knows Jenkins is soon to announce his decision. I smile. How could I ever leave Callahan's? He's been so good to me. Always. Even now, after the spectacle I've made of myself during this entire conference, he hasn't fired me. He's barely reprimanded me. No, I will not be browbeaten into leaving Callahan's by anyone—including Jamie.

With my mind made up, the next two hours pass in near agony as Jamie insists on pressing his rock-hard thigh along mine, no matter how many times I jab him in the ribs with my sharpened nails. In fact, it only seemed to make him enjoy himself even more and leads me to firmly believe he has a pain fetish.

At the end of the meeting we are told it is our final business engagement and the rest of the day is ours, to do as we please. There will be an optional barbecue at the back of the hotel if anyone wishes to attend later. I hurry from the room and head outside into the sunshine, ignoring Jamie's calls for me to wait. With Jamie's, Andrea's, Mark's and Mr. Baxter's faces flashing through my mind, I feel like I'm stuck on a fairground carousel. They spin around and around in front of my eyes until I feel sick. I quickly pull my phone from my bag and head across the vast lawn toward the privacy of the waterfall.

Dropping down onto a stone bench hidden from the view, I punch in Sam's number. It's almost one o'clock on a Sunday afternoon so I know there's at least a forty percent chance she's awake.

"Hi, Sweetie." She says in a happy sing-song voice.

"I let Jamie do everything bar shag me last night." It comes out in a verbal rush.

Silence.

"Sam, did you hear...?"

"Everything?"

"Everything."

"You mean he kissed you? Fingered you? Sucked on your tits? Licked you?"

"For crying out loud, Sam! No, he never licked me!"

She blew out a disappointing breath. "Oh, well, if you didn't see any lickedy-licking action, he didn't do everything, did he?"

I glance around me. "It's still wrong though, isn't it?" I hiss.

"Why?"

"Because, because..." I look around and then jab my finger in the air like I've struck gold. "...Mark turned up here last night."

"He did? Shit."

"Yep. While he's waiting in the bar, unbeknown to him, I am climaxing up against a tree."

Her screech makes me whip the phone from my ear but I can still hear her screaming from two feet away. I wait. She continues. I wait some more and then as I think she might self-combust, it falls quiet. Tentatively, I slowly put the phone back against my buzzing ear.

"Sam?"

She lets out a low whistle. "Jamie made you come? First time? Jesus, Hannah, hang on to this one, girlfriend!"

I cover my eyes with my hand. This conversation is not exactly going in the direction I planned.

"Do you know what? Just forget I rang, you are not helping."

"Hey, come on. Chill out. So you had a little fun with an ex, so what? No-one else needs to know."

"But you should have seen Mark's face when I told him Jamie touched me. It was horrible, Sam. I ripped his heart out." My voice cracks.

"You told him?"

"Yes."

"Why?"

"Because I had to tell him something!"

"Hey, hey, okay....let's rewind and start again. It's okay...it's not as though you slept with Jamie. It was a fumble. And even if you had, it has nothing to do with Mark. If he turned up there, he was asking to get hurt. Mark will see it for what it is eventually."

"And what exactly is it? Because I haven't got a bloody clue," I moan.

"It's lust, honey. What else?"

I swallow and the words stick in my throat. "Oh, I don't know. One minute I want to jump Jamie's bones, the next I want to punch him clean through a wall."

"And how are you feeling about him right now?"

I look up to find Jamie watching me from the other side of the water. The breadth of a river separates us, yet I feel my nipples tighten to iron arrows. If I look down, I'm convinced I'd see little flags hanging from them saying, 'please be mine'.

"Shit."

"It's not shit. I'm asking you a serious question."

"What?"

Sam blows out an impatient breath. "I said, how do you feel about Jamie right now? Lust is my superior department, you know that."

And with my eyes still locked on Jamie's, I say, "Yeah? But what about love?"

Chapter Sixteen

I snap the phone shut and slowly get up from the bench. He's walking toward me and part of me wants to run in the other direction, the other, to stay right here for as long as this 'thing' lasts between us. My behaviour is bordering on insanity and I have no idea why the word 'love' crept into my vocabulary just now. Sam's right. I can tell she's right by the incessant throbbing between my legs as he closes the space between us. This is lust. God, the man is so damn fuckable.

Lifting my chin, I wait until he's a couple of feet away from me and then raise my hand like a stop sign. He halts.

"If this is about working for you, I don't want to hear it."

He takes another step forward. "It's not."

"What do you want then?" I say, wondering if he can hear me over the sudden ear-splitting crackle of sexual fireworks.

"Mmmm?"

"I said...Jamie, will you stop that? I mean it, stop it right now."

"What? Look at you?"

"You are not looking at me. You're ogling me."

"No, I'm not. I would never ogle a future member of staff. You could sue me for sexual harassment."

"See? You did come out here to talk about me about working for you. Right, let me make this very clear. I. Will. Not. Leave. Callahan's."

He smiles, shrugs his shoulders. "Fine."

I frown. "That's it? You've finally got the message?"

"I give up. I want you to work for me but more than that, I want you to be happy and if that means you stay with Callahan's, so be it."

I watch him through narrowed eyes for a long moment before I nod curtly. "Good, because that's exactly what I want. You're all about money, Jamie and there are far more important things in life."

His smile dissolves. "You've got me wrong."

"I don't think so."

His jaw tightens and his smile dissolves. "Then tell me what it is you think you've got all worked out about me, Hannah?"

I open my mouth to tell him exactly what I've got worked out, when Andrea emerges around the corner of a hedge.

"Ah, there you are." She smiles, her eyes searching mine, silent questions burning in her baby blue gaze. "Is everything okay?"

"Everything's fine," I laugh, waving a dismissive hand in the air. "In fact, we were just coming to find you, weren't we, Jamie?"

"No."

My laugh notches up another octave. "He's such a tease!"

She glances at Jamie. "Are we still on for lunch?"

I turn but he isn't looking at her. He's looking at me. His eyes are ablaze with something I can't quite decipher. Anger? Fury? Passion? Whatever it is, it's clear Jamie is not a man to mock. He never was when I knew him before and it seems he's not very open to the idea now. He blinks and his smile re-appears.

"Of course." He holds out an arm to each of us. "Shall we?"

We walk out from the cover of trees and along the gravel path to the front of the hotel. Since coming here, I have managed to become an unwilling but very big part of a trio that has all the trappings of disaster. The sooner I leave this damn conference, the better.

We find Mr. Jenkins standing on the steps of the hotel, looking at his watch. Jamie drops our arms and strides forward, his hand outstretched.

"Mr. Jenkins, sir. I am so sorry to keep you waiting."

"Well, I must say, Mr. Young, it is not something I'm used to. But maybe I'll be a little more forgiving after a slap-up meal, eh?"

I smile. Mr. Jenkins may have enough money to buy the Taj Mahal but more importantly, he's an extremely pleasant and charming man. I send up a silent prayer he has chosen Callahan's. I cannot think of a nicer client to have on my presently empty books.

We take a taxi into town and Jamie leads us inside a pub with a billboard outside boasting of its award-winning home-cooked lunches. Andrea and I sit at a vacant table while Jamie and Mr. Jenkins venture to the bar. As soon as we're alone, Andrea takes my hand in a death grip.

"I can't believe you nearly told him," she hisses at me and I flinch as her spittle lands directly in my eye. "Sorry," she mumbles.

"But I didn't, did I?" I say, snatching my hand away and picking up the menu. "Don't panic. I promised I wouldn't say anything and I won't."

"But you almost did," she says, her eyes so wide I can see the veins in them bulging red.

"Look, after this meeting, I'm going back to the hotel to pack my bag and I'm leaving," I say, stealing a glance at Jamie's turned back. "I will not be seeing Jamie again, so there's absolutely no need for you to look like you're about to have a coronary."

She stares into my eyes for a long moment. "You're not staying for the barbecue?"

"No."

"You're heading home straight after this?"

"Yes."

"Okay, good." She exhales and sits back in her seat.

Jamie and Mr. Jenkins return to the table with two pints of bitter and a glass of white wine for Andrea and me. We touch glasses and drink. I watch Jamie over the top of mine and feel a painful kick low in my abdomen. I meant what I said to Andrea, I will be heading straight home once this lunch is over. Whatever happens with regard to Mr. Jenkins, my brief interlude with Jamie is over.

The next hour passes as we devour a meal, which wholeheartedly warrants the chalked claim of superiority as per the billboard outside. Once we're done, Andrea, Jamie and I simultaneously stare expectantly at Mr. Jenkins. The torture has gone on long enough. We're ready.

He finishes the last of his second pint and looks at each of us in turn. His intelligent eyes wander from each face to the next. At last, he clears his throat.

"You are all an incredible asset to your companies. Andrea, I have learned some pretty impressive things about both you and your career. You are a steadfast girl who knows what she wants and a firm favourite with your clients."

"Thank you, Mr. Jenkins. I..."

He holds up a hand to stop her and turns to me. "Hannah. What can I say?" His smile is warm. "You are like no-one else I have ever met. Funny, outspoken, honest and from the speed at which you have got to where you are, incredibly determined. Fine, fine attributes in any financial adviser."

Excitement races through my body. It's me. He's picked me. I shoot a quick look at Jamie whose jaw is clenching and unclenching like he's chewing on a lump of dung. Be afraid, Jamie. Be very, very afraid.

"And as for you, Mr. Young," continues Mr. Jenkins. "There is little else to say other than...Congratulations!"

Andrea and I exchange a look of disbelief before slapping smiles on our faces quicker than I can pick up a fork and stab it in Jenkins' eyes. "Wow. "Well, congratulations, Jamie," I say, the words almost choking me.

"Yes, yes, well done, Jamie," beams Andrea.

"Thank you, ladies." Jamie gets to his feet and he and Jenkins shake hands across the table while Andrea and I sit smiling like a pair of demented circus clowns. I feel so incredibly pissed off. I have failed to conquer the very first challenge Mr. Baxter set me as a new IFA and I can't help thinking, if I'd been a bit more focused on my presentation instead of Jamie's cock, things could've turned out differently.

I stand up, extend my hand. "Well, thank-you for considering Callahan's as a possible contender, Mr. Jenkins. It was wonderful to meet you and I hope our paths cross again soon."

"Oh, they will, Hannah, I'm quite sure of it," he beams, pumping my hand up and down.

I give a curt nod, first to Andrea, then Jamie. "Bye then."

Jamie stands up. "You're leaving now?"

"Yes."

"But..."

"Bye, Jamie."

And I stroll from the pub with my head held high but my ego in pieces.

****

Back in my room, I throw everything into a suitcase, suddenly desperate to get back home. For the first time since arriving at The Laurels, I haven't had a missed call from Mark and that speaks volumes. Finally, it appears the Mark episode of my life is over and so is Jamie. It's time to get back to reality…work, career and me. Nothing else matters.

Slamming the case shut, I twiddle the combination and then sit down beside it on the bed. I stare at the hotel phone. I need to ring Mr. Baxter. There is so much I should be saying to him. Explaining to him. I swallow the hard lump in my throat. Up until a few days ago, all I'd really cared about was proving my worth to him, myself and Callahan's. It has taken me two years to finally see the light with Mark and now I've backtracked six years, to the Jamie obsessed mess I was before. Inhaling a long breath, I pick up the phone and dial Mr. Baxter's room.

"Mr. Baxter? Hi, it's Hannah."

"Oh, my dear!" he exclaims. "I've been beside myself waiting for your call. Well? Did you get him? Is Mr. Jenkins the latest member of our close knit family?"

I squeeze my eyes shut. "No. I'm sorry."

Silence. Oh, bloody bloody, hell.

"Mr. Baxter? Did you hear me?"

"Which one?"

"I'm sorry?" My eyes shoot open.

"Which one did he go with? Lloyds or Young's?" His emphasis on the word 'Young's' does not slip by unnoticed.

I feel nauseous. "Young's."

"I see. And how do you feel about that, Hannah?"

"Sick. But Young's are so successful, Jamie is so…"

"Yes, Jamie. Mr. Young. He is just so…isn't he?"

It's as though Mr. Baxter has been possessed by a demon, his voice is strange and eerie, soft and scary. I swallow.

"I'm so sorry, Mr. Baxter," I say. "But next time I'll screw the target to the wall with my laser sharp gaze before he or she even has time to scratch their arse." I laugh nervously.

"Mmm, next time. How are things with your live-in boyfriend now, my dear? You disappeared up those stairs, faster than lightning last night."

Cold sweat breaks out on my forehead. "Mark? Um…we…"

He let out a manic laugh that freezes my blood. "I'm teasing!

There's no need to explain, my dear. I was young too, once upon a time. In fact, I still thoroughly enjoy a good dose of flesh on flesh action with Mrs. Baxter when she's willing."

My stomach lurches and I swallow down the bile that has seeped into my mouth. "I'm sure you do. Anyway..."

"Oh, God, yes. She's like a firework once her wick is lit, if you know what I mean."

I hurriedly clear my throat. "I'm really sorry about Mr. Jenkins, Mr. Baxter," I say. "But could we talk about this in more detail on Monday? I really have to leave right now."

"But why are you rushing away? Don't you want to bring Mark to the barbecue tonight?"

"No! Yes, I mean...I'd love to but I have some urgent family business at home."

"I see."

"Yes, it's Mum. She's not well and I..."

"Then of course you must go. As long as your leaving has nothing to do with Mr. Young, I am quite happy."

I never knew it before, but it is possible to actually feel the colour drain from your face. The blood sort of shifts beneath the surface of your skin and oozes over your face to your neck. "No, no, not at all," I croak. "Right, well, I really should…"

"Good, good. Because he seems to have spent a lot of valuable time bothering you somewhat."

I force a laugh. "Bothering me? No, not at all."

There's a long pause. "Well, if you're sure. Because as I've said before Hannah, Callahan's prides itself on family, commitment and integrity. I wouldn't want to think you weren't suited to us. That would be most distressing after all your hard work."

I hear you loud and clear, Mr. Baxter. Loud and clear. "Oh, Callahan's suits me, Mr. Baxter. That's why I want to go home, make sure Mum is all right before coming back on Monday, ready and willing to sit down and work out my next money-making strategy."

"Excellent."

The hammering in my chest begins to slow, everything is going to be all right. Situation under control. No more distractions, I still have a job. God is good.

"Yes, we have lots and lots to talk about, Hannah," he says. "So shall we say eight o'clock in my office?"

The phone buzzes dead in my ear before I have time to answer. I slowly replace it before falling back onto the bed, utterly exhausted. The tone of Mr. Baxter's voice leaves me in no doubt he has been watching Jamie and me like a hawk. And he'd just made his disapproval of our 'relationship' pretty damn clear. I let out an animalistic groan before throwing an arm across my eyes.

My boss clearly blames losing Jenkins on my association with Jamie. I slam my head from side to side. And as I do, it knocks the rational, intelligent part of my brain back into place. The clouds clear and I sit bolt upright. Jamie was scared. He saw my name on the attendee list and my God, he knew I'd be a threat. He's always known the level of my determination when I want something. And he knew I wanted Jenkins. He didn't even really want me to work for him at all. As long as I didn't get Jenkins, he didn't care about anything else.

I've got to get out of here. Now. Tears sting my eyes as I leap to my feet.

It is nearing five o'clock by the time I check out at reception. My plan is going well and it looks as though I'm going to escape without facing Jamie Jock-strap. I sprint across the pebbled courtyard toward the lines of parked cars, my heart literally bursting from my chest with the pure exertion of avoiding him.

I smile at the sight of my poor, unkempt Fiesta as she sits among the Mercs, Jags and Beamers. I slide into the front seat and gun the engine, breathing a sigh of relief when she starts first time in her unique emission burping way. I pull on my seatbelt and throw the gear stick into first. Hip-hip-hooray!

Then there's a tap at my window. I turn.

Andrea.

Her blonde hair is scraped back from her face in a neat, flawless chignon, her blue eyes are lined in soft brown and her lips are nude. Simple, no fuss, yet absolutely drop-dead gorgeous. Why the hell doesn't Jamie see what's right in front of him?

I wind down the window. "Andrea, hi."

"You weren't leaving without saying goodbye, were you?" She smiles, her pale-pink fingertips gripping the top of the window. "I thought we were friends now."

I release my held breath, manage a smile. None of this is about her. "We are."

"Then why the rush?"

"No rush, I just want to get home that's all."

But her eyes show her disbelief. Her smile slips. "What's he done?"

I turn away, look out the windscreen. "Nothing."

"Hannah..."

"It's nothing."

"Then look at me."

I snap my head round. "Fine. I think Jamie fucking Young had this entire conference laid out for me before I even got here. And on top of that, my ex-boyfriend turned up last night and I managed to smash his heart into mush. And that..." I pause to slap a hand against the steering wheel, "...that was all down to Jamie too. As soon as Mark looked at me, he knew something had happened with Jamie. It may as well have been written in black and white across my forehead."

Her hand slips from the window. "Wait a minute. You slept with Jamie?"

Red hot heat sears across my face. "No, no, of course not." I shake my head. "We just...um...just kissed."

Her eyes bore into mine long enough to make my scalp itch, before she blows out a breath. "Well, that's not so bad," she says. "Don't get me wrong. I'm not jealous or anything. The complete opposite, in fact. I just don't want Jamie hurting you again."

I sit up a little straighter in my seat. "He won't. He's a tosser. But then again, you know that only too well. He left you fucking pregnant."

"Hannah, sshh!" She looks left and right. "You have to stop shouting about that. It's ancient history. And I've told you, Jamie didn't know anything about it. Technically, he did nothing wrong."

"Huh. Accept shag you without a condom. Don't you dare let him off this, Andrea. The guy is a walking porn star."

She laughs. "It broke. As clichéd as it sounds, it does happen."

I look at her. She's telling the truth. My shoulders slump. "Shit."

"What? You want him to be guilty of leaving me? Abandoning me, crying and alone in a dirty slum in East End London?"

I narrow my eyes but a smile twitches my lips. "Okay, I enjoy a bit of Dickens now and then, what can I say?"

She reaches inside the window and squeezes my hand. "I don't think Jamie came here with any sort of agenda, Hannah. Not as far as you're concerned anyway. It was me who saw him crying into his bottle of Cabernet, remember? It was not professional."

I stare at our joined hands, they blur.

"You do know how much Jamie likes you, don't you?" she says, gently.

I force a laugh. "Jamie likes nothing but money."

"Does he know you're leaving?"

I meet her eyes. "No."

And then, just like that, I hear him.

"Hannah! Hannah, wait!"

"Oh, bugger!"

I look over Andrea's shoulder to see Jamie sprinting toward me. I look at her, panic threatening to choke me.

"I've got to go, I can't speak to him. Thanks for everything. I'll call you, okay?"

She nods before leaping back from the car in obvious fear of a broken foot and I skid away sending gravel flying into the air. With my heart hammering painfully in my chest, I look up into the rear view mirror. He stands with his hands behind his head as Andrea rubs a comforting hand up and down his back. I blink away my tears and turn back to the path in front of me.

The Sharp Points of a Triangle

Chapter Seventeen

I make it home in record time. Twilight is falling as I pluck my handbag from the passenger seat and get out of the car. And once I do, I squeeze my eyes tightly shut. There is high-pitched laughter and squeals of manic delight coming from next door, as well as the thump-thump of 1970's disco music turned up full volume. A party is the last thing I need right now. I walk to my front door and let myself in. The gratitude I feel for the blessed silence threatens to overwhelm me.

Tomorrow is another day. All I want to do now is run a long, hot bath and collapse into bed. But as I hang my bag on the banister, my phone starts to ring inside it. Rummaging around, I finally managed to locate it and even though I don't recognize the number, I press talk anyway.

"Hello?"

"Hannah? Can you hear me?" Mark bellows. "I'm next door. Get yourself sorted out and come on over. We're having a blast."

I press my hand to my forehead. "What the bloody hell are you doing next door? Have I lost my mind? Did last night not happen?"

"What's that?" he yells.

"I said, did last night not happen!"

"Whatever, life's too short. Get over here, we're having a ball."

"I'm not coming over there. What is wrong with you?"

"Oh, and just so you know, you may have to broaden your mind a little if you want to have a good time when you're here."

I frown. "What do you mean broaden my mind?"

He lets out a roar of laughter as a burst of female giggling passes by the phone before disappearing into the back ground. "You'll see."

And then the line is dead and I'm left staring at the phone. I am not going over there. Does he really expect me to do that? He's pissed enough to be slurring and despite the frivolity of his words, his animosity toward me had flowed down the phone line like an airborne virus.

I walk upstairs. Three short weeks ago, I'd felt as though I had the whole world at my feet. My biggest professional goal to date had been achieved, my dead-end relationship with Mark finished and I was braced for bigger and better things. But nothing, not one single thing has gone the way I thought it would and now I'm in a mess right up to my neck.

Walking into the bathroom, I drop onto the closed toilet seat and have a good cry until snot's running into my mouth. I take this as a gross sign to knock it off and with a flick of my wrist, send the toilet roll holder into a roly-poly frenzy. Tearing off a mile-long piece of tissue, I mop up my sodden face.

"Boo-hoo, poor old me," I say aloud. "That's it, that's the way to get yourself back into the game. What did you expect? Did you really think Mark was going to walk away quietly without a word? Did you really expect Mr. Jenkins to fall at your inexperienced feet like a self-made millionaire mug?"

The truth of the matter is, it's Mark's God given right to be angry. I may have told him I wasn't happy but he obviously wasn't ready to hear it and I know exactly how that feels. So he's pissed? So what? I should get my arse off this toilet seat and go next door. I should explain my feelings. Make him understand going our separate ways will be best for both of us in the long run. Last night was painful but I don't want him to hate me for the rest of his life.

Suddenly feeling energized and moderately positive, I stand up and splash water on my face. I rush into my bedroom and change out of my skirt suit into a pair of jeans and T-shirt. A dab of foundation and a brush of mascara just about disguises the blotchy state of my post-cry face, before I finish off by pulling a brush through my hair a few times.

Ten minutes later, I push open my neighbours' garden gate and inhale a shaky breath. Their front door is wide open and the house is so jam-packed, people are spilling out into the garden. I nod hello to guests averaging from the age of eighteen to eighty who raise their cans and glasses in semi-paralytic greeting. My progress down the narrow hallway is slow and no less distressing.

I have no idea what my new neighbours look like, so the bottle of wine I've brought as an offering, hangs limp in my hand waiting for someone to rush forward and claim it. I scan the living room, kitchen and dining room but don't see Mark anywhere. He knows how much I hate going to parties where I don't know anyone, and the fact he's not waiting close to the front door, is another indication of his loathing.

I risk stepping into the back garden and my breath catches in my throat.

No, no, no!!

I want to close my eyes. I want to turn and run before this scene of hedonistic debauchery scars my soul forever. But as hard as I try, my eyelids refuse to slam shut and my feet remain glued to the newly laid patio. My breath quickens. Laid out in front of me is an eight-seated hot tub, a steel triangular structure from which hangs a black leather swing, (I kid you not) and finally, a chaise-longue, deep and wide enough to accommodate the six, fifty-two to sixty-eight-year-olds lying there right now, butt-naked. It's as though a set from a 1970s porn movie has been plonked down, right next door to my house.

"Ah-ha, there you are!" I hear Mark's voice boom out beside me but I still cannot move. He slides an arm across my shoulders and squeezes. "Hello? Earth calling, Hannah."

Slowly, inch by excruciating inch, I turn my head. "How? How?"

"Great, isn't it? I hope you're ready to strip off and dive in the hot tub with me," he grins. "It's like a bloody sauna in there."

My eyes widen. "You've been in?"

"Oh, yeah. The ladies love it, baby!"

"Ladies? Bloody hell, Mark, what ladies?" I cry, emerging from my semi-comatose state with intense ferocity. I leap out from beneath his arm. "Do you mean the sixty-eight year old over there? Or the fifty-five year old about to climb aboard the swing?"

He'd brought me in here knowing damn well this is so far from my idea of a party that we may as well be in Outer Mongolia having high tea. I glare at him. "Well? Which one?"

His blood-shot eyes struggle to focus on mine. "Don't give me that prudish, holier than thou look, Hannah. We all know you enjoy a swinging session as much as the next person."

The Sharp Points of a Triangle

"What? What the hell do you mean?" I demand. "This...this orgy is insane!"

He takes a slug of his beer, swipes a hand across his mouth. "Come on, just admit it."

"Admit what?"

"Fine." He topples a little closer. "You, Hannah Boyd, fucked Jamie Young behind my back!" he yells in my face, pebble-dashing my skin with beer phlegm.

"Mark, for God's sake," I say between clenched teeth, looking around at the drunken stares and curious whisperings. "People are looking at us."

"So? I couldn't give a shit."

I turn to walk away and he grabs my elbow. "Where do you think you're going? We're only just getting started."

"I'm going home. I refuse to talk to you like this."

He tightens his grip. "What's wrong with me having a little fun, eh? You fucked Jamie Young, I thought I'd even things up a bit."

"I told you we kissed, who said anything about fuck...sleeping together?"

He tipped his head back, wobbled and laughed. "Do you really think I'm that bloody stupid? You stayed another night at the hotel. You didn't even come after me!"

"So? You left. We are not a couple anymore. Why should I come after you?"

"Bollocks! You stayed so you could fuck him again."

My heart beats hard in my chest, my mouth is devoid of saliva. One by one, I peel his fingers from my arm. "I'm leaving."

"That's right. Run away."

"I'm not running away, Mark. I came over here to talk to you. I didn't want to leave things the way they were between us. But now? Now, I couldn't care less how you feel."

As quickly as I can, I power walk back through the house and out the front door.

Sam. I need to see Sam.

****

She opens the door in her pyjamas, her eyes blurry with sleep, but God bless her, she's not the least bit perturbed to having me turn up on her doorstep at approximately eleven o'clock at night.

"He's turned into a monster," I say.

She stands back from the door. "Come on. In you come. I'll make some hot chocolate."

Sam's house is a small three-bedroom, mid-terrace show home. Unlike me who buys stuff on a whim and then has no idea of where to put it or what to use it for, Sam buys inanimate objects like a professional interior designer. I walk into her immaculate, shaker style kitchen and settle myself at her small but beautifully hand-crafted table, and serenity settles over me like a child's comfort blanket. This is where I can forget about both Mark and Jamie.

"How do you do it, Sam?" I murmur.

"Do what?" she asks, spooning cocoa powder into two mugs.

"Always know exactly what you're doing. Even when you do things on impulse, it's always the right thing. Somehow, I always, always fuck up."

"You are joking, right?"

"I'm serious. Look at the mess I've got myself into now. Mark's turned into a volatile alcoholic overnight, I'm sleeping on my best mate's couch..."

"You are?" she asks, raising her eyebrows.

"Sorry, yes I am. If that's okay?"

She smiles and places a steaming mug in front of me.

"Of course it is."

I drop my head into my hands. "Why am I such a walking disaster?"

"You're not."

I look up. "Sam, come on. Look at the mess I'm in with Jamie, with Mark."

She puts down her mug, sits back further in her seat. "Finishing with Mark was absolutely the right thing to do. You're only letting yourself feel guilty because of the state he's getting himself into. He's an arsehole, Hannah. Always has been."

"He looks like death, Sam."

"So? He would put you down and then cover it up as a joke. Take you out on your birthday and then get so pissed, you had to literally carry him into a taxi to get home. The guy is a moron."

"That happened once, twice at the most."

"Why are you sticking up for him?" Sam asks, her eyes wide with disbelief. "You know damn well I could come up with another dozen incidents if you gave me ten minutes. He's playing with your emotions. Can't you see that? And as for Jamie? I for one, am bloody glad you met him again."

"How can you say that? Look at what has happened since the first day of the bloody conference."

"You're single. You can do what the hell you like." She pauses, narrows her eyes as she looks at me. "Please tell me you don't feel guilty about that bloody orgasm!"

I shift uncomfortably under her scrutinizing gaze. "A bit."

"Sod that, Hannah! Why don't you ask yourself what made you do it in the first place? What happened to make you completely forget yourself? What was it that made Hannah Boyd lose her mind and climax with another man, two weeks after she's finished with her long-term boyfriend?"

"For God's sake, Sam!" But I'm smiling.

She grins. "Well?"

I cover my face with my hands. "Jamie."

She plies my fingers from my face and cups a hand around her ear. "Sorry? I didn't quite get that."

"Jamie! Jamie Young makes me want to drop my fucking knickers every time I see him. Satisfied?"

"Nope, but you were."

We both burst out laughing.

"Hannah, listen to me. What you feel for Jamie is special. God, I'd love to meet someone who does to me what Jamie does to you."

"I'm going to get hurt if I pursue this, Sam. All Jamie cares about is his business."

She shrugs. "Maybe he does, maybe he doesn't. But can you honestly say you'll be happy never seeing him again?"

The thought makes me shiver and a horrible queasiness seeps into my belly. "What am I going to do?"

"You found the courage to call things off with Mark and now you're free to take up with someone else. You like adventure and misbehaviour and it sounds to me as if Jamie's the one to give you that."

"But the last four days were not real life! Jamie's an extremely successful IFA with his own business. He didn't mention getting together again or anything."

"Did you give him a chance?"

The image of Jamie's stricken face in my rear-view mirror as I sped away from the hotel flashes in front of my mind. I reach for my mug. "No."

"Then you have to ring him and find out."

"Are you mad?"

"I'm not saying ring him tomorrow or even the next day, but at least think about it."

And later on as I lie in the darkness of Sam's spare room, I do think about it. I think about it until the sun rises and the digital clock tells me it's five-forty eight the following morning.

The Sharp Points of a Triangle

Chapter Eighteen

I wake to find the curtains open and a cold cup of tea on the bedside table. I look at the clock and groan. The house is silent and at six-thirty, I know Sam has already left for work. Throwing back the covers, I pad into the bathroom and turn on the shower to warm up while I sit on the toilet. There's a note stuck to the mirror opposite me.

Do what's right girlfriend. Love you loads, Ring me later, xxx.

I snatch the note from the mirror and give it a quick kiss—Sam is the best friend a girl could ask for. The power-shower is set to what should be called 'Skin Scorched by Needles' and I cannot figure out how to change it. Therefore, ten minutes later, I emerge looking like a hedgehog plucked naked of her spikes. I quickly dry my throbbing skin and pull on my jeans and top. It's seven o'clock and I need to be in work before eight, or risk Mr. Baxter firing me.

I hurry home, with the things Sam had said to me last night circling around in my head. Ever since I first saw Jamie standing in front of me in the Oak Suite of The Laurels, I've asked myself over and over again why I've given every relationship since him, no chance to work. Could he really be the one? Even though I was fifteen when we met?

I walk up my driveway. The aftermath of next door's party is wholly evident this morning. Beer cans, glasses, party poppers and, rather worryingly—underwear are strewn across the lawn like lurid confetti. A woman in her late fifties is making her way around the garden, inch by inch, picking up a piece of trash and then stopping to cradle her head for a second before bending down again.

As I put my key in the lock, she sees me.

"Woo-hoo! Ow! You must be Hannah."

I turn with a friendly smile plastered on my face, and walk over to the fence separating our two gardens. She's holding her head like it's about to break apart.

"Hi. Yes, I am." I hold out my hand. "And I'm guessing you're one half of my new neighbours. I did come over last night on Mark's say so, but I had no idea what you and your husband looked like."

She drops the bin bag she's holding and takes my hand. "Not to worry, love. There were so many people here last night, I only saw my Larry twice," she laughs, drops my hand, and extracts a squashed pack of cigarettes from between her gigantic breasts. "But then that's always a blessing, believe me. I'm Esther, by the way."

I try not to gawp as she pulls a lighter from the pack, pops a cigarette into her mouth, lights it and then returns the whole pack back to their nesting place in one swift motion.

"So, you and Mark been arguing, have you?"

I drag my eyes from her chest. "Mmmm? Sorry?"

She nods in the direction of my front door. "You and Marky-baby. He was full of chit-chat about you, well until he came back from that fancy conference thing you were on. Since then, he's been all over the place. Drinking and swearing. Yesterday he was walking down to the shops in his pyjama bottoms until Larry stopped him."

The first thing that hits me is Mark has been sleeping in my house as though he still lives there, the next is the realisation of how deeply imbedded his denial is—or was. "Really? Well, I can't think what could have happened to make him start acting like that," I lie, glancing toward my house in the hope Mark's not inside.

"Well, it was probably you sleeping with that other bloke that put a spanner in the works I would've thought, don't you?"

There's not the merest hint of disapproval in her voice, she's just stating a fact. I rub the back of my neck in increasing discomfort. "He told you about that?"

"'Course he did. Like that, me and Marky-baby," she says, holding two crossed fingers aloft to demonstrate how close she and Mark have become in the six short days I've been away.

"I see. Well, I didn't sleep with him, not that it matters..."

"You didn't? He's convinced you did, you know."

"Nope, never happened. But Mark and I had split up before I even left for the seminar so really even if I had..." I let the sentence drift off, peer at my watch in a rather obvious way. " Gosh, is that the time?"

She exhales a stream of smoke, carefully watching me through the grey-blue haze. "You sure about that?"

"Of course I'm sure," I say, a tad impatiently. "Mark's delusional and if you see him, make sure you tell him I said that."

"Not much chance of that, Hannah, love. Saw him taking some clothes and stuff from the house early this morning."

Relief drops my shoulders from under my earlobes. "Oh. Right. Good. It's better we don't come face to face right now. For both of us. Anyway, must dash. I've got to be at work in twenty minutes or I'll be out of a job on top of everything else. Bye."

I rush into the house and slam the front door behind me. Racing upstairs, I carefully dress in a cream cowl neck blouse and black trouser suit. Slipping my feet into high-heeled sling-backs, I put on full make-up as though applying protective war paint in preparation for my meeting with Mr. Baxter. Twenty minutes later, I jump into my car and reverse out of the driveway before Esther can hijack me again.

I'm sliding into the seat behind my desk when Miss Willoughby strolls into my office. Her self-satisfied smile sits upon her face like a shining beacon of torment.

"Ah, Hannah. How lovely to see you," she says.

I refuse to look at her and instead turn to the filing cabinet behind me. Pulling open a drawer, I extract a file and start to thumb blindly through the contents. "You too, Miss Willoughby."

"So, has all that business at the seminar been sorted out?" she asks.

Good God, does everyone know everything about my life? Slamming the drawer shut with a loud clang, I swivel around and face her. "What business?"

"The business between you and Mr. Young, of Young's Financial Management of course. Mr. Baxter has been beside himself with worry. He's convinced you spent the entire seminar utterly focused on being unfaithful to your intended."

I stare at her. "What? That's absurd..."

"And in doing so, you were unfaithful to both him and Callahan's."

"I was not unfaithful to anybody. Including Callahan's. And if I had been unfaithful to my boyfriend, I do not understand how my personal life has any bearing..."

"Mr. Baxter says you were carrying on like a pair of sex-starved teenagers, feeling each other up under the cover of darkness and frolicking in the bushes."

I'm gob-smacked. "He...he...wouldn't."

"He would and he did."

"But he hasn't said anything as direct as that to me. Surely, he would speak to me about my behaviour, not you."

She slowly shakes her head. "For reasons I cannot fathom, Miss Boyd, Mr. Baxter has become increasingly fond of you, and this debacle has caused him the utmost distress and concern. He needed someone to talk to and I was willing to listen."

"I bet you were," I mumble.

"Now, I suggest you think very carefully about your position here before you go in to see him. It's only fair you speak honestly of your betrayal, so that I can allay Mr. Baxter's fears of having to send you back downstairs to Tele-help," she says, walking towards the door.

"I don't need you to do anything for me. Mr. Baxter cannot send me back down-stairs, I'm a qualified IFA now, in case you hadn't noticed."

She laughs. "You've no idea how powerful Mr. Baxter is, do you, Hannah? You see, some people are not suited to the decorum expected of staff on the twelfth floor. Some people are destined to always remain on the lower levels — if you know what I mean."

She leaves the room and that's when I notice, at some point I have picked up a stapler and am now slapping it against my palm like a baseball bat. As much as I try to defy the niggling shame of other people knowing what went on between Jamie and me, the glaring truth of how much I've let Mr. Baxter down is literally blinding.

Blinking hard, I take a deep breath and stand up. I'll go into his office right now and talk to him. It's time to face whatever it is he wants to throw at me. I walk across the corridor and give a confident rap on his closed office door.

"Come in."

I push open the door.

"Ah, Hannah. Good morning."

I swallow and press my perspiring palms together in front of me.

"Good morning, Mr. Baxter. Are you ready to see me?"

He puts his pen down and leans back in his chair.

"Yes, yes, of course. Close the door, come and sit down."

I do as he asks; trying to gauge what he's thinking by looking deep into his eyes, but for the first time since I started working for him, they are blank. I clear my throat.

"Do you mind if I go first?"

"By all means, my dear. By all means."

I exhale. "Okay. About my behaviour at the seminar…the way I acted was not normal for me. It's not a reflection of either my personality or my…"

"Are you saying, the pursuit of a good-looking man like Jamie Young is not an everyday occurrence in your life, Hannah?"

"I didn't pursue him!" I protest. "You have to understand that Jamie and I were once in love. Well, I was at least. To see him again was a shock and as time went on shock gave way to something else, something so strong I had no choice but to act on it." I pause, waiting for him to say something but he continues to watch me. "I have no idea if I'll even see him again, Mr. Baxter, and that makes me feel stupid for acting as openly as I did, but I was happy when I was with him. That doesn't mean I was right to do what I did, but for that moment, I was just…happy."

Mr. Baxter steeples his hands beneath his chin and when I look into his eyes, they are shining with unshed tears. "Oh, Hannah…"

I fight the sting of my own tears. "I'm sorry. You want me to leave Callahan's, don't you?"

"Well, Mr. Young explained…"

I almost choke. "You've spoken to Jamie?"

"Oh, yes." He grins. "It must be two, no wait a minute, three times that I've spoken to him since leaving The Laurels. It's really quite sweet."

"What is?"

"The way he keeps ringing on the pretence of some business matter but really wanting to ask about you."

A fluttering erupts in my belly. "I really don't think…"

"He always finds a way to slip your name into the conversation. Quite adorable. At first, at the seminar, I thought the man was going to seduce you and then toss you away like a forgotten conquest, but I'm thrilled to be so completely and utterly wrong."

My heart bangs against my chest, threatening to stop completely in its ferocity. "And what exactly do you tell him when he asks about me?"

"That you are well."

Disappointment presses down on my throat. "That's it?"

He raises one fluffy grey eyebrow. "Is there more you wanted me to say?"

I wave a dismissive hand. "No, no, of course not."

The corners of his mouth twitch. "Well, I also might have mentioned you were looking a little bereft."

"Bereft?"

He nods. "I was young once too, you know. When I saw the instant sexual chemistry between yourself and Mr. Young, I thought to myself, 'Uh-huh, this could mean trouble' but not for one minute did I expect you to fall head over heels in love with him."

"I didn't say I was in love with him," I gush. "It's...well like you said, sexual chemistry."

His smile is sympathetic. He gets up from his chair and comes around the desk and takes my hands. He tips his head back to look at me. "You are in love with him, my dear. No-one has such pain in their eyes over unfulfilled lust. I watched you go through emotion after emotion in those five days. Yours is a classic case of tortured love. It is...just wonderful."

He drops my hands and flings his arms around my waist, pinning my arms to my sides. He then squeezes me so tight, I can feel the blood pumping through my constricted veins and his head is mashed painfully against my pre-menstrual breasts.

"Mr. Baxter? Mr. Baxter, I can't breathe," I croak. "You need to loosen your grip..."

"Oh, such pain, such agony, such romantic longing," he wails.

"Mr. Baxter, please!" I extricate myself from his surprisingly strong grasp by nearly catapulting him across the room. "This isn't helping."

He stumbles backwards and I grab his hand before he hits the bookcase behind him. "I do not need your sympathy," I say. "But I do need to know I still have a job."

"Ah, your job. That's an entirely different matter," he says, reaching over and pulling a tissue from a phallus-shaped receptacle on his desk. All thoughts of my job loss are momentarily forgotten as

I peer closer. Is that supposed to be a penis? And the white tissues are the…?

I shake my head and quickly turn back to Mr. Baxter. "You mean...?"

"Please don't look at it as losing your job, my dear," he says, dabbing at his eyes. "I hold my values for Callahan's very close to my heart and I cannot condone what happened between you and Mr. Young, just because of my fondness for you. What kind of message would I be sending to my staff?"

"But you said it was romantic!"

"And it was, but decorum is everything in this business, Hannah."

"Mr. Baxter, please. I've worked so hard to get here," I say, my heart racing. "I can't have messed up such a wonderful opportunity. Please."

"It isn't only your behaviour with regard to Mr. Young, though, is it? You lost the Jenkins account to him as well."

"I know but..."

"Mr. Jenkins told me, he really, truly wanted to come with you, but he expected more hunger from you in the principal presentation. He felt you were more concerned with impressing Mr. Young than him."

I hang my head. Jenkins is right. I did spend more time with my eyes locked on Jamie's, trying to show him how clever I was, how successful, rather than keeping eye contact with the man who could really send my kudos and career sky-high. What a stupid, stupid thing to do. Mr. Baxter gives me an opportunity most IFA's would kill for and I mess up in the name of a bloke. I deserve this. I deserve to be fired.

"You're right, Mr. Baxter and so is Mr. Jenkins," I say, quietly. "I'll leave. But I want you to know I have loved every minute I've spent working with you."

"Oh, Hannah," he cries and steps forward to grab me again.

I hold up a hand like a shield. "No. No more of that."

We both grin at each other, our eyes shining with tears. Mr. Baxter clears his throat. "It's not all bad news, you know."

"No?" I smile, swiping a hand at my moist cheek.

"No. Mr. Young is downstairs waiting for you as we speak."

"What?" He may as well as have dropped his pants and started dancing the fandango. "What do you mean, Jamie's downstairs?"

He continues to grin. "I only meant you can't work for Callahan's anymore, my dear. I would never see you jobless, would I? I telephoned Mr. Young and he confessed how he'd already attempted to head hunt you from underneath me but you resolutely refused out of loyalty. But now? Well, that's a different story, isn't it?"

"But..."

He gently grips my elbow and leads me toward the door. "No more buts. Go pack up your desk and I'll phone down and tell reception you'll be with Mr. Young in twenty minutes okay?"

I smile. "Make it ten."

Chapter Nineteen

It's raining as I struggle to walk rather than run, across the gleaming asphalt of Callahan's car park. I see him before he sees me and take this advantage to just look at him. He's leaning against a sleek black Mercedes, one hand stuffed into the pocket of his trousers. He's nervous. I can tell by the way he rubs his other hand back and forth across his jaw. His hair has turned darker from the rain, the shoulders of his grey suit jacket almost black. He looks magnificent. I press a steadying hand to my stomach.

"An intelligent man would sit in their car," I say, slowly walking toward him. With each step, I become more and more scared. Terrified of what will happen when there are no more steps between us.

He looks up and his welcoming smile makes the rain disappear. "Hannah." He says it like a breath.

My cheeks are red, I just know they are. I smile, suddenly shy. "Hi."

And then with no further words, he opens his arms and I step into them letting my head fall to his chest. The weight of his chin settling gently on top of my head makes breathing a little easier. We fit perfectly and I have no idea how long we stand there, just holding each other before he gently breaks the silence.

"So you want a job, do you?" I can feel his smile against my hair.

I lift my shoulders. "If you know of one going."

"Mmm...I might be able to find a place for you somewhere," he says, stepping back and running his gaze and fingers over my hair.

He dips his head. His lips are warm and soft against mine. I lean into him, my tongue seeking his. His hands slip to the small of my back and I lift my fingers into the smooth silk of his hair. The kiss is long and deep, soft and tender. The urgency of what we shared at the seminar has gone, it's as though we both know there is every possibility we could have all the time in the world.

"Can we get out of here?" I ask softly.

"Sure, but there's something I want to ask you first."

I frown. "What?"

He brushes the hair from my eyes. "If you feel this way about me, why did you leave the seminar without saying goodbye? Andrea said you were in a hurry to get back."

I look away, embarrassed, self-conscious. "I was scared."

"Of me?"

I meet his anxious gaze. "Yes. But not in the way you think. I'm scared now," I laugh. "Terrified."

He runs a finger along my collar bone making me shiver. His eyes cloud with desire. "Everything's going to be all right, you know."

I squeeze my thighs together to stop the throbbing, but I can't do a damn thing to prevent my nipples from leaping to attention. I smile. "So…your place or mine?"

He grips my hand. "Mine."

The hour's drive and separation in our different cars is agony but when we eventually pull into his driveway, every second was worth it. I park my Fiesta beside his Mercedes and get out. Jamie's house is a Victorian masterpiece. Three-stories of architectural splendour stretch high above our heads, the red brick glistening from the rain and a small welcoming light burning in the arched porch way. I turn to look at him.

"It's beautiful."

"I'm glad you think so because now you're here, you're not leaving. Ever."

"Jamie…"

He lifts his shoulders. "What? You can't blame a guy for trying."

We're grinning at each other like we did as teenagers and I feel free of responsibility, like I did back then too. He takes my hand and leads me inside. The interior of the house has been decorated with the exterior in mind but there is not a hint of dreary brown anywhere. Everything is cream and walnut and caramel.

"Please tell me someone helped you with this," I moan, throwing my arms wide to encompass the beautiful living room. "If you say you did this, you'll never ever come to my house."

He smiles. "Why wouldn't I have done it?"

I arch an eyebrow. "Because you're a man and men don't think about colours and fabrics and...oh, God..." I pause and reach toward the settee, grabbing a luxurious cashmere cushion and pressing it against my face. "...cushions."

"Okay, fine," he laughs. "It was an interior decorator. Does that make me an upper class snob?"

"Nope," I say, fingering the heavy velvet cream drapes. "It makes you sensible."

He pulls me into his arms. "I am so glad you're here."

I smile. "So am I."

"Going to that seminar may have been the best decision I ever made." His eyes hover at my lips, his voice as soft as butter. He looks up and what I see in his gaze is unmistakable.

"Shall we?" he murmurs.

I feel a sharp, tangible pull between my legs. I moisten my dry lips with the tip of my tongue and he follows the gesture with his eyes. "Shouldn't we at least talk first...?"

"Later. We'll talk later. Right now, I need you upstairs in my bed. Just us. Alone."

His words tickle my skin, make my heart beat faster and my hands turn clammy. And that's when it hits me right in the centre of my brain. I didn't come prepared for this. And I don't mean mentally. I can't possibly let him see me naked! Oh, no, not now. Not today.

At the seminar I was aware of him all the time and although I'm loath to admit it, I dressed as conscientiously beneath my clothes as I did on top. But here, now, after spending the night at Sam's I pulled on what I call my 'illusion' underwear and headed out the door. There's no way I can let him see what I have on underneath my suit.

I step away from him. "I can't, Jamie. I'm too nervous."

"Nervous? With me?" He closes the space between us. "Come on, Hannah. Relax. Please." He presses a feather-light kiss to my ear, starts a trail down my neck. "Let me make you feel like you did at the hotel. Let me make love to you."

Panic crawls up my body from the very tips of my toes. "I can't."

"Why?"

"I...um...I..." I press my hands firmly against his chest and he stumbles backwards. "...need a drink first."

He rubs at his thigh where it struck a walnut dresser. "A drink?"

"Uh-huh." I swallow. "White wine would be perfect."

His brow creases. "Okay," he says, slowly. "I'll open a bottle of wine."

I clap my hands together and then proceed to roll back and forth on the balls of my feet in a decidedly virginal manner. All this is done convincingly, despite wanting to strip my clothes off, lie on my back with my legs in the air and have Jamie pump me all the way to heaven.

I smile. "Great. We can catch up on the last six years."

His eyes widen. "Six years? You want to sit and discuss the last six years now?"

I feign disappointment. "Well, if you think I only came here for a wham, bam, thank you, ma'am, type of thing, you are way off the mark, mister."

He narrows his eyes and studies my face. I struggle to keep my eyes on his. Jamie will know I'm lying. Mark never could, but Jamie always, always knew.

He grins. "Bullshit."

I cross my arms. "I beg your pardon."

"Bullshit. Now, get your arse upstairs."

"Jamie!"

"Now."

My brain kicks into overdrive. I cannot go upstairs, knowing I have enough scaffolding on to support the Empire State Building. If I can just get him to sit down so I can consume a bottle of wine or two, my underwear might not matter to either of us then.

I demurely avert my gaze. "No, Jamie. My show of wanton abandon at the seminar was out of character," I say, lowering myself onto the butter soft leather sofa. "I can't have sex with you like this. Please. One glass, that's all I'm asking."

He lifts my knuckles to his teeth and growls. "Fine. Maybe you're right, if I ply you with enough alcohol, you'll have to stay until morning."

Once he's left the room, I drop my head back against the sofa. Avoiding sex when you want it more than anything, is exhausting. Excitement churns along my nerve endings along with every other emotion in the universe. In less than a month I've gone from a super-studying, exam passing twenty-four year old living with a reliable, but totally crass, TV fitting boyfriend, to the youngest IFA in South West England who's been felt up by her long lost love in the bushes of a hotel.

Talk about evolution.

"Here we are," Jamie announces, walking back into the room.

I take the huge bulbous wineglass from his hand, suddenly feeling a whole lot better about the underwear situation. I take a mouthful.

"Mmmm, Pinot. My favourite."

He sits down beside me and clinks his glass to mine. "I know."

I giggle, chuffed he remembers. "Go on then, you start," I say.

He takes another gulp from his glass. "What do you want to talk about?

"You, me...us."

"Okay....." He puts the glass down on the table in front of us and settles back into the sofa. "I left the love of my life, you, to go after a high-flying career in the city. I went from company to company until I landed a position on the UK stock market. I earned a fortune working night and day until I had the capital to start my own company. Then I left." He drew in a long breath and started again. "Once the business was up and running, I was able to work more sensible hours, even managing the odd date here and there."

"Just dates?"

"Well, I've allowed a few maidens to share my bed along the way." He lifts his eyebrows rapidly up and down, which causes me to swat him up the side of the head with one of the many sofa cushions. "Ow! And then one day out of the blue, an invitation arrives on my desk to attend a seminar in the Cotswolds. I had absolutely no intention of going until I saw a particular name on the guest list and the deal was done."

I look at him. "You honestly saw my name and knew you were going to go? There wasn't any other reason?"

He frowns. "Your name? No, no. Mr Jenkins' name."

For a split second I think he's serious, but the mischievous and super sexy smile that curls his lips sends my groin into another burst of activity. He takes my glass from my hand and presses his lips briefly to mine. "Of course it was you. It's always been you."

"Jamie..." His lips make a slow progression down to my jaw, my collar bone and my eyes drift shut. "Oh, that's so not fair."

"You were wearing a skirt and a thin white blouse when I first saw you at The Laurels," he says, his breathing warming my skin. "I could make out the outline of your lacy white bra..."

I sigh. "I was supposed to look professional."

"And your legs." He gives a low moan. "I had to adjust my trousers before I could even think about approaching you."

I giggle. "You naughty, naughty boy."

Talk dissolves as he pushes me onto my back, his weight solid and welcome against me. We kiss and it's hot and heavy. And when I feel my blouse being inched from the waistband of my skirt, my mind is telling me to say something to stop him but it feels so good...his hands glide over the bumps...no, it's no good. I can't do this.

I sit up, flinging him back to his side so hard he almost tips over the arm of the settee. "Oops, sorry."

"What are you doing?"

"More wine?" I ask, reaching for the bottle.

"Hannah, look at me."

The wine bottle trembles against the rim of my glass. From nerves or arousal, I'm not entirely sure. I turn and plant a smile on my face. "What?"

"Why won't you let yourself go like you did at the seminar? I'm serious about this, you do know that don't you? As soon as I saw your name on that list, I had to see you. I had to know if you forgave me. I didn't expect..."

"To be bringing me to orgasm up against a tree?" It's my turn to smile mischievously. He looks so sombre, so worried. Like a little boy who's lost his best friend and girlfriend all in one go. I lift a hand to his stubbled jaw and he turns to press a kiss into my palm. I watch him. Why am I wasting this precious time? Why deny what's inevitably going to happen?

"Shall we go upstairs?" I whisper, aiming for the romantic moment of surrender.... but as soon as the words are out of my mouth....I'm screaming.

He leaps off the settee and lunges at me, throwing me over his shoulder like I'm a featherweight. "Grab the wine," he orders. My entire body is shuddering with great guffaws of laughter as he leans me down towards the table so I can swoop up the wine bottle in one hand and the stems of the two glasses in the other.

And then we're heading for the stairs.

Thankfully, his bedroom is in darkness and for the first thirty seconds, I make the stupid mistake of thinking I'm going to get away with doing it in the dark. But then he carries me to the massive—I mean, bloody gigantic bed and we fall on top of it. He then reaches over and flicks on the bedside lamp.

"Can't we have the light off?" I murmur as his lips get busy doing that thing he does to my neck.

"No."

I reach over and flick it off anyway. He stops nuzzling me. "What did you do that for? I've touched you pretty much everywhere before, remember?"

"Yes, but not like this."

His brow creases and he props himself on an elbow to look down at me. "So the memory of the soft skin of your thighs trembling against the back of my hands as my fingers thrust into your beautiful, sexy pussy is all a figment of my imagination, is it?"

"Jamie!" I slap him. "Don't use words like pussy!"

"Why not?" He grins. "Don't you like it?"

"No, I do not."

"Liar."

And then with his eyes locked with mine, his fingers are on the buttons of my blouse, snapping them open one by one. The smile dissolves from my lips when he slides an eager hand inside the cup of my bra and circles my rock-hard nipple with the most delicious, agonizing strokes. I know I'm already wet and waiting for him.

Sexual anticipation ripples across the surface of my skin as he touches and teases my tongue with his, our lips not yet touching. His hand travels down my torso and I automatically suck in my stomach. If he notices, he doesn't say. His hand slips beneath the waistband of my skirt and I squeeze my eyes tightly shut. Here goes nothing.

The rock-hard erection pressed against my thigh is going to rapidly deflate with one touch of the support knickers that reach from the middle of my thighs to an inch below my belly button. I hold my breath. But it doesn't deflate, it stays pert and performance ready. Oh, God bless Mr. Winky!

And he really does try his best to manoeuvre those clever fingers of his a little lower but support pants are designed to suck fat in like it's vacuum-packed. There isn't enough room between my stomach and the pants to slip a cracker bread, let alone Jamie's manly hands.

"Could you give me a minute?" I mumble from beneath my hands which are now pressed hard against my face.

I feel the weight of his hand lift from my belly and then he's gently pulling my fingers away from my face one by one.

"A minute? You've got ten seconds to get those things off and be back on this bed. Go!"

And with no shame whatsoever, I scramble out of my skirt and pull down my knickers like they're on fire. And it's in this moment, this glorious, liberating moment, standing butt naked in Jamie's beautiful Victorian bedroom that I realise for the second time in the past fortnight, I'm in love.

I walk back toward him like a Femme Fatale, my hips swinging, my pout so exaggerated I could give Victoria Beckham a run for her money and his grin widens. This is what it's supposed to be like. Trust, fun, excitement—my body is humming beneath his hungry gaze and I can't wait for him to feed upon it. I lift his T-shirt over his head and allow myself a few blessed seconds to appreciate the beauty of a man who works out.

Leaning forward, I feather delicate kisses across the breadth of his rock hard shoulders and up to his strong neck, until I come to rest at lips as hot as the desert. We share a long, sensual kiss before I step away and intertwine my fingers with his. I pull him to his feet and drop to my knees.

Above my head I hear, "Oh, Jesus."

Satisfaction skips along my lips. There is nothing quite like feeling in complete control. I'm choosing the pace for the first time in two years. The sex between Jamie and I isn't going to be the smash and grab I'm used to with Mark. My fingers work the buckle of his trousers, then pop the button and lower the zip. I slide his trousers over solid buttocks and muscular thighs, leaving them pooled at his feet. His erection is waiting beneath a tent of black boxer shorts. He's trembling as I lower them and his cock springs forward, quite obviously eager to play.

I tease my tongue around the moisture at its tip. He's musky, masculine and meant totally for me. Opening my mouth, I take him deep to the back of my throat, my fingers curling around the shaft easing him deeper and deeper. I close my eyes and his hand slides gently through the hair at my crown. I begin to move back and forth and a low guttural moan escapes him. My own excitement is moist between my legs and I squeeze my pelvic muscles tightly together.

After a few seconds, I feel him getting bigger, straining hard against the inside of my mouth. Shall I? Can I?

"Hannah?" he pants. "No, not that. I want...I need..."

I ease him gently from my mouth, letting my tongue linger at its tip for a few seconds longer before pushing to my feet. His kiss is urgent.

"I love you." He says it once. "I love you." He says it twice.

The words send a jolt of electricity through my chest but I daren't say them back. Not yet. I can't, I daren't. But Jamie isn't worried about that right now and I screech with delight when he pulls me down on top of him.

"Mmmm, now what have we here?" I murmur.

And then I'm rubbing my clitoris up and down the length of him and it fills me with acute pleasure to see his eyes close and his jaw tense. He's actually concentrating on keeping control, worrying about me and when I'll be ready. I shudder involuntarily. The man is so unbelievably sexy, real and dare I believe it? Mine.

I study the handsome contours of his face, as I shimmy up his body until I'm hovering above him. He grips his hands either side of my waist and leads me down over him and his penis slips effortlessly into my wetness.

"Oh, yes." I whisper out the words on a breath. "Oh, yes."

We move—our rhythm as natural as two people who've spent their entire lives together. I lean my hands back on his thighs, my breasts on parade—jiggling and bouncing around for his pleasure. I feel like a slut, a queen, a God damn vixen! And then, and then—yes, yes, yes!

The Sharp Points of a Triangle

Chapter Twenty

The next morning, I wake at first light. I wait for the wash of regret to sweep over me but it doesn't and when I look across my pillow and watch Jamie breathing softly, my heart swells. There's no going back. This is it. This is where I want to be. Throughout the night, I've considered where I am and what I'm doing. And the upshot is—I want none of it to change. The only concern I have is whether it is a good idea for Jamie and I to work together—but there will be plenty of time to discuss that later.

I languidly stretch my arms above my head and glance at my watch. It's just past seven o'clock but already the morning sun is seeping through the thin cotton of the curtains and the birds are singing my happiness. I need to pee. But as I move to get up, Jamie's arm comes across me, pinning me unceremoniously to the bed.

"Don't even think about it," he mumbles into the pillow.

A girlish thrill bolts through me. "And why not?"

"Because you're staying right there, naked as the day you were born until I say otherwise," he says, turning over so one perfect sea-green eye watches me from between the pillow and the duvet.

I smile. "And what if I can't stay here? What if Mr. Baxter hadn't asked me to leave and the idea of going to work filled me with insurmountable erotic anticipation?"

"Mmmm, so Baxter's bald, shiny head does it for you, does it?"

"Oh, no, it's not just Mr. Baxter's," I smile. "It's any bald, shiny head"

And then I scream as he launches himself at me, growling and snarling. We wrestle and kiss, kiss and wrestle until we both emerge from beneath the duvet, panting for breath. I lie my head down on his chest and listen to the beat of his heart. It feels incredible to be here alone with him after so many years apart.

A solitary tear slips down my cheek. I'm so happy. Jamie would pop into my conscience whenever Mark and I had a row, or when I felt afraid or lonely. He was there when I picked up the keys to my first house, again when I passed my Financial Planning Certificate. I love him. I always have.

He strokes gentle fingers over my cheek. "Are you all right?"

"Uh-huh. Just thinking."

"Want to share?"

I hesitate. "Have you thought about me over the years?"

"God, Hannah, countless times. I told you, as soon as I knew you were going to be at The Laurels I had to go. Had to know one way or the other."

"But there have been others?"

"Yes...but nothing like this."

Andrea thrusts to the forefront of my mind. I swallow hard. "But we're in the first throes of good old-fashioned lust, Jamie. What happens when we get back to normal day to day life? Then what?"

"I want this for keeps, Hannah." He moves and I'm forced to look at him. He touches a finger to my chin, his eyes confirming the sincerity of his words. "If you want me, I'm here. I started this with every attention of getting back into your heart. It was a long shot that it would ever happen, mind you. In fact, I couldn't believe you would even look at me again."

"I believe you. It's just..."

Andrea, say something, anything about Andrea. Please. Just tell me you respected her, liked her. Just so I know the abortion was all her decision—and nothing to do with you walking away from her and a new baby.

"What, Hannah? Talk to me."

I squeeze my eyes shut, locking him out. "I don't think I'd get over you breaking my heart a second time."

There's a long silence. I wait and then I feel his warm lips against mine. "Open your eyes."

We pull apart and I open them.

"I'd never consciously hurt anyone, let alone you," he says. "It's impossible to imagine, two intelligent, hard-working people hankering after a teenage romance for six years, unless it was meant to be. I'm not the most romantic guy in the world, so why would I even believe it would work unless it was a foregone conclusion, eh?"

He's trying to sound blasé, confident even, but I know Jamie and I recognise the anxiety, the genuine worry in his eyes. He's as scared of rejection as I am. But I need to know, I need to know he's here for keeps. Nausea flows thick and fast through my stomach—we've had unprotected sex. Will he be around for me if I fall pregnant? Or will I be forced to take the same decision as Andrea? I open my mouth to ask him and then shut it again.

I promised Andrea. I promised I wouldn't tell him. How can I tell him something as big as him fathering a child with her, when we are both naked in bed, talking of a future together? I shamefully push her to the back of my mind—for now. I force a smile.

"You are romantic, Jamie. God, you have no idea how romantic you are."

"I love you, Hannah. I mean it, I really do."

I look deep into eyes I've never forgotten. "Could you take the day off work?"

"I'm the boss, aren't I?"

"Good."

A whole day. We can shut the door and forget about our responsibilities for twenty-four hours. And then we'll talk. I turn over and press my face into the pillow, my fingers clutching the corners. "Mmmmph!"

He laughs, "What are you doing?"

"Mmmph!"

"What?"

I lift my head. "I love you too. So bloody much!"

"Woo-hoo!"

And then he flips me over onto my back and covers my body with his and we're kissing and teasing, touching and tasting. His hands are in my hair as I score my nails over his muscular back and shoulders. His teeth nibble deliciously at the curve of my neck and I smooth my hands down to cup his rock hard arse.

"Me thinks someone's ready for some more lovin'," Jamie whispers against my ear.

The little hairs all over my body stand to attention and I shiver with anticipation, but instead push my hands to his chest (Oh, God, his chest!) and I slide out from underneath him.

"Before this gets any more heated, I need to check my phone," I pant. "I haven't spoken to Sam since last night. She'll be worried sick."

He groans. "Now look what you've done."

I lift the sheets and see his erection ready and willing. I grin. "He's just going to have to wait."

As I get out of the bed, his fingers grip my wrist. "Hey, where do you think you're going?"

"To get my phone."

"There's no way you're putting one foot out of this bed, Missy. Here." He leans over and passes me the phone from the bedside cabinet.

Taking the phone, I start to dial Sam's number and stop.

"Can I talk to her alone? If she knows you're lying right beside me, I'll get no sense out of her at all."

He kisses the tip of my nose. "I'll go downstairs and make some tea."

"Fab."

I shift to the side and happily watch his rock hard buttocks for a few pleasurable seconds when he gets up from the bed and pads across the bedroom floor. I sigh with disappointment when he spitefully covers them with a pair of boxers. He turns and gives me a wink before leaving the room.

I quickly dial Sam's home number hoping to catch her before she leaves for work. It rings and rings before the answer phone kicks in. I cut the line and then dial her mobile number. Nothing. I leave a message on the answer phone.

"Hey, babe, it's me. Just to let you know I am still alive and blissfully happy," I smile into the phone. "No prizes for guessing who I'm with. I'll call you later. Love you."

I hesitate for a second longer before putting the receiver down and collapsing back against the pillows. There will be plenty of time to tell her I've lost my job and Mark seems to be losing his mind later. Right now my bubble is fit to burst. And just when I'm starting to feel his absence, Jamie's head appears around the bedroom door.

"Coast clear?"

"Yes." My stomach flip-flops at the delicious sight of him.

He strolls into the room and I burst out laughing. He has wrapped a tea towel around his neck in what I can only assume is supposed to be a tie, and a half-dead dandelion hangs from between his teeth. In his hands is a tray laden with tea and chocolate biscuits.

"Wow, I'm impressed," I laugh.

"For you, Madam." He lays the tray on the bedside cabinet with a flourish.

I watch him as he tries to wrestle his way into the packet of biscuits. My gaze wanders over his face, his back. I am in serious, serious trouble. I swallow.

"Jamie?"

"Mmmm?"

"You know what you said to me earlier?"

He glances at me furtively. "About cutting your pubic hair in the shape of my name?"

I swat him up the back of the head. "Nooo."

"What then?" he laughs.

"About loving me."

He stops rustling the biscuits and stares deep into my eyes. "I meant every word, Hannah."

I lift my hand and slide my fingers through the short soft hair above his ear. I gently kiss him. "I believe you. And no matter what happens from here on in," I say, softly. "I'm glad this happened. I haven't felt this happy since the day you left."

The tea is forgotten as he throws the biscuits behind him and takes me in his arms. He kisses me so deeply, that eventually I have to pull away just to take a breath. He brushes the hair from my eyes.

"This is really going to happen, you know."

I smile. "I know."

But as he leans into kiss me again, a horrible, unwelcome sense of foreboding skitters along my skin causing my hands to tremble.

****

"Hey, sleepy-head."

I open heavy lids to the sound of his voice deep and husky against my ear and his hand cupped over my breast.

"Well, good morning," I say, stretching my legs. "And how long have you been groping me without my consent?"

"Pretty much most of the night. In fact, you had two extremely selfish orgasms."

I look at him doubtfully. "You may be good, but you're not that good. Ow!"

He releases my pinched nipple. "Serves you right," he mutters, before turning to nibble my neck while sliding his hands up my body.

My mobile beeps somewhere in the room, I glance at the bedside table but it's not there. Groaning, I reluctantly shuffle away from Jamie. "Did you bring my bag upstairs? I know I really should talk to somebody after disappearing under your duvet for the last…" I pause. "….thirty-five hours or more but I really, really don't want to."

He lifts a hand, shakes it in the general direction of the left-hand corner. "Over there, on the chair."

"It's barely seven, who could be texting me at this time in the morning?" I wonder aloud as I get out of the bed.

"It was beeping when I went downstairs to check the post so I thought I'd better bring it up."

"It was?" A dart of icy cold dread pierces my stomach. "Why didn't you wake me?" I ask, unzipping my bag.

Jamie gives a loud yawn. "Jealousy."

"What?"

"It's probably Mark, isn't it?" he says, "If the guy came all the way to the conference to get you back, you can pretty certain he'll be ringing you a few more times before he accepts you two are over…"

But I'm not listening. I'm staring wide-eyed at the display. Seven missed calls and seven messages. Unease ripples through my belly. I dial playback. Four messages are from Mark — all along the lines of he's sorry and won't I come back so we can talk? He sounds either pissed or crying on each of them.

And three from Sam.

By the time I have listened to the third, I'm shaking so much Jamie leaps from the bed and pulls me tightly into his arms.

"What's the matter? What is it?"

"It's Mark. Oh, God. I've got to call Sam."

I scramble from his embrace and rush into the en-suite bathroom and slam the bolt. With my blood thundering in my ears, I dial Sam's number.

"It's me. Tell me you're winding me up, Sam. Please."

"I'm so sorry, babe. It's true. He's in St Alban's Memorial. Where are you?"

Too guilty to admit I am still here after I left her the message an entire twenty-four hours ago, I ignore the question. "Is he going to be all right?"

"There's not a lot I can tell you. His mum rang me at one o'clock this morning asking if I knew where you were because Mark had been involved in an accident."

"Oh, God, oh, God." I cover my face with my hands.

"Hannah, listen to me. He'll be all right. Do not blame yourself for this. Do you understand me?" Sam says. "I won't let you do this."

"But it is my fault, Sam," I cry. "I've got to get to the hospital. Will you meet me there? I need you."

"Of course I will." She pauses. "Are you still with Jamie?"

I swallow. "Yes. See you there. I'll be twenty minutes."

I snap the phone shut and then throw up over and over again in Jamie's snow-white toilet. What if Mark dies?

The Sharp Points of a Triangle

Chapter Twenty-One

Sam is waiting outside the sliding doors of the hospital. I rush into her open arms and then hand in hand we run inside. The reception area is in organised chaos. Gurneys are being pushed back and forth, a guy who is more plaster of Paris than skin, sits alone in a wheelchair waiting for someone to notice him, while a brother and sister are pencilling a tattoo on their sleeping father's face.

We descend on the circular reception desk and Sam instinctively takes the lead.

"Hi, we're looking for Mark Hardy. He was brought in earlier after being involved in a car accident."

Giving us both a sympathetic smile, the receptionist turns to her computer. "Mark Hardy, Mark Hardy..."

I bounce from one foot to the other, my gaze darting left and right along the bright white corridors.

"Mark Hardy, Mark Hardy..."

I cross my arms to stop from reaching forward and shaking the information from the gaily dressed receptionist. I exchange a glance with Sam. She too, looks dangerously close to exploding.

"Ah, here we are." The receptionist says at last. "Mark Hardy, Caucasian male, age 29. Is that right?"

"Yes," says Sam through clenched teeth. "Is he okay?"

The receptionist narrows her eyes. "And you are?"

Her superior tone does nothing to calm the hysteria building deep inside of me. I stare at her. Obviously the St Alban's hospital reception area is her domain which she rules with a possessive blend of brightly coloured tent dresses and half-moon spectacles. Sam presses a thumb into her own chest.

"I'm little Miss Nobody, but Hannah here is his live-in girlfriend."

I open my mouth to correct her, but then realise this is the only way this woman is going to give us any information whatsoever. She looks past Sam to me. For a moment, she just stares at me and I think we haven't got any chance of seeing Mark, then her eyes soften and the suspicion turns to sympathy. I swallow the bile that rises bitter in my throat.

"You're his common-law wife?" she asks, gently.

I'm about to respond when Sam steps in front of me, blocking my view of her.

"Yes, I just told you she is. What aren't you telling us? Is he dead?"

I freeze.

It feels like three hours pass before the receptionist ekes out a response. "No, he's not dead but he is lucky to be alive," she sighs. "It says here a copious amount of alcohol was in his bloodstream when the car crashed."

Sam fists her hands at her hips. "He was drunk? Oh, for the love...."

I push forward, grip my fingers around the edge of the desk. "So he's alive? He's going to live?"

"He's out of danger, yes. Just a few cuts and bruises..."

Sam nudges me out the way. "Well in that case, there's no need for you to tell me or his girlfriend what a prick he is for drinking and driving. We already know how big a cock he is. That's why she..." Sam pauses to jerk her thumb in my direction, "...spent the night shagging another bloke."

Silence descends on the reception area like a freeze-frame in a movie. Everyone stops what they're doing to turn and stare, at the adulterous slag visiting her boyfriend who was involved in a near fatal car crash. I step over the tumbleweeds and place my hand back on the desk to steady myself.

"Thanks, Sam."

She shrugs. "You're welcome."

I want to throw up all over the white tiled floor but know I have to face this. I have to see him. He could've died. Pulling myself up straight, I tilt my chin. I lock eyes with the receptionist. She looks back at me as though I am giving off the smell of a horses' turd left to dry in the mid-summer sun.

"Which room is he in?" I say with as much authority as I can muster.

She looks at me over the top of her glasses. "You were with another man?"

"Yes. Which room is he in?"

She sniffs. "You. Were. With. Another. Man?"

Sam steps forward and I grab her raised arm in my hand and hold it there.

"I said, which room is he in?"

Her gaze wanders down the length and breadth of my body. "Room forty-two. Turn left at the lifts and it's the fourth door on the right."

I smile until my jaw cracks. "Thank you."

With my fingers still pressed into Sam's wrist, I propel her in the direction the receptionist indicated. Once we are around the corner, she turns on me.

"Why the hell did you stop me smacking her?" she cries. "She deserved a slap looking at you like that. Who the bloody hell does she thinks she is?"

I look up at the suspended ceiling and slowly count to five before meeting Sam's angry gaze. "Calm down."

"No. She...."

"You're scared, I'm scared."

Tears turn her eyes glassy. "Scared? Over Mark? Give me a break? It's you, Hannah. I know what's going to happen once you walk in and see that selfish prick."

"Selfish? Selfish, Sam? It was me having sex with another man while Mark was skidding along the A432 in case you'd forgotten."

She rolls her eyes. "Oh, here we go."

"What?"

"I know what's coming next."

I fist my hands on my hips. "What's that supposed to mean?"

She flings out her arm, pointing her hand along the corridor. "You're going to go in there and let Mark spread the guilt on you with a fucking trowel. And then you'll take him back."

"Sam, for God's sake. He could've been killed."

"I rest my case."

I feel the sting of tears. "I could really do with a friend, right now,

Sam. The last thing I need is you looking at me like that."

She crosses her arms. "Right, well that's it then."

"What is?"

"I'm going to be your friend," she says. "And your friend says you're out of here. You're going to turn around, walk out of the hospital and go straight back to Jamie's house."

"I am not leaving here without seeing Mark. No matter what you think of him, we shared our lives for two years."

"And?"

"Sam, come on. That counts for something surely? This isn't a soap opera, its real life. I know him...and I care about him."

Sam huffs out a breath. "I give up. I don't know what you want anymore. In fact, I don't think you even know yourself."

"I want Jamie."

"So don't go in there." Her eyes soften as she steps closer and takes my cold, cold hands in hers. "Listen to me. You know Mark's alive. There's no need for you to do this."

I glance at the closed door of room forty-two. "I didn't ask for Jamie to re-appear in my life, or for Mark to ruin what we had by becoming such a selfish son-of-a-bitch, but I have to at least see him in his hour of need. Yesterday was amazing, fantastic, the best twenty-four hours of my life even, but right now, Mark is lying in a hospital bed." I shake my head. "I have to see him, Sam."

"You won't change your mind?"

"No."

She lifts her shoulders. "Fair enough, just wanted to make sure either way. Shall we go in then?"

"That's it?"

She links an arm through mine. "That's it. I kind of guessed you'd have to see him, but I thought I'd at least try to stop you making a colossal mistake. Isn't that what friends are for?"

"I'll make sure he's going to be all right and then I'll go."

She shakes her head. "That won't be it, Hannah. And you know it."

I swallow. "Yes it will."

"Fine, just do one thing for me, okay? Take a second to think before you say anything once we're in there. Promise me you won't lose sight of what's happened between you and Mark...or you and Jamie. Please."

"Okay, okay."

But as I push open the door and see Mark lying on the bed, I feel my promise fall to the tiled floor and smash into a million little pieces.

"Oh, Mark."

My hand is welded to my mouth as I approach the bed. His eyelids are swollen shut and purple with bruises as is the rest of his abnormally bloated face. His bottom lip hangs limp and slightly to the side. A big square of gauze is stuck to the side of his reddened neck.

"Oh, Mark," I whisper again and feel Sam slip her hand into mine.

My eyes travel the length of his still body and my eyes hover at his cut hands and broken finger nails. There's a patchwork of dried blood and lacerations on each and every finger. But it's when my gaze halts at his suspended, cast-covered legs that the first hot tear slides down my cheek.

"Oh, God, Sam, he's a mess. What have I done?"

She snatches me around to face her, her hands gripping and pinching the flesh on my upper arms. "Stop it. Right now. I told you, this is not your fault. Mark decided to get behind the wheel all on his own. This had nothing to do with you."

"How can you say that?" My tears are in free fall now. "How can you believe my ex-boyfriend lying half-dead in a hospital bed has nothing to do with me breaking his heart?"

"Because, because..."

"Hannah?"

The sound of Mark's cracked and croaking voice silences us and I throw Sam's hands off me and rush toward him.

"Mark? Mark, I'm here."

"Get me a drink will you, babe? My throat's like bloody sandpaper."

I quickly reach for the plastic jug and fill a cup with shaking hands. I ease the straw between his dry lips. He takes a few sips and then drops his head back against the pillow.

He tries to smile. "I'm glad you're here."

"What were you thinking?" I say. "You could've been killed."

Sam steps forward. Her arms crossed. "Or killed someone else."

I spin around. "Sam, for God's sake!"

But Mark slowly shakes his head making the pillows rasp beneath his bloody hair. "Babe, she's right. I was stupid. Why the bloody hell did I think I was going to find Jamie's gaff, after drinking six cans of beer."

"Six cans of beer? My God, I thought you might've been stupid enough to drink a couple and think you could drive. But six? Are you mad?" I stare at him, incredulous.

"About you? Yes. I'm an arsehole, aren't I?"

I drop my gaze to the bed, suddenly finding it incredibly hard to look at him.

"You said it," mutters Sam.

I continue to stare at the sheets covering his torso. I purse my lips tightly together for a second, giving myself time to think what I actually want to say.

He reaches for my hand. "I was wrong, babe. I know that now."

I snap my head up. "Wrong? Wrong, Mark? Do know something? I want nothing more than to smack you right in the face right now!"

"But it's all right, the doc says I'm going to be fine. Apparently this shit all over my face is just superficial and the casts will be off my legs in a few weeks."

"I'm not even talking about you," I spit. "Didn't you think about anybody else before you got in that car?"

My question hangs in the air of the silent room. I look from Mark to Sam and back to Mark again. "Don't you understand how bloody selfish you are?" I ask, blinking back another deluge of tears. "Can't you see what could have happened?"

"Don't cry, babe. No one else was hurt."

Sam gave a low whistle. "You are unbelievable. I've always tried my hardest to put up with you for the sake of Hannah. But now she's found herself a decent bloke? Fuck you, Mark!"

I stand still as Sam strides from the room, slamming the door hard behind her. A heavy blanket of exhaustion drapes across my neck and shoulders. I glance around and pull a plastic chair to the side of the bed and sit down.

Mark lifts his arm and pulls the hand covering my eyes down from my face. "I'm sorry, Hannah. Really I am."

I stare at him. "Why, Mark? Why did you do it?"

But then his tears scorch my heart like liquid acid. One by one they stream over the bumps and craters of our relationship, burning holes through the fragile scraps that are making me still feel responsible for him.

"I love you, Hannah. I've loved you since the day we met. I can't lose you. I can't."

I sigh. "But you lost me a long time ago."

"You wouldn't be crying if you didn't still care about me."

I brush the traitorous tears from my cheeks. "I'm crying because I wouldn't wish death on anyone, Mark. My tears have nothing to do with still loving you."

He squeezes his eyes tightly shut. "Come back to me, Hannah. Come back and I promise things will change. Please."

"No. I can't force myself to love you."

There's a discreet knock at the door and a guy in his mid-forties walks into the room. He extends his hand to me.

"Hannah?"

I nod. "Yes. Hannah Boyd, Mark's...friend."

"I'm Doctor Phil Gardner. I'm the psychiatrist looking after Mark while he's here."

"Psychiatrist? But..."

Dr Phil looks from me to Mark. "Have you told Hannah the reason behind the accident, Mark?"

Mark bows his head like he's just been reprimanded by a head teacher so I stand up. "Why don't you tell me, Doctor? Clearly Mark isn't a mature human being," I say, coldly.

But the doctor's gaze remains fixed on Mark. "Would you like me to tell Hannah, Mark?"

Mark nods and the doctor turns to face me. "Mark's accident was not actually an accident."

I frown. "You mean...?"

He blows out a breath. "This will be difficult for you to hear, but there is no easy way to say it, I'm afraid. Mark attempted suicide last night."

The words echo around and around in my head, bouncing off the ventricles of my brain like ping-pong balls. "But I thought you ran into a tree?" I say, turning on Mark.

But it seems he's now lost the use of his tongue, so once again Dr Phil steps in. "He was heading toward the edge of Suttondown Hill but misjudged his steering and so in effect, a tree saved his life."

I look at Mark. "Is this true?"

He finally meets my eyes and nods.

And never before have I wanted to rip somebody's head from their shoulders, like I did Mark Hardy's in that moment.

****

I march straight out of the hospital into the car park, my breath rasping and burning my throat. I jump when Sam's fingers clutch my elbow.

"Hey, what happened?" she says, turning me to face her. "What did he say to you?"

"He...he...he tried to bloody kill himself, Sam!"

"What? That was a suicide attempt?" Her eyes teeter dangerously close to the edge of their sockets.

"He meant to drive straight off the edge of Suttondown Hill, but misjudged and ended up crashing straight into a tree. Can you believe it?"

We both stare at each other in bemused shock for a long, long moment and then—God forgive us, we both burst into uncontrollable laughter until I have to slap a hand to my crotch, to stop myself from peeing all over the grey asphalt. Sam holds a hand to her head.

"Only Mark could miss a great big bloody cliff face and hit a tree instead!" She screams. "Oh, my God, oh my God, this is it. This is how I'm going to die."

It's at least another ten minutes before we get ourselves back under control and face the reality of Mark attempting to end his life. We sit side by side on a vacant bench.

"So, what happens next?" Sam asks, quietly.

I look at my friend's beautiful face and take a deep breath. "I'm going to stick around. At least for a while. I can't just leave after this, can I?"

"What? Of course you can. What are you going to say to Jamie?"

I lift my shoulders. "I haven't thought that far ahead, yet."

"What if he won't sit and wait, Hannah? I can't stand by and let you lose a bloke like that over Mark. No way..."

"If he won't wait, it wasn't meant to be." But I feel nauseous just saying it.

"He shouldn't have to wait, Hannah. Mark was drunk, Hannah.

Drunk! The selfish bastard doesn't deserve you fussing over him. You don't even love him anymore." She pauses and fists her long blonde hair back from her face. "It's not right."

She sighs, slips an arm around my shoulder. "You tried over and over again to make it work. You know you did. It wasn't meant to be. People grow apart, they change."

I squeeze her hand. "Not us though."

She grins. "No, not us."

We sit for several seconds in silence but I inhale a long, shaky breath and release it. "You're right."

"I know."

I swat her playfully on the arm. "I'm not risking losing Jamie after this. Mark did this all by himself, didn't he?"

"Absolutely. Good girl. Thankfully, he's just a sad psycho who messed up his own suicide but he could've have been a sad psycho who'd killed someone, Hannah. Forget him. Forever."

I smile. "I will. I have."

And then the bright morning sun falls behind a shadow and when I look up, Mark's mother is staring down at me. Sam's arm slips from my shoulder, leaving me feeling incredibly cold.

"Maureen, hi," I smile. "Is Mark sleeping?"

Even in the best of circumstances, Mark's mother and I had merely shared a sufficiently civil relationship. There was never any hugging or cheek kissing, but we didn't beat each other about the face and body with insinuations and challenges either.

"Yes. Yes, he is," she says between pursed lips.

"Good, good. I...um...was about to leave actually." Mark is his mother's problem.

"Will you be back shortly?"

I stand up, hitch my bag onto my shoulder. "No..."

"I know about what happened at your so-called seminar, Hannah," she says, the words loaded with an unspoken threat. "I recommend this sad time is used to let bygones be bygones as Mark so generously suggested."

I slowly nod my head as though contemplating this suggestion. "Really?"

"Well, yes. He's still willing for the two of you..."

"I won't be getting back together with him, Maureen. Mark and I are over."

"Now you listen to me, young lady, you've had your fun. Gotten rid of what ever itch you felt needed to be scratched, but now it's time to grow up."

I stare at her in disbelief. "Me, grow up? What about Mark? He's..."

"Men are boys, Hannah. Now, he needs clean pyjamas and a wash bag. I'll be happy to sit with him until you come back."

I can feel Sam's eyes burning into my temple but I refuse to look at her. "Maureen, you're not listening…."

She turns to walk away and I'm about to gesture rather succinctly behind her back when she turns around. "You know he loves you very much, don't you, Hannah?"

And I nod because I do know, but it doesn't matter one tiny little bit anymore. She continues to stare at me, "He only ended up in this hospital, battered and bruised, and unable to walk because he thought he'd lost you."

The air around me is so oppressive I'm finding it hard to breathe. I clamp my hands together so she cannot see them shaking. "It's not my fault this happened, Maureen."

"Maybe not. But you could at least ease my burden for a little while." She pauses, wipes a finger under her eyes. "Just for a few days?"

I glance beseechingly at Sam who gives a curt shake of her head. I turn back to Mark's mother. "A few days?"

"That's all I'm asking, Hannah. Let him get over the worse of it and then you can do what you want. But you owe him a few days."

"But surely in the long run…."

"Please, Hannah."

Her voice cracks and I feel my resolve weaken. I blow out a breath. "I'll be back as soon as I can."

And with that she walks away, her shoulders slumped and suddenly looking a lot older than her fifty-eight years. My stomach lurches. She's only doing what she can to help her son. Sam gawks at me.

I hold up a hand. "Don't."

"She has to understand you and Mark are over."

"Did you see her?"

"Yes, but..."

"What, Sam? What should I have said?" My voice is close to

hysterical.

"He did this for attention. Pure and simple," Sam says, waving a dismissive hand. "No-one, not even Mark could miss going over Suttondown Hill. This entire thing was for your attention."

"Do you think I don't know that? As soon as Dr Phil told me, the truth slapped me square in the face. That's why I walked straight out of there without a backward glance." I wearily pull my car keys from my bag. "Look, I'm going home to get him some clothes from the pile he's left behind. I need time to think."

"Fine, get him the clothes and then you tell him...and Maureen, it's over."

The Sharp Points of a Triangle

Chapter Twenty-Two

I pull out an overnight bag from the bottom of the wardrobe and toss it onto the bed. I then throw in the last pair of Mark's pyjamas, a couple of T-shirts and some clean underwear. As I zip it shut, my eyes are drawn to the bedside clock. It's nearing midday and almost five hours since I left Jamie's. I take out my phone and see he's tried to ring me three times. I then scroll down the contact list to Andrea's name. I stare and stare at the name for a few seconds. Life is too short for deceit. Too short for lies and false starts. I hit the talk button.

"Hello?"

"Andrea? It's Hannah."

"Oh, hi. It's so great to hear from you."

"How are you?"

"Great, great."

I inhale a breath. "You might change your mind about that when you've heard why I'm ringing."

There's a long silence. "It's about the pregnancy, isn't it?"

I look to the ceiling. "Yes."

"Oh, Hannah! I knew you wouldn't be able to keep it from Jamie once you fell in love with him." She pauses. "And you are in love with him, aren't you?"

I nod. "Yes. Yes I am. And if he finds out I knew about the pregnancy and never told him..."

"But it's not your place to tell him," she protests. "It's mine and I see no reason for him to know. It's finished and I want it to stay that way."

"Andrea, please..."

"No, Hannah. I mean it."

I can tell by the tone of her voice it will be a hopeless endeavour trying to change her mind, but I can't have this secret hanging over our heads, waiting for the axe to fall. Or worse, Andrea deciding six months, or a year from now to call Jamie and come clean.

"I can't promise to keep it from him anymore, Andrea. It's feels as though I'm lying to him every time I look him in the face."

"It's for the best. Trust me. There's nothing he could do then, and there's nothing he can do now. Why does he need to know? I know there are things he's keeping from you."

"Sorry?" My heart leaps into my throat.

I hear her blow out a breath. "Look, all I'm saying…"

"What did you mean? He's keeping things from me?" I ask. "What things?"

"Hannah, open your eyes. Jamie is a force to be reckoned with and nothing ever stops him from getting what he wants."

I stand up a little straighter. "And? What? He wanted me and he got me. I don't think falling in love is the worst crime he could commit, is it?"

"He's a business man, first and foremost."

The insinuating tone of her voice is beginning to piss me off. "I thought we were friends, Andrea. Why are you being like this? Are you jealous? Is that it?"

"I wish you both all the happiness in the world, it's just I think you can be incredibly naïve at times."

Heat sears my cheeks. "Why? Because I happen to think it's the right thing to do, to tell Jamie about the abortion? God, Andrea. It's called integrity."

"I appreciate that, but Jamie is not going to care one way or the other about your integrity. All he cares about is his work."

I smile smugly. "You're wrong."

"Really? And have you agreed to work for him yet?"

I narrow my eyes. How the hell did she know about that? "What?"

"Have you?"

"No."

"But you will?"

"Maybe. Whatever I decide, it has nothing to do with you."

I hear her inhale a long, deep breath and brace myself for

whatever's coming. I have an overwhelming feeling I am about to be pole-axed by something so devastating, I'm going to want to disappear for a very long time.

"He's told you Jenkins couldn't decide between Young's and Callahan's, hasn't he?"

"Of course," I lie.

"And he told you he had to think of a way to swing it his way."

My silence speaks volumes to both of us.

"I didn't think so," she continues. "Jamie told Jenkins he would do whatever was necessary to get you to be part of his team. Jenkins liked you personally, but Jamie's business ideas more."

The first splinter is shallow but still painful. "You're lying."

"I'm sorry to hurt you, Hannah, but I'm telling you this so you let the abortion thing go. Jamie is not the caring sensitive soul you seem to think he is."

"You're lying!"

I disconnect the phone and throw it onto the bed. I'm trembling, my heart beating so fast I press a hand there, scared it will smash its way through my ribcage. She's lying. She has to be lying. Could he have done that? Would he have done that?

Grabbing Mark's bag, I snatch up my car keys. Rushing from the room, I run downstairs and straight out the front door. Slamming the car door, I pull away with such urgency that I leave skid marks down the length of the drive. I can't stay here. I can't stay another minute on this driveway or even in this country.

When I push open the door to Mark's private room he's sitting up, watching a Friends re-run. He laughs at something on screen as the door clicks shut behind me and he turns.

"Hey, you're back!"

I give a small smile. "Yep. Here, I brought you a few things."

The canned laughter of the TV sounds too loud in the room. I pick up the remote and press mute. The atmosphere instantly turns heavy. I know from the way he's watching me that Mark feels it too.

"Mum said she spoke to you outside and you were coming back. I'm glad."

I look at him. "Where is your mum?"

"She went back home to get some sleep. I told her I'd be okay until you got back." He pauses and then tilts his head to the side. "What's happened?"

"What?"

"Something's happened since you left here," he says, carefully watching me. "Something bad."

"I'm fine. I brought you some stuff and now I'm leaving."

I dump the bag at the end of the bed and turn.

"You're leaving?" he asks. "You're leaving for good?"

I turn around. "Yes, Mark. For good."

He looks toward the ceiling and I see his lips mouthing the seconds. When he looks at me again, his eyes are shining. "Can I ask you one last question?"

"What?"

"Is it just sex between you and this Jamie?"

I lift my shoulders and blink away the tears burning my eyes. "Who knows?"

"It's not, is it? You're going to leave here and go to him, aren't you?"

"Maybe," I whisper.

His brow furrows. "What does that mean?"

My tears blur his face. "It means I don't know."

"Oh, shit. Has he hurt you?"

I hold up my hand, the last thing I need is his sympathy. It's so much easier when he's acting like a selfish idiot. "I'm going, Mark. Look, just promise me you won't try anything stupid once you're discharged from here? This is a new start, okay?"

He falls back against the pillows and lets out a long, deep breath. "I won't. I'll be fine."

"Mark, promise me. Please."

He smiles wryly. "You know me. Always brush myself off and get back in the game."

I give a wobbly smile. It's true. Mark is one of those people who always seem to remain untouched by the chaos going on around them. I suppose that's why, when I look at the shining streaks of tears drying on his cheeks, I know he still loves me despite everything negative that's happened between us.

Leaning over the bed, I press a kiss to his battered forehead. "Take care."

He puts a finger to his lips before pressing it to mine. "Live your best life, Hannah. I love you."

And then I turn and leave the room as fast as I can. I run down the corridor, through the reception and burst outside. I bend at the waist and breathe in great gulps of air to cool lungs that feel as though they are on fire.

****

I've been sitting in the hospital car park for just over an hour now. My head is sore from resting against the hard rubber of the steering wheel and there is bound to be an imprint of it against my forehead, when I finally muster the strength to sit up. I look about me and see the car park is slowly filling with visitors who've finished work for the day. Men and women dressed in suits carrying young children still in their nursery sweatshirts, head for the sliding doors, eager to see their sick or convalescing loved ones.

Why am I wasting time sitting here waiting for someone to tell me how to fix this? I pull my bag from the passenger seat and take out my phone. I scroll down until I find Jamie's number. He picks up on the second ring.

"Hannah? Are you all right?"

"No."

"I don't know what to say. Is he okay? What happened?"

"He tried to kill himself."

"What? Shit!"

"That's just the reaction he was going for. He changed his mind at the last minute, he's going to be all right."

"Thank God."

I start the engine. "Listen, I'm ringing to tell you all bets are off and I never want to lay my eyes on you again."

He laughs. "What time will you be back?"

"I'm serious, Jamie. Have a nice life."

"What? What the bloody hell are you talking about?"

My stomach begins to quiver. He sounds genuinely panicked and it's easy to see how I, and no doubt Andrea and every other bloody female he's shagged, can fall for his shit.

"I know, Jamie," I sigh. "I know about your little agreement with Jenkins."

A long pause. "What agreement?" he asks, slowly.

"Don't, Jamie. Don't be a bigger shit than you already are."

"I honestly don't know what you're talking about. What

agreement?"

"The one about getting me to leave Callahan's so Jenkins can have the representation he wants, i.e., yours truly and the added bonus of your business strategies. Sound familiar?"

"Who told you?" He more or less growls. There's a distinct drop in the volume of his voice and the tiny hairs at the nape of my neck stand to attention.

I swallow. "It doesn't matter who told me."

"Who, Hannah? I want to know."

"So it's true?"

Silence.

"My God, you haven't changed at all, have you?" I say. "I will never, ever forgive you for doing this to me again, Jamie. Never."

Tears slide down by face and my hands tremble but I still can't put the phone down. I desperately want him to tell me I'm wrong, that he loves me but he doesn't, and I don't know what else to do.

"Yes, I wanted that account but I wanted you more," he finally says. "I told Jenkins that I'd try my utmost to convince you to work with Young's but I never promised him anything."

I squeeze my eyes shut. "Why didn't you tell me? Why didn't you tell me so I could be a part of the decision?"

"I told you I wanted you to work for me."

I roll my eyes. "But I thought you were impressed by my resume, by ambition, not by the fact that Jenkins loved me getting pissed and dancing the funky chicken!"

"It wasn't like that."

"Bullshit. Why would she lie? What would be..."

"She? It's Andrea, isn't it?"

His voice shakes with anger, making my heart pump harder and harder.

"No. No, it wasn't."

"Yes, it was. Andrea told you."

"Jamie..." But it's too late. The line's dead. My eyes dart around the car park looking for someone, anyone to stop this. To stop this horrible drowning deep inside me.

I've got to go. Get out of here. Leave. Go away for a long, long time.

Throwing the phone onto the passenger seat, I slam the car into first and leave the hospital. I drive through the town centre and out the other side. I drive and drive. My mind racing with ideas of what I'll do next and then it dawns on me like a breaking sunrise.

I have no job. I can leave the country with no explanation to anybody. That's what I'll do. I need to get away from here. Take some time alone. I turn the car around and head back into town and the nearest travel agent I can find.

"I want to go to Paris," I beam at the highly effeminate, fuchsia-pink shirted, man behind the desk. "Today!"

"Ooh, la, la!" he says, flipping his hands up. "C'est oui, mademoiselle."

I force a smile and hope it's not too obvious I want to reach across the desk, grab his turquoise tie and fling him through the plate glass window behind me.

"Give me a teeny-weeny, little, bittle second here," he says, in his stupid sing-song voice, tapping away on his keyboard with his long and if I'm honest, ridiculously dexterous fingers. "And I'll see what I can do."

I lean back in my seat, my leg bouncing up and down on the carpet like an out of control pogo stick. I press my hand against it and feel my jowls wobbling so immediately lift it away again.

"Ah-ha!" He glances at his watch. "Mmmm. Maybe not."

I lunge forward to have a look at his computer screen. "What is it? What have you got?"

"Well, I could book you in for the midnight flight but that would mean you'd have to be there by ten. It's nearing six now."

I rummage around in my handbag, extract my purse and pull out my credit card with a flourish. "Book it."

"But don't you at least want to know where you'll be staying first?" he says, arching an eyebrow, which to my expert eye looks suspiciously plucked. "The only available room is, well, let's just says pretty luxurious with a price tag to match."

"Luxurious? I can do luxurious," I say, beaming wildly. "Stick it on there. I want three nights of pure luxury. I don't care what it costs. Just do it."

"But Madam, really..."

And then I'm leaning over the desk and my fingers are gripping his tie. "Book it! Book it now!"

His Adam's apple jerks hard in his throat and his eyes are so wide, the veins are bulging. He holds his hands up in surrender.

"Okay, okay. Simmer down."

"Simmer down? Simmer down?" I hiss between clenched teeth. "I want to get out of here. Do you understand me? Today. Now book the damn flight, hotel, transfer, every bastard thing I need to get me from A to B. Got it?"

Tears brim at his lower lids and his bottom lip is trembling by the time his colleague and glamour model wannabe, appears at his side.

"Please could you remove your hand from Bryan's tie, Madam," she says, "Or else I'll have no choice but to call the police."

"Jesus," I mutter under my breath. But I let go of a quivering Bryan and sit down.

"Thank you," she says, sliding her size six arse onto the side of the desk beside Bryan.

I don't know why she's acting like his great protector, as one swift karate chop to her waist and the skinny bitch would split in two.

I meet her eyes. "Sorry. I need Bryan," I smile graciously, "to book this Paris trip for me if he will."

She nods and taps Bryan on the shoulder triumphantly. "Are you okay to look after..." She glances at my naked wedding finger. "...Miss...?"

"Boyd," I spit.

She smiles. "Boyd, Bryan?"

He nods but looks far from okay. "Yes, yes, of course."

****

I step from the taxi and my breath catches.

"Oh, my God," I gasp. "I'm staying here?"

The cab driver smiles, "This is the Plaza Athenee, Mademoiselle. You like?"

I turn and push some Euros into his hand. "I love it!"

He laughs as he tips a finger to his hat and turns to get my suitcase from the boot. I follow him through the double doors and into the gold and buttermilk lobby. He leads me to the reception desk and I find it hard to not grin, like the virgin luxury hotel visitor I am.

I fill out the reservation form with a shaking hand and I'm led to my room. It's costing me six months wages to stay here, but I truly don't care. When the porter opens the door to my room, I tip him and slowly close the door. With my back pressing into the wood, I slap both hands over my gigantic grin and stifle my scream. The double bed is dressed in bronze and cream, with thick and sumptuous cushions placed just so against the pillows. The crystal bedside lamps glint and shine under the chandelier high above me. I drop my hands and slowly walk further into the room. It is beautiful, absolutely beautiful. I circle around until I come to a stop by double doors leading to a small balcony.

It's past half past two in the morning and the street below me is still abuzz with traffic. I breathe in the air. God, it feels good to be away. Away from everything. My stomach rumbles reminding me I haven't eaten since the coffee and muffin I had at the airport. I turn back into the room and throw myself on the bed clutching the leather bound folder containing the delights and services of the hotel. I order a sandwich and mineral water before flipping myself over on to my back. I'm here. I'm in Paris.

Scrambling to my feet, I hurry over to my suitcase and start to unpack. I was in such a mad rush to leave, I literally grabbed what I could before heading straight to the airport in a determined attempt that nobody, especially my terrifying neighbours, caught me leaving. I unpack, pleased as well as surprised with my choice of various vintage dresses, soft floaty skirts and vest-tops. I pull out my only pair of Jimmy Choos with a flourish, followed by my only pair of pink strappy Manolo Blahniks. What more could a girl need in Paris? Once I'm unpacked, I reluctantly turn on my mobile phone. I need to at least let Sam know where I am, she's probably already rung around the hospitals and alerted my mother that I'm missing in action.

When my mobile re-sets to the Parisian service, I am greeted with the beep, beep, beep of ten missed calls — equally split between Sam and Jamie. Well, the former I can cope with, the latter will never hear my voice again. I ring Sam despite the time difference knowing she'd want me to. She answers the phone on the second ring.

"Hannah? For Christ's sake!"

"Well, hello, to you too."

"Where the hell are you? I leave you at the hospital telling you not to go back to Mark, then next thing I know your phone is turned off for a gazillion hours. Are you with Jamie?"

I inhale a breath. "Nope."

"Mark. You've gone back to him, haven't you? That's why you turned your phone off. Where are you? At the hospital? No, you can't be seeing him at three o'clock in the morning. Where are you?"

"Paris."

"The bloke's an absolute cock, how can you be so blind? Paris? You're in Paris?"

I grin with the absurdity of someone else saying it out loud. "Yep, I'm in one of the deluxe rooms at the Plaza Athenee."

"Shut up."

"I am!"

There's a long, long pause. I wait. And I wait. And then hold the phone away from my ear as Sam lets out the longest, highest pitch scream in the history of womanhood.

"You. Are. Fucking. Kidding. Me!"

I fall back onto the bed laughing, "I'm serious."

"Oh, my God. Are you with Jamie?"

"Nope."

"But you can't afford to stay at a place like that. Are you crazy?"

"Maybe. But I'll worry about the money when my credit card bill arrives next month. Right now, I'm actually bloody doing it!"

"But how did this happen," she laughs. "Actually don't answer that. Just tell me why I'm not there with you?"

I laugh. "Maybe I should've rung you but I had to get out of Bristol, out of England. I can't take any more. I need some time alone."

"Because of Mark?"

"Partly." I swallow. "But mostly because I found out I was a pawn in Jamie's grand game of chess."

"Game? What game?"

I close my eyes. "Remember the account I was supposed to secure at the seminar but lost to Jamie?"

"Jenkins?"

"Yep. It turns out it was between Jamie or me, but when Jamie promised him he'd get me to come to Young's, the decision was made that much easier for him."

"Bastard. And Jamie told you this?"

"No, not exactly. His ex did."

"Andrea?"

"Yep."

"Did you speak to Jamie?"

"Yes, and he didn't deny it. In fact, he hung up on me."

"Oh, Hannah," she says, softly. "I'm so sorry, babe. I really thought..."

I force a smile into my voice. "Listen, it doesn't matter. Look where I am. I don't care, Sam. Seriously, it's just another life lesson, that's all. I should never have jumped into bed with him and I should've never believed he could change. It was stupid."

"But why say he loves you? He did say that, didn't he?"

"Exactly. Why the hell would I ever want to be within ten feet of a bloke like that ever again?"

"I'm going to track him down and kill him."

"Sam, don't..."

And then there's that dead line again.

The Sharp Points of a Triangle

Epilogue

People talk about how romantic Paris is in the Spring, but as I sit here sipping ice-cold Chardonnay on the banks of the river Seine, I can't help wondering why Paris in the summer doesn't take precedence. It's the second week in August, the sun is heating the streets at a rather pleasant eighty-two degrees and I'm thinking, even without Jamie, life is looking pretty good. I stretch my legs out in front of me and slip off my shoes. The flagstones are warm beneath the soles of my feet and the river sparkles with diamonds of sunlight. I reach for the menu sitting in the centre of the wrought iron table.

Aw, shit. It's all in French. I wrack my brains trying to remember my limited French. Jambon — Ham. Fromage — Cheese. Boeuf — Beef. Fries — Frites. Okay, I can do this.

"Oui, Mademoiselle?"

"Oh, right, yes," I say as the waiter — or garcon approaches me. "Puis-je embrasser les frites, le boeuf...um...petit pois, s'il vous plait?"

He smiles. I smile back. He smiles some more.

"Oui?" I say doing the whole eyebrow raised thing to no avail.

He tips his head back and laughs. "Faites vous avez bien envie de boeuf, Mademoiselle?"

Okay, now he's completely thrown me. I shimmy forward on my seat. "Pardon?" See easy.

"Faites vous..."

"Elle voudrait des frites, un boeuf et des petit pois, s'il vous plait."

The waiter and I turn to look at the owner of the delicious French accent and deep, rich voice but I doubt very much the waiter's heart lodges in his throat like mine.

"Jamie?" I croak. "You're here."

He doesn't look at me, only continues to address the waiter. "Et le meme pour moi, s'il vous plait."

The waiter gives a curt nod. "Mon plaisir, Monsieur."

Jamie pulls out the seat opposite me and picks up my hand which is lying limp on the table top. "Hi."

"What did I ask him?" I say, tears burning the back of my eyes.

"You asked if you could kiss the chips, beef and peas."

I struggle not to smile. "Well, damn Mr. Reynolds, he was my French teacher. Always knew he fancied me."

Jamie smiles and my heart turns over in my chest. "What are you doing here?" I ask quietly.

"Andrea told me about the baby."

Our eyes lock. "Oh."

"I was shocked, then mad, then a little sad before finally, relief kicked in."

"Relief? That could've been your child." I pull my hand from underneath his. "How can you say that? I thought this would matter to you. God, I really don't know you at all, do I?"

I look away from his beautiful, beautiful eyes, as I feel another piece of my heart break away and look at the laughing, smiling faces on a tour boat out on the water. And feel as though they are laughing at me.

"It would have mattered if I'd ever loved Andrea, Hannah. Or maybe even if she'd have told me at the time. But now? Now it's done? I'm relieved. I'm relieved because I want that with you. Nobody else."

I turn to look at him. "What do you mean? You want that with me?"

"I want to marry you, Hannah. I want you to have my kids, my life."

He looks as though he hasn't slept since I left his bed two days ago. "Jamie, you can't mean that."

He takes my hand and presses a kiss to my knuckles. "I mean it more than anything. I asked you to work for me because I wanted to see you every day. It had nothing to do with Jenkins. I didn't know any other way to keep you close. I asked you to work for me before

Jenkins even told me about his indecision, remember?"

"But..."

"Once I saw you at the seminar, I knew my life would never be the same again. I felt my career slipping through my fingers. I knew I would spend the rest of my life making you mine if I had to."

"But Andrea said..."

"I know. I know she did. And she doesn't know why. Do you really believe someone of Jenkins' stature would make a business decision based on emotion? Of course he would go with an adviser with more experience, a reputation built from years of informed and brilliant decision making."

I snatch my hand away and cross my arms. "And of course, I have none of those things."

His cheeks flush. "I'm joking. I have no idea what tipped it for me, Hannah, and I really don't care. You're fantastic and you're going to be an amazing IFA. But please, let me be a part of that. I want to go there with you. You don't have to work for Young's, you can work wherever you want. I just want to be with you."

"Fine. I'll work here then."

"Where? Paris?"

"Uh-huh. Are you going to stay with me now?" I challenge.

He looks around him like a little boy lost. "You want to stay here?"

I throw my arms up in the air. "Why not? It's a beautiful place. I could be happy here."

He hesitates for just a second before his sexy, sexy mouth stretches into a grin. "Good. That's great. It's just as well I extended our stay at the Plaza Athenees for another week then, isn't it? Especially, if we're going apartment hunting."

"So...come on then, what do you think of that, mister I'll follow you to the ends of the earth..." I stop. "What did you say?"

He stands up and pulls me to feet. "I love you, Hannah Boyd, and we're going to stay here and figure out how we're going to spend the rest of our lives together."

"You're crazy!" I stare at him. "You've extended our stay for a week? What are you? A frigging millionaire?"

"Yep. That's exactly what I am."

"Holy shit."

And, as he takes me in his arms and slips a hand beneath my

shirt and up over my back, a long, contented sigh escapes my lips. Oh, yes, here we go again.

About the Author

Rachel Brimble has been married to her own romantic hero since 1998. They have two daughters and a Labrador. She lives in the UK and writes in a log cabin at the bottom of her garden. Her loves are simple—friends, family, books, wine and laughter. The preferred order can change throughout the day. She began writing when she became pregnant and hasn't stopped since. *The Sharp Points of a Triangle* is her first book with Eternal Press.

Please visit her at…
www.rachelbrimble.com

The Sharp Points of a Triangle

Available now from Eternal Press

That Taste of Orange

By Valerie J. Patterson

Can the taste of orange rekindle their passion?

If ever two people were perfectly suited for each other, it's Sabrina and Chas. Both pastry chefs. Both excellent cooks. And both love the taste of orange. But the Christmas season has been a very busy time at their pastry shop, and they're both feeling the weight of the long hours, the lack of personal time, and the stress of the holidays.

Sabrina wants nothing more for Christmas than to regain the wonderful relationship she once had with her husband. The very traits that drew her to him in the beginning are now driving her crazy. Chas loves his wife, but he's overworked and needs some down time. When he suggests they need time apart — and neglects to tell her where he was one evening — Sabrina thinks the worst.

Will the end of the holidays signal the end of their union? Or can one juicy little orange bring them back where they belong?

She got up and went downstairs, wondering where Chas was. As she stood in the kitchen doorway, she smiled. He was wearing the bottoms to a pair of pajamas she bought him last year. They had candy canes all over them. His dark brown hair — which reminded her of dark chocolate when wet—was damp and a crescent-shaped section hung over his forehead. It was clear that he'd taken a shower while she napped. She wondered how he'd been in their bedroom without her knowing. Used to be, she could just sense when he was around her.

His chest was bare save for the bib apron he wore. In the front pocket of the apron were a hand towel and a potholder. Tucked into the waistband of his pants was another hand towel. On the counter were several small glass bowls containing various ingredients circling a large mixing bowl, a carton of eggs, and the bottle of Amade ChocOrange liqueur. He picked up a wooden spoon, twirling it like a drummer would a stick, before using it to mix whatever was in the bowl. She watched him, unable to take her eyes off his biceps…watching them pump up and down as he reached for the little glass bowls one at a time, dumping ingredients into the mixing bowl. Exchanging the wooden spoon for a stainless steel whisk, he hummed as he expertly whipped the chocolate-orange velvet cream to a light, delicate fluff.

He grabbed a teaspoon from the drawer, which he dipped into the cream. Her eyes followed the spoon to his mouth, eagerly watching his tongue as he licked the remains of the cream off the stainless steel. Her body heated up. She really wanted to go in there, rip off the bib apron, and smear his chest with that cream.

The Sharp Points of a Triangle

Available now from Eternal Press

Heaven in Her Eyes

by Wendy Stone

From the #1 Best Selling Author at Eternal press for the year 2008 and 2009, Wendy Stone and Eternal Press presents Heaven in Her Eyes - Book two of the Romus trilogy.

Shanna Hunter-Clinton is on the run from her Senator husband. She's had all she can take of his abuse and the terrible things he made her do. She flees to Texas and straight into the arms of Special Agent Brandon Austen. But can Brandon keep her safe from a husband who just doesn't want to let her go? Or will he get lost in the Heaven in her Eyes?

"Oh God," she hissed, staring at the old-fashioned stand mirror in front of her. Her hands went up to cover her breasts, as if hiding them from herself.

"Shh," he whispered, bending his head so he spoke softly in her ear. "You don't know how beautiful you are, I want you to see you like I do." He put his hands over hers, slowly dragging her hands down her body to hang limply at her sides.

"You have the most sensual hair, Shanna," he said, still speaking softly, letting his cheek rub against the softness of her hair. "Do you know how much men love long hair? Especially like yours, it's so thick and almost seems to have a life of its own. It makes me wonder how it would feel wrapped around me, draped over me, against my naked skin." He lifted handfuls and let it run out of his hands like water.

"Your skin is perfect," he whispered, his fingers coming up to trace across her cheeks, feeling the heat of her blush. "Creamy silk," he moaned. The back of his hand tracing down her throat and across her collar-bone, then barely brushing the hardened tip of her nipple.

The Sharp Points of a Triangle

Available now from Eternal Press

Witch's Brew

by Tabitha Shay

Witches, wizards and magic!

Saylym Winslow regains forgotten magical powers, but is determined to ignore them. No way is she a witch; magic brings nothing but trouble.

But when Talon, Waken Prince and assassin of witches is assigned to terminate Saylym by stealing her soul, she discovers being a real, spell-casting witch is only the beginning of her problems.

Talon is enchanted by Saylym's beauty and charm and refuses to do his duty. He is given a choice by the powerful Waken Guild: Handfast with the trouble making witch to keep her in line or they will send Drayke, the most ruthless waken assassin, to hunt her down.

Sparks fly in this bewitching, sexy battle of the sexes-witch-style.

The hairbrush in Saylym Winslow's hand came alive, wiggling worse than a worm on a hook. With an earsplitting scream, she flung the brush across the bathroom and pressed a hand against her runaway heart.

Unfortunately, the brush landed in the commode with a

distinctive plop. Water slapped over the sides of the porcelain rim, splattering onto the worn tiled floor.

Biting her lip, Saylym tiptoed to the toilet bowl and peered over the edge, then jumped back. Her breathing rattled to a dead stop in her chest. "Ohmigod! I don't believe it!"

The brush had inched its way up the side of the white porcelain as if it had suddenly sprouted hands and feet to pull itself up the wet surface. It reached the top, tottered for a second, then toppled over onto the floor and flopped like a fish out of water.

"No more," Saylym moaned. "Please. I can't stand one more inanimate thing coming to life."

Made in the USA
Charleston, SC
26 January 2010